OUTLINE

Laura

Michael

1. Moving In, *Resolve*
2. Prior Ties, *Inspiration*
3. Smoking with Dan, *Individuation*
4. Interview, Lottery, *Confidence*
5. Visiting Meghan, *Amplification*
6. Home Alone, *Discovery*
7. Training, *Trust*
8. Fired, Drinking, *Expression*
9. Getting the Car, *Empowerment*
10. Groceries, *Structure*
11. The Club, Malik, *Consolidation*
12. Cocaine, *Satisfaction*
13. Voices, *Solution*
14. Seeking a Job, *Articulation*
15. The Hospital, *Grace*
16. Reasoning, Doctor, *Grounding*
17. Another Day, *Mastery*
18. Home, *Innocence*
19. The Father, *Artistry*
20. The Drive Out, *Current*
21. Drinking, *Modulation*

PARALLEL OPPOSITES

A coffee and cigarette story

RIAN Meir

DISCLAIMER:

This author does not promote the use of drugs and alcohol. Additionally, he recommends caution or avoidance of caffeine and nicotine, as they are dangerously addictive and can also undermine a person's health, as illustrated in this narrative. As readily available as legal substances are, they require moderation if they are to be used at all. Characters either interact with voices or experience psychological trauma in this story, and the author takes no responsibility for any damages. Reader discretion is advised.

CONTENTS

This book is dedicated to:

Mom and Dad

Maurice

And Everyone Else.

CHAPTER 1

"An individual has not started living until he can rise above the narrow confines of his individualistic concerns to the broader concerns of all humanity."

- MARTIN LUTHER KING, JR.

Translation

August 10th, 2003.

The afternoon sunlight wavered through the trees and invited her to the view outside the kitchen window, where she took a glass of water without hesitation, as if wanting, demanding, a moment's pause to silently revisit whatever used to happen here. Maybe, also, this was something she often did, without someone else in the room to see her.

The soft glow on the counter shone on her face and the painted metal flag from July at the side of the cupboard as something remarkably unexpected and vivid—a side of her privacy rarely glimpsed at, her whole livelihood summarized in an instant--as the shadows of leaves danced (menaced?) around her. She could suddenly leave and abandon the moment before she'd cry over something compiled with all the rest of it. It seemed rare to see her like this, within the routine of a day, at an unspoken interval maybe common for her.

Here at the farm again for the weekend, Laura wanted more to be said. After many failed attempts at speaking her mind with even the people closest, trying had only proved useless. Visiting her parents, she should feel free to say anything, yet what more was there than the television always being on and seeing her mom give so much time to it?

So, she remained at the window, speechless and with a sharp pain in the heart of her back. The trees past the road swayed together. The pear tree out front had grown, its peacock shape having intensified since the last she noticed, and the locust tree had also grown so immensely, children could no longer climb it. The yard was freshly mowed, a quiet sign of her father who was gone.

Just past the trees across the road, the cattle gathered at the water, as if wanting to remain under the sun, always arriving at spring rather than fall, to bring children to smile, but there were no children now. Tension gripped Laura's back. She couldn't possibly get herself to talk over the television but glanced at her mom and hesitated.

"Don't you think TV's a problem?" she said.

"Oh, I don't know," her mom said, to say the simplest thing because it always mattered to Laura, to team with her, whatever it could be.

Laura chomped down on some ice, the cattle having her attention again. There was a momentary silence before the television blasted into a commercial.

Renae didn't know where to begin. Laura—in a daze, thinking to herself—wanted to talk. But now? Had the last guy been calling her again after all that? And why not go shopping sometime with her? She had to breathe. "So, what are you doing today?" she said.

"When I get back to Omaha, I'll probably have a drink; there's a place downtown." Noise penetrated the room. "I won't be out late," Laura said, "So...." They glanced at each other. Laura had to think. "...if you wanna call, after seven I should be home."

"You could stay for dinner," Renae said.

"Yeah--."

"--We hardly see you anymore with you living out there. *Why* don't you?"

If Laura could say the right thing, her mom would think about it for weeks, maybe even years. She said, "I just don't think I have time." Laura put her glass down and turned to leave the kitchen. In the grace of any moment given to say something, she said, "I brought the camera so I could walk with Siva before I head out."

"Oh, okay," Renae said, alert and cheery with a half-spent cup of coffee getting cold somewhere. After all, her daughter had the same spirit as the kindergartners, herself, and the people on TV, to be happy.

In the living room, the day shone through the curtains, dust hovered in and out of its sunlight, and the old wooden floors creaked and echoed to the basement below. A new floral sofa had no matching rug, and boxes loaded for transport to her mother's kindergarten class were piled on the floor just as any other year, though seemingly permanent like revisiting here a year ago again.

Laura glanced at her reflection in the curio as she left the house. She was only certain she should get her back checked.

Outside, Laura stood confused. Was she forgetting

something? The slender cross between a German shepherd and a pointer, Siva approached Laura, wagging her tail, positioning herself to be petted, and maybe wondering if now Laura would say something different as her ears lifted.

These days, Laura felt people were superficial. Over time, ideas related to this changed, always with more hold on her than they already had. Too often, nothing mattered, and she wanted to believe this wasn't true. Despite this, Laura wanted to get back with friends and noticed more and more how no one would call or respond to emails. Siva had a noticeable scab on her ear.

She had a heavy feeling of apprehension with a mere walk outside, faced with all this. Early on, she'd distanced herself from her family, yet they had great importance to her. Renae, often in good spirits, was sometimes frustrated by the things people said, and at rare times, appeared to have doubts about how to handle things. Laura's father had a quiet presence, fighting restlessness through difficult thoughts or unrealized aspirations. Alcohol was both a reward on the good days and a therapy on the bad days. Like many, he was an underappreciated hard worker. Her brothers were normal, though in their development, too attached to what the other kids in school were, while maybe losing sight of who they'd started out as. At least these things often appeared to Laura on the surface.

Laura's instinct growing up was essentially to differentiate herself from others, for individuality's sake. In this area of the country, people seemed too likeminded. All this, and her family hadn't spoken much; moments came to pass to the next forgotten ones. It seemed they didn't desire getting closer to anyone than what it had been. Everyone still knew Laura to be a child, because in like mind, they were also.

There'd be times going to movies, to malls with bookstores and coffee, until it was beer parties, to the country roads with friends to drink or get high, to come home to a family she deeply felt was hers, but at the same time, she barely knew them. Maybe they didn't know her as well as she thought, either. Time given to school may have been more crucially given to her family, because here and now, pieces were missing.

The dog's eyes expressed gratitude for this and every moment with people who cared enough to keep her around and provide for her, as if only by chance, after waiting while they were gone. Often when the family was away, Siva felt abandoned, only to sleep and forget.

Laura left the house. Her mouth was shut as if it always was. She could've carried the attitude her situation wasn't fair at the same time the experiences brought some level of self-esteem.

Siva walked ahead, perked. Her smile showed she longed for these walks.

Laura came to where her car was parked, not far from the old, white barn, which stood upward to a worn, seemingly forward-slouching peak with the lengthy grass swaying below it in the breeze. Through the vigorous wind, Laura opened the driver's side, leaned in, and grabbed the tote from the passenger seat. In a restless childish demeanor, she left the carved box of her supply underneath as she made sure it was there.

Whether it'd been family or friends, or anyone else significant, her ties felt better with distance, yet this was getting to be a breaking point. There simply was no going back to what it all used to be.

Siva, curious and wagging her tail, wanted Laura to stay and not leave inside the car...

Oblivious to Siva, Laura came out of the car and shut the door. When she turned around and caught her breath, Siva stood on her hind legs with her paws outstretched just to touch her, reminding Laura of how everyone had tried with her and how innocent they were.

"No, Siva," Laura said and started to walk.

They began following the lane to the back, between the white and ocher machine shed and the two pale, weathered sheds soon to collapse, the old metal piled between, including the beloved tricycle, all rusted and bent now. Above in the trees, robins called out their always-so-abrupt, temporary dominion.

Impatient, Laura knew something was meant to continue with the friends she lost touch with. But what could she do?

The grove rustled its uppermost leaves through the wind above. The farm had been her only true home, was now something of her youth and her past, and wouldn't outlast the passing of time. It felt strangely unknown, like an old friend whose personality shifted to an unrecognizable state through illness and other misfortunes. Memories couldn't conjure up, as if something had occurred here and secretly removed them.

She wanted to remain with family and friends who'd together keep to their youth and not give up on what their hearts knew of each other. She only knew she wouldn't give up on the past, but maybe she had been for a long time.

Weeds and junk overwhelmed the area. She moved forward past the machine shed with a glance at an older barn, recently fallen after a storm. Just then, the snap of the electric fence at another shed alerted her attention further, like someone snapping their fingers. To her right was the burn pile, its dried twigs, branches, weeds, and trash ready to burn, only the weather was too hot.

Each step in her walk came with the persistent emotion of never having landed after long flights of responsibility to people, to school and work, to Jae, and here she was only in her early twenties. She had almost already done all she could.

Beneath the shade of the mulberry trees, ditch weed and other numerous plants, some taller than Laura, were enough to have to step down to clear a path at the thought of turning around to give up. Eventually, she came through the last of it where the trees met the field.

In and of the grove, a silence, aside from the surrounding breeze, felt new to her after years away from this spot. A person could feel softly blanketed by the trees from the outside world here.

But being alone was marring her wherever she went. She couldn't remember what the last time was, yet here again, it was the same stubborn boredom and curiosity with no end. Other times made her think she needed people to help her, but no one understood. The pain it brought was far from what life had been. Where would it go? It was taking her nowhere.

The dirt around her had a padded softness, patched with lengthy crabgrass, foxtail, and nettles. The breeze lifted her senses with the field she was about to walk, and Siva watching her obediently also urged Laura to come back home.

As if mindful of people around her, she took out a cigarette where she stood, and lit up. Smoking, she glanced down the path as if waiting for someone to arrive here, as if waiting for taxis or buses, and as if about to check her watch. There were times spent with Rebecca, times with anyone, and the last of it given to her last relationship.

Laura, who was often so serious, sometimes had no visible admiration for people. As for Jae, she cared about him through all of it, but he accused her of being useless and threatened her when she behaved as though she wasn't listening while he kept them up at night during his frustrations. Lack of money often angered him. Lack in her ability to be more supportive or even interested had set in after the first fight.

Laura had just gotten out of a hospital when they first met, disoriented with drug treatment he convinced her to discontinue. At the apartment, she was with someone she met by chance on the street, though they both came from good families.

Laura exhaled at the plants below her. She was nervous

at the thought of him, but it always meant he deserved to be happy. Once, snow melted from his worn-out sneakers at the door to their studio while he cooked, another sign of his urban upbringing amid the speed of everything carried from their youth to the point of knowing each other, colliding them into money trouble together, because it seemed an uphill battle for him and always a potential, downward spiral for her.

She only once cried about the obvious anger he had with anyone. It wasn't just her: he had a deeply-set fear of people on various outings, and he felt they were to fear him. An offensive disposition was uncalled for. He always insisted it was assertiveness, not aggression.

Another time, she suddenly cried at the computer as he watched TV because it was painful to understand how much he tried in face of what tormented him, and how well he represented himself despite his off-and-on aggression. God knew he was more proper than Laura. And she was supposed to try, too, with him, at the same time she wanted to escape and go it alone...

"Now what?" he said.

"Nothing. Don't worry about it, it's nothing."

"Won't you tell me?" With a heavy silence in the room, Laura was about to say she didn't know how to say it. "Oh, my god. The thing about you I can't stand, Laura, is that you don't talk!" He put his cigarette out. "Laura, do you know what I think of this ashtray?"

"What?"

He said nothing. Then he calmly poured the ashes out onto the trunk before violently hurling the metal hubcap ashtray almost at her head and denting the wall of the apartment.

Laura lost her patience with the surrounding grove. She always expected she'd instead meet someone who'd share the same respect she intended. She went to an old piece of farm machinery to sit, and Siva lifted her ears at whatever sound it could make. Maybe the old contraption would finally collapse.

December Seventh, 1978. What now was the significance of her birthday?

The cigarette was halfway done, and Laura put it out on the heel of her shoe. She stood calmly aware of her surroundings again and looked toward the house, wondering if her mother was thinking of her.

Whatever led her away from what life offered others was unfair mostly to her parents. She owed them the success of her life. There would've been times after she first got her driver's license for her to decide who to hang around, and it rarely ever was her family. Despite all signs of how much they cared for her, she wasn't noticing. She wanted to continue knowing them as the family they always had been, but in the grove alone, she feared the experiences wouldn't last. She needed a better relationship with them, yet so much had passed her by.

What was an oppressed look on her became one of disgust as she and the dog went into the bean field and the bright sunlight. She ran her hand over the leaves as she walked, believing her efforts with people had failed. She'd become quieter with everyone in whatever moment she couldn't reach out.

Laura stopped to look around.

Barn swallows flew closer to the grove, and past the fields to the southwest, an eagle or hawk--possibly an owl-- flew to a tree at a bend in the creek. After Laura had her camera turned on, she took a picture of herself looking to the side with the open field behind her. Her memory wasn't the best, but pictures provided a glimpse into certain memorable days. With a half-smile, she could admit to some happiness.

She walked further in long strides with her head down, to be done with this. The clumps of dirt made the path difficult, so she moved to a tire track row.

Several minutes later, she slowed in her walk and let the bag drop to her hand as she approached two large marijuana plants. Only two of the five she planted had grown. As they swayed in the wind, it seemed as if they'd been waiting for her, but then the leaves, through the wind's vigor, were forbidding her to even look at them. They had bunched together and stood high among the beans as something hidden only until a person came to them, in a place no one had reason to be.

Laura let her bag down finally. She took out her scissors and began collecting. She could just as easily pull at them instead of using scissors. Of course, she'd never done this before.

Siva smiled since this allowed her to rest for a moment. She sat buried in bean plants with her head sticking out, panting. Then, ears perked, mouth shut, she looked at something moving in the distance behind Laura. Possibly a deer. Laura turned to look.

Nothing.

Again, Siva smiled through quick breaths with her tongue out, and Laura passed a grin before returning to the plants.

It had been a long time with nothing to do, as was common for many people in Nebraska. Generally, people were preoccupied, but as if they'd obtained their personality through someone derived from the first. It probably meant they always sought inspiration, in a place often dry of it.

Driving through the cemetery one Friday, high as ever, a friend told Laura to go down a hill on a maintenance road. Laura had turned onto it only to see more graves, and once the car was turned around, the shift cable broke. With the car stuck in reverse, she drove backward down the hill, running over graves to get back on another road.

Laura smiled. Maybe she'd smoke with Meghan.

Besides reuniting with friends, not much else was important to Laura lately, other than an attempt at writing a novel. Already, she had ideas of making a living as a writer to provide a home for herself and someone close.

She believed few people would ever be closer to her than Jae. Even though they separated, she felt committed to him. She could admit he had had both a shady side with the friends he chose, and a more responsible side with other friends he chose, but both sides Laura either put all or no trust in, whether it assured her he was the only guy for her, or if he truly was as disappointed as he acted sometimes. In her young mind, he was the one for her, and for him to also see her this way had given them a sense of belonging to each other for life. Things didn't come together when the increasing challenge with money came between them. They could no longer live together if he'd continued fighting her about it, and he would've.

At this time, she had no one, and he didn't either. Laura pulled a few of the smaller portions and worked with haste to move on. After some light-hearted reflection on what seemed to be the answer to her writing and a final gust of wind, she was done. She tied the plastic bag and put it in her tote.

"You ready to go?" she said, as she got her bag over her shoulder, tired of it all. It wasn't fair to assume much of a person coming out of their formative years, and she was one to notice.

She started in another row of beans, ignoring the bag. Despite some of the doubts about the family, none of it bothered her as she walked. Everyone was easy to accept, and she had what she needed to remain alone as if everyone preferred it this way.

As she walked, she no longer realized she finally had what she'd been waiting all this time for. Of course, maybe it would help the writing or getting back with people again. But the sense of rejection was getting worse; she was often alone to her thoughts and worries. Being home at the farm, she could acknowledge this but never in her place as it was happening.

Then, she simply had what she came for. All to hear was the wind and her padded steps over the dirt, and of course, Siva walking ahead within the bean plants.

Laura soon approached her car and left the bag in the back seat. With her box, she came to the house, passed through the living room, and entered the kitchen. "Mom?" she called.

"I'm downstairs!"

"Okay," Laura replied.

Here she hesitated for a moment, not knowing her next move, then evaded her mom by going upstairs. The first room was missing a TV after one brother took off with it. Spiderwebs clung everywhere, and the floor's dust moved as she passed through to her old bedroom, though even with the warm air, this was all pleasant to her. Of course, she was alone, time got ahead, and just as it was for others, maybe it meant she needed people. With the pain Laura felt, she suspected she could do nothing to fix her back herself.

In private, she sat at a desk in her old bedroom and opened the box. Soon, the marijuana from her supply, the papers, and a small screwdriver were out in front of her. She could see for herself she had the impatient nerve of Jae running through her. So, she gathered her patience, and she couldn't help it: she had no one.

Without further hesitation, she prepared the paper with pinches of weed spread from end to end until rolling it. She wanted to talk but didn't know anything to speak of yet. In no time, she finished packing the joint, twisting the ends, and licking the gummed edges.

Laura then came out to the roof where the landing was. She didn't want to rush, so she stood watch and waited. The town at the horizon still had the little white church, and the church still had its services. Only the elderly people went each Sunday. Many things had happened in her life, and even the church could not remind her of it. However, she remembered her aunt playing the church's old piano, but nothing else came to memory. It was painfully vague.

She sat on the roof and began smoking, then stopped. She didn't want to waste any of the smoke but looked at the joint, wondering if she may already be feeling it. She waited, then held a few puffs and leaned back while the high set in. After everything settled, she calmly smoked until she was done.

A couple of sparrows began chirping as if they'd been watching her in silence, and Laura wanted to sit out for a minute. A sort of glow came to her, and it was happiness to be out on a warm afternoon when the high and the sunlight would last a while. The sounds satisfied her enough she even smiled. Everything was alive.

Laura stood and turned in a simple gesture and returned inside. With a push from her body, she managed to shut the stubborn door, then locked it. Silence in the room both welcomed and warned her, and she shifted to her side before standing straight, reminding herself of what just went down. At the desk, she packed up her box and soon passed through the first room before knowing it. Slowly, she made her way down the steps as her mom was preparing something to eat.

"You know you're welcome to eat with us," Renae said, as Laura entered the kitchen. "How was the walk?"

Laura readjusted, almost to saying she didn't know. "Good," she said, "I'll be right back."

When Laura left for the door, Renae asked, "What's in the box?"

"Photographs." Laura went to her car and hid the box under the seat. "Fuck," she whispered. The birds still went about their routine, and Siva was elsewhere. Laura returned to the kitchen in speed. "I have to get clothes from upstairs."

"Okay," her mother said, giving a questioning look. Laura couldn't ignore this when she turned to go upstairs. It seemed reckless to smoke here at home with her mother around if her mother even knew.

In her bedroom at the dresser, Laura found herself absorbing the moment and recalling someone from her past again. She couldn't focus on the task but knew what clothes to bring. It'd be difficult to talk with her mom.

With a small pile of clothes, Laura retreated into the bathroom at the bottom of the stairs. She washed the smell off her hands, then brushed her teeth and put lotion on her face and hands as if dreaming it. Her mother was like a stranger in the house. Maybe it was Laura who was a stranger. She couldn't decide, but the thought was troublesome.

Laura placed the pile of clothes in the living room so they would be ready to take out. Then, she breathlessly sat at the table with her mom. Everything had a stigma, but the television was off.

"So. What's up?" Renae asked. "How was the walk?"

They shared a glance. "Well, it was just a walk," Laura said, shaking her head, taking a deep breath. The moment slowed to a standstill. She said, "I'm all right. I don't know. I keep thinking it's too difficult to talk to people. People always just bullshit each other." She tried smiling despite this, to show she wouldn't always give in to doubt. But then she was serious. She said, "It just doesn't mean anything."

"You know, if you keep that perspective, that's all you might see in people."

Laura thought. To open up about this side of herself and say it—would mean she'd have to stand by it this moment? "I keep questioning things because most people are wrong," she said.

"No, Laura, you will find people have good intentions."

Laura felt distant. She said, "Sometimes, I just think it's too easy to forget everything." Now it appeared Laura was giving up, though she was trying to say something. "I think people don't have as strong of a purpose as your generation because we're distracted by the most insignificant things. I mean, most people don't care enough about anybody; they'd rather just watch people BS each other on TV."

"Well—"

"Too much of real life passes. There are things we should know."

"Like what?"

Laura's eyes were glazed and emotional. She couldn't get herself to say anything. "I don't know. We don't know who we are? Things just pass us by like all we do is die?"

"Do you think this often?" This was new to Renae, and she was concerned.

"It's just something I *know*." Laura could see the change in Renae. She was about to talk slower, and this was wrong to talk about. Nothing was right to talk about.

"I believe other things will help change your mind. A more positive attitude *will* help you." Renae was happy to say this because it could finally bring Laura closer to her. She always pushed people away.

"I try," Laura said, shaking her head.

Renae got up to check the dinner at the stove. "Look at me, I've lived this long, and nothing's bothered me. You'll be okay."

Laura hesitated. "Are you going to Omaha this next weekend?" she asked. Laura lost her reach, saying this, or she lost her reach by perceiving her own mother as an acquaintance who had just left the table.

Renae remained cheerful. "You know me; I'm always going to Omaha. Maybe I *will*. Oh, what's Saturday?"

"Saturday's good, we can walk downtown." Laura focused on the time on the microwave: four-fifteen. She nervously stood. "I better go now." She was almost too quiet to hear.

"Are you sure?"

"Yeah." Laura went to the living room and remembered her pile of clothes, and Renae followed her to the door. Laura hesitated. "Sorry I can't give you a hug," she said quietly.

"Oh, it's okay. I'm fine. You know we'll miss you at dinner." The room was quiet. They almost interrupted each other. "Come back any time you feel like it. Okay?"

Laura refocused. "Yeah. I will." Laura hadn't looked at

her mother for a while. She sometimes had trouble with her hair, but it had a nice cut now.

"Let me get the door for you." Renae had a mind to say she cared about Laura then, but it was not what people did, and she was unsure of herself about how Laura would consider it. They said their good-byes.

Laura entered the sunlight again, to the freedom of being on her own. Or what sunlight suggested of it.

After situating the folded clothes over the marijuana, Laura finally entered the car and sat still as she held the wheel. The bar was downtown, and she wouldn't be out late because it'd be even more people with nothing in common but living in Nebraska, which would mean less to them than it did to her, or something far different. Or perhaps it was far different and much less than what she knew. People were annoyed with each other. Actually, as of late, they often said without saying, "You're not the best friend, so I'll ignore you from now on because I deserve more. Besides, life is short, and I don't want to spend my time with you if I can find someone better."

Laura started the car and drove down the lane. She imagined herself looking like someone violently shook her by her shoulders.

Through the kitchen window, Renae watched Laura leave. She sipped her coffee as Laura was almost out of view. She wanted to have said something more, anything to make Laura happy or proud.

Renae didn't know what to think of Laura smoking. There was always doubt about drugs, but Laura was doing well; she'd had a job for a while already. Renae put her cup down.

Laura slowed and stopped at the intersection, gazing one direction much longer than the next, hunched forward with both hands on the wheel. She could almost cry, knowing how nervous she normally felt about moving on, away from what used to be. Whatever the destination, in her car she was by herself. She'd give her passenger seat to Jae any day, not to be alone.

Soon, she rolled the window down to listen to traffic of the highway. Over a hill on the meandering part, and past an open expanse of fields, she later merged onto another highway, heading southeast. By now, the high enveloped her within the heavy heat of her car and the light of day.

As an added sense of defeat, she realized the missed opportunities to understand more of herself and what her family actually meant to her. As an adult, growing apart was the only thing ahead, just as it was an ongoing thing of her past, and everything she could feel with anyone now. Nothing stopped the necessity of the job and living on her own. But maybe it was just another distraction… She wasn't ready for this to be a long time.

Back home, Renae still stood at the window, sobbing. Maybe Laura was right, but to understand her through this was difficult. Renae didn't know about these things. For Renae not to know what it was, it seemed to be something she needed to. Questioning where Laura was going and what she would do, she regained herself, but she feared she never had anything important to say to people. And she couldn't think like Laura, as if somehow she wasn't the influence Laura needed. At least Laura was growing up, but her departure this afternoon further marked a time she wouldn't remain the kid she once was.

Laura checked her speed as she passed through a small town. She'd be in trouble if she were pulled over with the marijuana in the backseat. Here, this place had no other purpose for outsiders than to fill up with fuel; she didn't just think of pollution, but realized it when she passed the only living, breathing icon on this road: none other than a gas station and its corporate branding of the whole town.

She sped up as she left. Oncoming cars roared by with a following silence, and her high quieted everything. Passing a marshland along the highway, Laura slowed for another town and started to speed up on her way out before noticing she'd been through Hooper. She then drove the divided highway, and the sound of cars continued. In a daze with the noise of wind and traffic outside, she knew nothing.

* * *

Resolve

The sun glared heavily down on weathered pavement and rooftops, all the yards were cut, and the folks of Fremont kept themselves hidden in neatly--though sometimes radically--painted homes. Despite no one in sight, their presence surrounded him. This wasn't a place he wanted to find himself.

Michael Brown was moving into another apartment leased by his cousin, a dreadful ocher duplex with a worn roof, likely built in the seventies as these other homes were. This street may have been borne through much happier times, but it was shameful to live with these people, who drank and watched television in some crude, self-serving ritual of giving up on anything else when they were overworked or couldn't find a job. He got a feel for the place a week ago when he signed the lease and paid, though nothing about this duplex would remind him of better days. Still, Michael was determined to live on his own again.

Time in the hospital brought him to undermine his original trust in people, though he'd never stop being as kind as he always had been. People had the wrong ideas, and he thought they got it from the media, from attitudes thrown around haphazardly at times.

He was born on the Ninth of February, 1980, Aquarius.

Fremont wasn't a place he cared about anymore since his time in Chicago. Everyone here was in a rut. The town, and others like it, were sometimes pure only in their neglect. He went with a half-tuition scholarship and made friends, but after dropping out, he was no longer in touch with even the closest ones. After Chicago, he moved back with his parents until attempting to live on his own in a place closer to home. Of course, it didn't work out as expected; his illness had resurfaced quite dramatically, here in this town.

Michael was unloading the truck, and his brother, Kevin, was helping. Michael remained hopeful but often expected more out of life than whatever time spent at an old, forgotten apartment in Nebraska could offer. He could admit he missed West Point and everything he couldn't turn back to. His family had abruptly moved to Fremont, and it wasn't the same. Luckily, Dan's mom moved to Fremont, and Dan was also in town.

Both right and wrong attitudes about people made him indecisive, and either attitude distracted him from recognizing deeper significance in himself. It didn't prolong his relationships, because he came across as having mixed ideas, which confused people. It was increasingly difficult for him to tell if anyone thought much of him anymore, so he was starting to doubt what all had been. Often, this made him vague and lacking confidence.

Having hauled in most of the furniture, he sat and looked around the living room, deeper in the summer heat, as if even the presence of a furnace was enough to smother him with dark carpet, blank walls, and stark light. His furniture had been carried along from place to place.

He scratched his arm at the thought of heat within the walls, then glanced nervously around the room before staring out the window until his head hurt. A little over six months ago was when he attempted suicide with pills, and the apartment's unknown, suspected past of pornos, parties, and whatever else could only remind him: the more he tried to make things work out at the last place, the more his attention went with everything spinning around him. People were moving out, and he still couldn't find a job toward the end of it. Upon release from the hospital, everything returned to normal.

At times, he stared at something and hallucinated, and his responses had not been normal with people, being overly self-aware much of the time. It was crazy, looking back. His focus was long, in response to noises and loud voices. While he tried ignoring it, he concentrated too hard, cycling the illness, and he often backtracked his thoughts and changed their meaning. He would break from it only to have it follow him wherever he went, anxiously adjusting himself. There was less opportunity for people to pull him away from it since he gave no mention of it. Sometimes he had the idea he was reasonable enough that the rest of it would pass. He simply wanted to be on his own.

Michael quickly developed a poor response to television during this sickness and wondered if somehow it pertained to him. Since he was used to watching television regularly, he'd watch even though his thoughts would follow along rapidly, from one point to another as if queued at times he was left alone, all the while losing any sense of privacy. TV was the craziest thing.

He had given up on his medication. Following statements with the doctor, Michael didn't know his diagnosis, but the medication treated psychosis, a term he also wasn't familiar with. He couldn't remember if they'd even been addressed, but enough of what he said leveled off before they let him go. He spoke clearly and had a way of defending choices made, and if he could ever grasp the better side of himself socially, he'd be a good actor: he spoke well, used common-sense gestures, and made appropriate eye contact, while in tune with his day-to-day responsibilities, even if just seemingly.

Although the diagnosis may have been worse than he knew, he'd settled to the fact he'd never threaten people or even try to cause harm, yet the idea behind any questionable possibility with an illness was enough to make it difficult to be at ease with, especially when he believed other people were causing his problems.

He had wondered his way into believing he could have more interaction with the world, and nothing was certain. Everything became an obstacle, and no one would show themselves to him. He often worried about worse things happening, even if they weren't. Eventually, he decided if he were anyone else, someone would've helped. Already, he had nearly forgotten all of it, except now the memory came back for a minute. It was the entirety of his old fears, in summary.

Though mostly everything was hauled in from the truck, Michael swiftly left out the back to bring in the last of it since he almost forgot what to do in all this thinking. He was well-journeyed, but this duplex severely marked an end to it all. They were times he didn't want to let go of.

Outside, a tree blanketed him from the sky and the sun. Having been immersed in the heat inside, out here he had some clean air, cooler to breathe in August. He'd have to go outside more often.

During the last few years, he drank some of the time. He and his friends drank all through high school. It felt lazier and unmotivated, but over time, he didn't notice the difference from one sense to another.

For the past few months, he was used to sleeping late but expected to work somewhere early in the day at a place nearby. The bonus would be less smoking since he'd had more cigarettes in the past six months than he thought he could handle. An interview was scheduled for the next day, which was a perfect Monday for ups and downs.

After bringing in the last of the stuff, Michael returned

out the back to smoke again. He sat on the step at the door and began to adjust his pants so his ankles wouldn't show so much.

Among his troubles, probation committed him to the town for procuring alcohol, despite his innocence. The idea of staying here for a year swayed his attention at the little stuff in and around the place, and the smoke dizzied him miserably.

His brother came out of the back of the truck. Kevin was different, mostly keeping up with more responsible people. "You want me to take the truck over to Dan's?" he said. Kevin understood things were okay with Mike.

"You can stay here and talk while I have a smoke."

"What do you want to talk about?" Kevin said.

"Heck if I know." Michael looked at the ground and back at Kevin. "You're lucky you have your license," Michael said.

Kevin promptly responded. "Yeah. It sucks."

"Yup." Michael continued smoking toward the ground. Maybe even Kevin had issues with alcohol.

"It's not fair," Michael said. Confusion took hold because he thought of the drinking, but he didn't mean this. He almost forgot what he was thinking when he got back to the issue of the license. His eyebrows maddened as he looked at the ground in what was another opposition to himself. "Everyone should have their license suspended if I do," he said, smiling.

Kevin was blankly perceptive, knowing nothing from before. He was one of the kids moving out of the last place Michael rented before the suicide attempt. "Yep," he said. Michael was too smart to end up in the hospital, so Kevin stared in doubt for a moment. The idea was new to him. "How much are you guys paying for this apartment?"

"Two hundred each."

"Cool." They refocused, and Kevin gave a thumbs up. "I think I'm gonna go now. Gotta work tonight," he said.

"Okay." Michael would be alone, and he didn't know what would happen. He quickly took a drag from the cigarette and blew it out in the same speed, only to hide the next one, which would come when his brother turned to leave.

"All right. See ya, Mike." Kevin left.

Michael finished the cigarette and put it out on the pavement. At the harassing sound of trains to the near south, he retreated to the apartment. The phone was already hooked up, but he decided to check it...

After some brief hesitation, Michael spent slow work putting dishes away. Then, he started the coffeemaker with some decaf his mom bought him. While he sipped it with his back to the counter, he noticed once more the apple-and-leaves wallpaper he wanted to take down. It was sort of reminiscent of women in a kitchen, and Michael wouldn't want people thinking about it if they visited. In the end, it was more work to do than he should have to. Finally, he remembered the phone, called home and sat.

"Hey, Dad? It's just me...No. Michael. I'm checking to see if the phone was turned on. Okay, bye. Wait. Do you want the number?"

Michael gave the number. He and his father spoke rarely and informatively.

He hung up with the push of a button as he looked at it, then checked the dial tone. He had already given up on any patience with the kitchen, which might've outlasted all his time here when he put the dishes away.

From the table, he looked past the living room at the front door. For it being the afternoon, the room was dark with north windows and a solid door where tapestry hung over an opening with the appeal of a ghetto he stayed in with a friend and her brother in Las Vegas one summer. The TV wasn't set up yet, but the last experience was horrific enough he wasn't wanting to watch anything. Every attitude on television was a different scheme or some crude life-and-times of a money-driven stranger living close enough they were everywhere. Opinions were thrown into people's homes with enough influence to warp everyone toward a feeling of mindless comfort, or discomfort.

From the kitchen table, Michael watched out the window, still shaken by his time in the hospital and the commitment he had here as he anticipated someone passing by. All to see was pavement, lawns, trees, and other surrounding duplexes. Everything was lucid. This moment, he had never felt more away from people, and now his friends weren't calling—. He snapped out of his thoughts.

In the living room, Michael opened the thick front door to let in light and arranged the sofa diagonally, so it faced both the TV and the window. He'd have the distraction of cars passing by, but he preferred this arrangement anyhow. He sat to get a feel for the room by just looking at the blank TV. At the sight of this black void, Michael felt hesitant about his past.

He sped through high school with a handful of friends he'd often drink or get high with. Having been brought up one way or another had its limits, and maybe they were catching up to him.

Mike had a far different appearance when he wore glasses. For now, he wore contacts because he didn't want to be perceived as someone critical or deceiving, and this should be a time to get to know more people. With glasses, his eyes seemed to put people, or himself in the mirror, under ridicule. Without glasses, he could read in him a vaster understanding and less of a narrow, intellectual demeanor. He had grown, even matured, in looks if not in mind. If someone were to see him without glasses, he felt more at ease and less to be judged. Though for the summer he had his hair buzzed, it was growing out. He recently shaved and appeared undoubtedly what people remembered in all his tired and stressed postures, careless words, and lanky body language. He was a victim of circumstance no more deserving than the next person but somehow reaching higher ground than some, or such was Chicago, now just a thing of the past.

Nebraska often seemed mundane, and from this, his

expectations of the public were low. He didn't understand how he could be far behind most others when he planned for more to happen sooner. Money was always short, and the days were too quickly passing to feel he could ever catch up. Somehow, Chicago was easier than Nebraska.

To retreat from the heat upstairs, Michael made his way to the basement as if harassed to do so. He came to the sofa and laid down, to find himself staring at the ceiling. Briefly, he anticipated noises again. After holding still and calming himself, it seemed everything he would face in life would be in the same way he approached things now, from boredom and anxiety, only to stare at a ceiling without a job and with rent to pay.

Although he wasn't supposed to smoke in the house, he sat up and lit a cigarette, noticing the urge to smoke too soon. He needed a cup to ash in, so he paced up the stairs for one in the kitchen and returned to the sofa in the basement. Back in the hospital, patients mirrored his past behaviors. Their laughter, though, was their own.

This was his first attempt to live somewhere since before the hospital. At the time, he'd been smoking a pack a day and even smoked with the sickness until being hospitalized. Even after he'd taken all the pills and most of the alcohol, he thought he needed one more smoke.

At the Fremont hospital, after waking up, he pulled an IV from his arm to leave the room when no one was looking. He took the stairs up a floor, left down the east elevator, and went outside around the back to a truck, where he waited in his clothes. From inside the truck, he watched police cars arrive and was somehow convinced he still needed a way to die. He'd simply get to an apartment complex and wait all day before walking home to drink more alcohol, but they caught him when he returned outside and drove him to Omaha.

Some ash fell to the floor, and Michael wanted to forget the past. Someone began knocking loudly.

Whoever it was, they opened the back door and stepped in. Michael sat up straight, thinking it must've been the police, an intruder, or even his cousin to see him smoking inside.

"Michael?" Dan called, diffident, his back turned to the basement.

"Hey, I'm down here."

"Hey, you want a drink? I bought a six-pack."

"Sure." Dan came down the steps and handed Michael a bottle, with the energy to pace through the time here instead of feeling dead to it. They were often victims of boredom. "Thanks, Dan." Michael grinned as they would often mock each other.

Michael put his cigarette out. While the event was enough to take his thoughts from the worst of things, it was lazy. Day by day, this could be a routine. But it was great to see Dan for a change, who remained standing near the wall, opposite the pool table, as if Michael would be the one talking.

"Some kids in Omaha mutilated a cat with fireworks yesterday," Dan said.

Michael had to think. He said, "That's about as sick and wrong as it gets."

"Yeah, fucked up is what I thought." Dan was always posed as if either unsure of himself or sure of himself, though no one could tell what he knew.

"So, you're moving in *tomorrow*?" Michael said.

Dan fidgeted and looked around. "Yeah. This bedroom is mine, right?" He peeked into the basement bedroom.

Michael hesitated. "Yeah. Hey, you got any bud?"

"Nah. Not yet." Dan was checking out the closet.

They had nothing to do. Dan looked around some more, a little absentminded. Above on the street just outside the window, a car passed while they drank, and the following silence held them.

Michael was aware of himself and stopped smiling. "My grandparents are in the nursing home now," he finally said.

"Yeah?"

"Yep." Michael stood at the pool table opposite Dan. "How many things do you have to move in?"

"Uh, my computer's down," Dan said. Other than my bed and TV, not much. Also, my clothes...my bike. I don't know; I need a new bike chain."

"You should get the computer working so you can play games. Otherwise, it's going to be boring as hell in here." Michael shook his head. "This apartment? I'm not sure about."

Dan nodded.

Michael later added, "I should hook up some music." On the floor, Michael took a small AIWA sound system from a box and started wiring it together.

"I heard you were in the hospital. You really tried killing yourself?" Dan said.

"Yes." Michael hesitated with the wires.

"Why?"

"Everything was ridiculous. It was like dying was the only thing, and I couldn't find a way."

"Yeah? I didn't believe it when I heard it." Dan didn't want to see another episode happen. It would cause him to also worry.

Michael continued. "I couldn't sleep, and everything was too much," he said, making eye contact. "If you'd have been around, things would've been different. But still, I wouldn't have made any sense." He said this shaking his head. "Everyone was leaving, and I had to come up with the extra money, only no one was hiring.

Michael had Meghan's attitude, saying this in a way to move on without being overly affected. It didn't add up, though. Now Dan wondered if Michael just wanted the attention, as what was commonly believed. He couldn't see the connection between what had been and why he would want to kill himself. But for Michael to attempt it meant something was wrong. And for Michael to be in a mental hospital?

After starting the music, Michael set up a game of pool. It appeared he couldn't handle sitting down, unlike what Dan remembered of him. They were on the same side to bring this place up, or Dan perceived it this way initially. At least the music was good.

"Pills and alcohol don't work, though," Michael said, standing at the pool table.

"What was it like in the hospital?"

"Well...I was able to smoke in there. Just normal people. Some were in there for aggressive shit. Nebraska is just boring. You know?" Michael was discreet now.

"Geez."

"The doctor told me they'd have to keep me longer if I did it again, so I told him I'd just admit myself."

Michael took a swig of beer. He felt he was showing off like it was another accomplishment. He shrugged, knowing it wasn't a good time.

"Good," Dan said.

Michael took the word the wrong way, as he questioned himself. The pool table was ready. "You go." Michael's attitude lifted with the music.

Despite whatever confidence, Michael believed he'd return to the hospital, because even though things were relatively normal, the usual lack of confidence, the hesitation, and the habitual worry was severe. Nothing came to impress him in others, and if it did, it wouldn't change him, as determined as he was against most people's ways he was exposed to.

Mostly, he didn't want to believe he was vain.

He was reminding himself of the interview set up for the next morning. If the job failed, Dan would get a new roommate, and Michael would owe his cousin money. Drinking wasn't always the right thing, but in any situation with drugs and alcohol, no one was stopping them.

Michael rushed his beer. It was as though he couldn't see into real matters. Nothing here was remotely near to the reality of some people. At least the buzz calmed him enough to forget his troubles when his thoughts finally rested. To recover lost time, they played pool and talked some more.

CHAPTER 2

Compassion

L aura made her way east on Dodge. Driving among this
many people presented a challenge while coming down
from the high. The only solace was talk of the war on
the radio.

Cars passed until Laura caught up with the people ahead
and allowed herself to speed with them. She had the look of
someone between carrying the tradition and giving up on it.

At a stoplight, she ignored much of what was here at
Seventy-Second, a commercial district often bringing her into
Borders or Barnes & Noble, or Crossroads Mall. Again, traffic
was busy, and people were oblivious to each other...

She remembered a time walking across Dodge late at
night. It was difficult to breathe with the day's pollution
hovering at the bottom of a few hills, which made this area
something more of a concrete valley. She was certain it wasn't
just her smoking. The air had been unusually thick and fueled.

Earlier, she had given thought to her book.

She relaxed enough to gaze at the lights of the intersection,
then a pedestrian crossing Dodge. After the light abruptly
changed, she mindlessly drove through the intersection. The
overwhelming traffic posed itself as a part of the world

dominated by money as if it were a race where she had somehow been in the lead, and people were advancing to leave her behind. As she passed through a stretch of lights as they turned green, she wondered why society had to be the challenge it had been for her, not having time to catch up to everyone else.

The further Laura drove, the traffic on the opposite side got heavier as people went home from a long workday. She was between belonging to the town and still being an outsider. Within today's traffic, no one would notice either way, much like the public on the streets when she walked. Of course, anywhere away from home brought her the same estrangement. With a glance at the rear-view mirror and then at the road, she was ready to be downtown where she belonged.

A while later, she parked the car on the opposite side of the street to her apartment, then took the box, the tote, and her bag inside with a sigh of relief. She walked swiftly to catch the elevator while blowing hair out of her face. When she was in her apartment, she locked the door and let the marijuana out on the dining table. Eventually, she'd have it all in baggies in the freezer, but she still wasn't sure whether it was useless ditch.

As she left the apartment again, no one occupied the stairwell to give her the typical looks of a stranger, the kind of look as if to know what she had in her apartment. With every loud creak of the boards, it was on her mind.

To leave for downtown, on the other hand, was the original freedom she had known when first on her own, though she'd admit nothing was drastically changing lately. These days, she was too much of a kid, and as a kid, she had carried too much of an adult attitude. Most people perplexed her with their oblivious happiness.

Outside, she walked through a part of town remaining older than much of Omaha. After letting a car through at Howard, Laura continued her walk into The Old Market, a place of old buildings with shops. Laura could almost see herself meeting people here today, though she could never tell. Unless she were to make friends with someone, she wouldn't stay for much longer than a drink she'd craved all day.

Laura covered her mouth, yawned, and smiled when she came to the doorway, briefly browsed the flyers, and went in. As she stood and waited at the bar, she admired the woodwork, brick walls, and sparsely-lit areas until the bartender returned.

"Can I get you something?" The bartender had the smile of having laughed at something a moment ago.

Laura was hesitant. She said, "You know, I just live up the street and come here sometimes. Do you own the place?"

"Yes, I do, actually."

"It's nice," she said as she nodded. She heard her voice, and it sounded like something hurt. "But there should be more places like it in Omaha," she added with a new-found brightness in her eyes.

"I agree," he said, understanding she was one of those too often alone and left to her thoughts, but he nodded with a smile anyhow.

"Yeah," she replied. "I'll have a pineapple vodka." She then sat at the bar since it was empty.

A moment later, Laura found herself staring at her drink before she dug into her bag.

'It's just three dollars; don't worry about a tip,' he had said.

Laura gave him a five and insisted he keep the change. The man handed her the change anyhow, then acted as though he didn't hear her over the music when she said thanks.

Not much later, someone sat next to Laura. The instant they made eye contact, she knew it would be a welcome acquaintance; if she'd know him beyond this, he'd be someone to understand in the same light she knew at first glance. Maybe she gave her trust too quickly. Maybe it was the vodka. It was all in his eyes, not unlike when she first met Jae.

"I'm Laura," she said, much too aware of herself.

"Sup? I'm Marcel." He folded his hands. Marcel was handsomely young but older than her. "Is someone with you?" he asked.

"No." She shook her head.

"Okay." He looked down. Laura found it urgent for the bartender to come back and get Marcel a drink. The two bartenders were busy on one side of her, while on the other side was Marcel, who possibly wondered why he was even here. Maybe he hadn't been here before, and here it was white. He had some build on his body, was well-dressed, appearing to belong to a family strong in tradition with a broad knowledge of people, including the likes of her. She wasn't even looking at him, and these ideas were all new to her. This moment, Laura had to say something, but she was speechless at the thought of her thoughts.

Marcel leaned back and scratched the side of his neck. Here was Laura, looking around, clearly hesitating. For now, she leaned over her glass, glancing down at her drink and up at the mirror as if nervous or upset. She leaned back and gave him a glance with the slightest smile when he chose to stay seated with her. And he couldn't help but ask: "You mind if I sit here with you?"

Laura said, "No, I don't mind at all."

The bartender switched over from the music to the television because the local news was on, and it leveled the place to a typical early evening with fewer people. "Be right back," Marcel said as he stood and went for the restroom. Laura watched him head to the back, and a few people had taken notice of her when she glanced around. She returned to her drink and ate some ice.

A guy approached Laura and asked if anyone was sitting with her, though he must've known someone already had been. "Yes," she said, intimidated.

"You sure?"

"Yes, of course." She placed her bag on Marcel's seat. Then the guy went back to his table behind her. Too many white people were what they were.

Marcel, who could've been thinking of what to say, returned and ordered a beer. Laura was too eager to talk, so she watched the news show flooding out west. If it wasn't flooding in California, it was on fire. She wanted to say anything for Marcel not to leave.

"Little mixing going on," the guy from earlier said from his table.

Laura glanced at Marcel, then glared at the guy. She said, "You're number one, aren't you?"

The guy finished his beer and left without another word. Marcel had laughed first.

"Are you from North O?" she finally asked.

"I'm in Dundee. Actually, I'm from Chicago."

They were in a stare. They were here, the same place, no other time but now to know each other for the first time, if at all. "Some people," he said.

"I know," she said, posturing herself. Laura returned to her glass. She said, "They just think life is some competitive sport." She was motioning with her hand on the table. "As if life's only purpose is to win over some girl, prove their manhood, and ride off into the sunset, marking their territory before they die." She looked at Marcel. "So no one will think they're gay," she said, smiling. "So, I guess their lives are determined by how they go about all that," she added.

"You single?" he asked.

"You could say I am. Recently split." For whatever reason, it felt urgent to tell him how it'd been without the people she used to share time with. She could see into Marcel's apparent commitments, but he seemed he had enough curiosity to know her the same way she'd want to know him: they were different, and they knew different things, but they were the same. Also, he could end up disinterested and they wouldn't see each other again. But they had common ground for now.

"What have your relationships been like?"

Laura thought for a moment and half-smiled. Although it was bold of him to ask, he didn't mean it as if they'd be hitting the bed tonight. Then she was serious. "I was first with a guy who talked over me like he was more intelligent —I was convinced he was. He was just beyond me, a Pisces: moved like fluid, thought with emotion. And I guess they're all so far above us. I felt really stupid. He always gave me silent treatment. Then, I was afraid he'd been involved with someone the whole time, so I couldn't handle it." She thought for a moment. "Then I went back to school, quit school, and met a guy who I lived with for a while, but he was violent. I once needed stitches over some money thing." She adjusted herself again. "We never had enough money. All we did was drink and smoke." She contemplated her drink. "I cared a lot about those guys."

Marcel said, "I could tell you've been through some things. You shouldn't bother with guys like that." Laura said nothing but nodded. He said, "I have a kid," his face a glow.

"Oh. I got the impression you were single," she said.

"I am."

They continued drinking. "So, what's the job like?"

"I work as a CNA," he said, nodding. "It's good. Been a quiet year so far." It was as though he could say this to anyone. He was proud in the least to say he had good work and for her to know it if it'd only be her to appreciate it with him—right now.

"Good." She finished her drink and sat up out of a slouch.

"Would you like another one?" the bartender said.

"A beer this time," she said. "Thanks."

Laura hesitated over what to say to go further with Marcel when this could be the same moment she'd lose her chance. There wasn't anything wrong with him.

"I got high today," she said. Maybe this was wrong to

mention. She covered a slight smile. "I took it to the farm because I wanted to see what it would be like to talk to my mom."

"Ah. You shouldn't do that too often. I used to smoke, but with the job, you know—."

She got her beer over a napkin and paid. "Yeah." She didn't know how to say it. "I'm trying to write a book."

"What's it about?"

Laura had the same insecurity anyone seemed to have. After this chance encounter, he'd wonder about her. With the pace at home and at the hospital, he couldn't see this working out, but he wanted it to this time. Together, they had already shared...something.

She found it a challenge to describe the novel. "Well, it features two characters followed separately. Totally unrelated other than the two of them—at the end." This wasn't what she wanted to say.

"How far are you?"

She adjusted to not appear bored with him. "The concept came to me a few months ago, but I'm putting notes down for an outline."

"Good luck. Is there a moral to the story?" He seemed surprised but either brave or a coward. Whatever was vulnerable about him appealed to her because already she cared. Quickly, she decided he wasn't a coward, and he maybe saw himself to be in the world where being brave wasn't the thing. It could work out anyhow for people like them. Probably, he knew many people during his workday and everything else. He seemed deserving of a normal life because maybe he hadn't reached it yet. She was surprised to see this much in him already.

"It's like we're blindsided by a system that no longer functions, we don't see past money, and we no longer understand what matters."

He said, "I guess you could write that."

"How would you know?" she said and smiled.

"I have a pretty good judge of people. But it sounds ambitious." Moments later, he spoke calmly with a light buzz. "My parents separated, but I talk to my mom. She had a stroke."

"I'm sorry to hear that."

"Yeah. My brother's in jail, and I think that's what it was. Chicago can be high stress."

"Well, I'm not close with my parents, but I care about them." She dug into her bag. "Don't get the wrong idea. I'm not a chain smoker."

"Ah. Same here."

"You wanna try one of mine? They're natural."

"I've heard of those."

Maybe something was on his mind he couldn't talk about. He simply smiled, short of laughing.

"The smoke's good," he later said.

"There's a store around the corner that's got 'em."

"Uh, yeah," he said, "Was just thinking of that place."

Laura felt the alcohol. People were coming and going. Then, she felt her youthfulness, and she had more instances to glance at him. His kindness with her was the same kindness he'd have with his mom, and he'd go further if she wanted to.

Here and now, the two of them were together without speaking. Marcel was on his second beer, and they both watched the broadcast and its commercials while they smoked. The more she smiled, the more he could tell she liked him. There was something in his mother's tone when she said he'd meet someone, as though she already knew who it would be. He wanted to tell Laura this.

Laura said, "I study astrology."

He said, "I'm actually a Leo; it's my birthday tomorrow."

Her whole face brightened. "Really? Everyone's different because the planets are always in different places--that, and genetics. Happy birthday!" It was some shy confidence she had.

"Sure, thanks. What can you tell me about me?"

"Well, I read tarot. Do you want a reading?"

"Sure."

Laura put her beer aside and took out her deck of playing cards. While she shuffled them, she wanted to see the things he knew. It was a simple layout.

"Okay...Things may come easy for you. When they don't, you are content. You also seek change in relationships. Some things you want met aren't working for you, but you have good opportunity and luck coming from your speed with things."

They gave each other a glance. Then they stared back at the cards.

"The changes you want make you happy when they are reached, but you also feel good when you have time between things." She looked at him again. "Nothing overwhelms you." She returned to the cards. "You have emotional freedom from trusting things when everything becomes blocked or when there isn't anything you can do to change a situation."

"Sure."

"You approach people with some challenge, but that is part of why you want change in your relationships, as it is a cycle. See how it goes from these two cards to this one?"

"Yes. I see."

"You may be happy with your home. This card here is related to the whole overall reading." She pointed to the queen of diamonds. "All of these cards are interrelated."

"Good reading," he said.

"Have you ever had one done before?"

"Only if I ever felt like paying for one. A lot of people are into that in Chicago."

She said, "Yeah? This layout follows the I-Ching. With every reading I do, it usually tells something in common with me, so it's a reading for both of us."

"Cool. Ever think of doing it professionally?"

"Actually, I only know vague terms. Everyone wants to know about people involved who I can't see in it, so I'm not good enough yet."

"I think you're good."

"Thanks."

"Thank *you*."

Laura collected the cards and put the deck away, happy to have shared it because it could enlighten her as a matter of common sense. She drank again. Getting involved with people maybe took away time she had for her mom.

Throughout the following minutes, Laura knew there'd be no promise of meeting again in this place if he didn't come back. She took out her paper and pen and was writing her number down for him.

"Do you want my number?" he asked.

"Yes."

"555-7493."

"Okay." Then, she split the paper and gave him the half with hers. She looked at him and took her beer back, drinking again.

They met another break in the conversation as they focused on the television, drinking. Cars passed slowly outside, and people still came and went as their feet creaked the boards of the old floor. Nightly, people came here to get away from the heat. Though everyone seemed to be talking, the place had no echo.

Marcel could see something prevented Laura from talking more. She seemed to have some adverse private reality--probably had a few friends. "I've enjoyed meeting you," he said.

"Yeah. I'm glad we met." She seemed shaky.

He said, "Will I see you here often, or do you want to hang out?"

"I'm not here often, so we should do something," Laura

said. She wondered if life was easy or hard for him. She wanted to know life could be easy.

"Okay."

She was quiet when she said, "We should smoke sometime. You'll like my place." Again, she was nervous.

"Well, do you want to go somewhere and eat when we're finished?"

"Sure, I guess," she said. "There's this great Arab place down the street."

✳ ✳ ✳

Inspiration

Dan and Michael had already quit playing pool after a couple of rounds. It was obvious Michael didn't know the rules. With nothing in mind but getting some herb, they listened to music. They shared a lighter, to smoke so they wouldn't have to say anything. It would ruin the buzz, whatever it was.

Michael was easy to respect. Never in his life would he fight with someone, yet people never sympathized with him at even his lowest of times. While he wanted a closer connection to people, this apartment could isolate him.

Time spent without marijuana was often restless. Even though they were drunk and had their smokes, it was never enough. He and Dan got high since their freshman year in high school, and there was no stopping it.

"Maybe Rick can hook us up?" Michael said.

"'Hick Rick' or 'Rico Rick?'"

"Rico."

"Yeah, maybe. Where's your phone?" Dan would've preferred to do nothing.

"Hold on, I've got the portable upstairs."

"Uh. I'm gonna smoke the rest of this outside," Dan said.

Moments later, Dan returned downstairs, and the music was off. "RJ. It's Dan. You got any? We need a quarter and a dime... Yeah...Okay, bye."

"So, he's coming over?"

"Yeah; I don't know. He might smoke with us."

"Isn't that funny how he goes by 'RJ?' Like 'Our J?' 'Oh, RJ. Where's our j, RJ?" They started laughing.

"You know what Meghan's doing lately?"

"Don't know. You could try her cell phone."

Michael took the phone and saw himself swaying from one foot to the other. This was great, drinking, getting high, to be here a while, and have it last. People would come over; they'd always have weed. Michael dialed the number and went up to the kitchen. The last time he saw her, they drove around West Point on the country roads, drinking. The phone picked up.

"Hello?"

"Hey, Meghan. It's Mike."

"Dude, what's up?" Meghan was somewhere in West Point. Michael had said he hadn't heard from her in a while. "Yeah. Hey, I don't know your number," she said. "Okay. I'll try to remember that." After a moment, "So have you fallen off the face of the Earth?" she asked with cheer. "You tried to, huh?" Meghan was somewhat ignoring him. "Well, then for sure we gotta hang out," she said. They were buddies and somehow still with younger years after having met in sixth grade. She was coming up a stairway to an apartment downtown where a group waited for her. *I'm moving into an apartment with Dan here.* "Yeah, that's what I heard. Dude, I've gotta go. I'll call you sometime if I remember your number." She hung up and turned her phone off, then knocked. Roger opened the door, and two other guys were inside, sitting on a sofa.

"Hey, chicky," Roger greeted with a grin.

Roger shut the door behind her as she walked into the middle of the group and turned. "Do you know how much it *reeks* in here?" she directed at Roger, smiling. They all laughed except Meghan. "It's all in the hall!" she said louder. "Did I miss out?" Her humor ran deep.

Jon got out the bong from behind the sofa. Slowly, he said, "You're just in time. We were about to smoke again."

"Dude! Give me that." Meghan smirked and swung her hair back as she took the bong and sat in Roger's chair. Roger sat next to her on the floor. "I've got this one," she said, grinning.

She lit the bowl and filled the chamber with smoke. Inhaling, she pulled the bowl out and cleared the pipe. Then coughing deeply, loudly, and wetly, she let go of the smoke.

"You'll go stupid doing it like that, Meghan," Roger said. He was once in a car wreck with Meghan and Ron in the backseat and Michael in front. It was far out of town on a freezing night, and they'd been drinking. As Roger was looking for tapes on the floor, the car rode into the ditch at about forty-five miles-per-hour, into the opposite side of a culvert, throwing them all forward from their seats. Two large webs were on the windshield where Michael and Roger were thrown, and the car was halfway up the ditch on one side. They climbed out and walked in the January cold to a utility shed where a man was working. Otherwise, they'd have had to walk much further. Michael passed out and later came to on a stretcher after the ambulance arrived. A nurse dug glass out of his forehead for two hours at the hospital while another stitched Roger's tongue. They were all in high school at the time. Michael was sixteen. The reason they left the highway for the backroads was because Michael had to pee. He was always peeing. On the highway, they would've all died.

Roger glanced at Meghan for a moment with this memory.

"No, dude," she said. "I'll only get higher this way. You've done it before, shit." Meghan always had to test the waters herself, and she was lucky.

For a brief time, he and Meghan were seeing each

other and separated as friends. He was recalling the time and following her cues. "Whatever," he said.

Almost forgetting, she said, "Guess who I was talking to."

"Who?" Roger said.

"Michael."

"No shit?"

"Fucked up!" She was now jovial.

"I heard that dude was in the hospital."

"Yeah, dude; that's what I heard." She passed the bong and lighter to Jon.

"Did he really try killing himself?"

"Yeah, dude. I bet he would try something like that." She shook her head.

"Maybe he was crying." At this, they laughed.

"Oh, what the hell," she said. In her mind, things were bound to return to normal.

The other guys both coughed, and it went back to Roger. He held his in before blowing it all out and adding to whatever room buzz they could get.

The room had nothing more than roughly used furniture and a television with some exposed game and movie disks. Instead of being lived in, the place appeared somewhat ready to move out of. The windows had no curtains up, but it was still darker, facing east. Also, an old coffee table was centered in the group with Meghan's bag and an ashtray full of cigarette butts.

They continued smoking until the bowl was done. Moments later, Meghan was loading it once more from her supply. The mood had leveled off, and the group was greatly subdued. Soon, she was ready for her next hit but moved much slower, as if in a cloud with no worries, not even of herself. From everyone else's perspective, a quiet surrounded Meghan and filled the room as she passed the bong. She wasn't doing anything to further habituate an attitude.

"Woah, Roger, I'm so high," she said as she looked from the ceiling to the group and leaned back. Roger grabbed a chair from the retro dining table. He absentmindedly started some music with a remote, and the abrupt sound was a harsh enough change to the room, Meghan was stunned. She held to the armrests and went swimming for something to say. Everyone was sitting still when Meghan said something to Roger. She then repeated herself over the music: "Are you high?"

"Yeah, Meghan. Totally baked," he said slowly under the music. As they were still doing things they were determined to do in high school, they were under the impression everything would remain the same for them. They'd always be getting together and driving around.

She looked at Jon and the other guy, who both gave her the thumbs up and a smile. They'd share a clumsy demeanor if they went outside at this time, the energy anchored them to the apartment, they had no plans to leave yet, and their priorities were straight, as they had none.

Meghan was staring at the blank TV.

"Oh, you wouldn't believe what happened to me today," she continued.

"What?" Roger said.

Her high kept her leaned back, and she almost forgot what she was remembering... "I *ran* into a parked car on *Main*, and some *people* at the *bank* watched me just *sit there* before I made a run for it. I was drinking a beer."

"No shit?" Roger said.

"No shit!" she said, laughing. Jon laughed while the other guy smiled.

"That's fucked up."

"You know I wasn't laughing, though," she said. "I thought for sure a cop saw me."

"Wow." Roger pictured it and smiled.

Meghan laughed with a full grin, reminded of when she

cussed as she drove off. At certain times alone, she didn't have the same humor, but a day never ended without laughter for Meghan.

They waited for a moment.

"What have you all been doing today?" Meghan asked.

Roger shook his head, and the question nearly passed him. "Just cruising."

"Man, this town is so fucking boring," she said to the group.

"And getting high."

"Yeah, dude."

"Guess what," Roger said.

"What?" It appeared she was sick of hearing 'guess what' time after time.

"We've got enough 'shrooms here for all of us."

"No shit?" She had the urgency of stealing something, with a narrow window of getting caught. "Get them out!"

Roger then went to the freezer and grabbed a plastic bag with equal parts stems and caps, saying, "You've gotta pay your share, though," and he put them out onto a plate and carried it carefully as if it were baptismal water to the coffee table.

"Should we wait?" Jon asked.

"Man, we'll take 'em now and go up to Wilderness after they, you know, take effect." They each picked out their share.

"Stoned and trippin'," Meghan said, smiling. "Gotta love that."

CHAPTER 3

Release

Marcel and Laura sat under the shade of trees at a table outside the small Arab restaurant. The place was at the edge of The Old Market, near slow traffic. People randomly were in and out of buildings and walking the sidewalks, quiet with each other just as any other day for them here.

"You should do a reading on yourself," he said. "I might learn more about you."

"It's nothing special," she replied, "but I'll read one for you." Laura shuffled the cards. Nothing of interest came to her, but she wanted it to translate well for him. Immediately, the queen of clubs lay in the middle as she started to lay the cards down. After it was down, she noticed how complicated it would be.

"It looks like I'm exploring things. It's a spiritual card, and I am cautious with people or think twice...I continue to question things with this card here. The ace matches with this row, and I don't know what that means other than a healthy outlook. I have grounding from not being misleading, so it's saying something about my honesty." She looked at the jack of hearts. "This card starts a line with these other two, and it means I like the world around me."

"And these two cards?" as he pointed.

"These two mean I have strong spirituality, though I would differ with that. But this other card means that what I want from whatever relationship--friend or family--has to matter spiritually."

"I get some of that impression. Not bad," he said, somewhat awestruck.

"Usually, it tells me things I already know, but it's interrelated in a way I wouldn't otherwise know by myself." She put her cards away again. "I'm using it for my book, but I'm afraid it's going to be a big mess. I keep worrying it'll be too many notes."

He could tell. Her people, at the same time they were everything to her, they'd have maintained only common ground without much going beyond it. "What's it called?" he said.

"'City Limits', I think."

At this, Marcel didn't want to share the fact he was in a homeless shelter after school, but it was on his mind. She wouldn't understand, and it'd only disturb her if she was looking for someone secure. "I think you'll do well," he said.

"Here." Laura handed Marcel one of her cigarettes. "I hope I can average about twenty pages a day once I start writing and be done after a few months."

"You'll make it." As he wanted to stand his ground in the conversation, Marcel sat to gain his luck in charm, inviting more to the conversation. He had assumed less of the people in town, sometimes getting needlessly harassed. "You said something about a farm earlier?"

"Yeah." She shifted. "I grew up about an hour away. I can't remember all of it--you know, there are bits and pieces, funny memories a person always remembers--it's just when I'm with my family, I'm happy, but it doesn't show. These days, I hate being alone." She shook her head.

"Well, I lived in a part of the city kinda like a small town where people in the area knew each other. But you quickly learn people don't have time for games out there. Here, it's different."

"Did you go to church?"

"Yes," he said, nodding. "We had a church. Up north."

"So did I, but I didn't believe in God, at the time. Now with tarot, I wonder."

"Oh," he said. "You mentioned earlier you didn't have a close relationship with your mom and dad?" He smoked.

"Well, it's mostly my mom who I talk to anymore."

"Same with me," he said as if he could chuckle. They both wanted to believe they had a lot in common.

The alcohol no longer affected them. Their food arrived. "This is so good," Marcel said, remembering food at the shelter.

"Yeah? I can't remember if this is what I ordered the last time."

There were instances when they made eye contact, but they didn't talk much throughout most of the dinner. No one was aware of this new pair of friends...

Laura soon just wanted to be done, to drive around with him and talk. She had eaten somewhat quickly, and he tried to keep up while they both wanted badly to say something.

Afterward, she said, "You wanna get high and drive around?"

He couldn't decide. But following her lead, he gave in with a grin. "I've got plenty of time. But I gotta tell you, I usually avoid that stuff."

After paying, they walked up the sidewalk toward her apartment. It was a distance. People looked at her with him more than they would've looked at either of them alone. It brought her to think she deserved to open up more, faced with this opposition. "I like you," she said. "Right now, I only have one friend at the building. No one has been around for months, and it's messing with me quite a bit."

"Thanks." He hardly ever had an easy mind to the whites in public. He didn't like their influence because he believed himself to be better in some regard. He accepted Laura more than he accepted many people at first. Sharing time with her helped, but she was maybe the one needing someone this time...

They had arrived at her loft. When they came into the apartment, he said, "You have a lot of space."

"Yeah, but I wish I could afford furniture of my own. Most of it's all hand-me-down." She was walking further in before she turned to him. "I've just gotta get the stuff, and we'll smoke."

"Sure." He came into the main room where the marijuana was spread out on the table. "Oh, God. Laura?"

"Yeah, don't tell anyone," she said, as she got her supply from the tote. Laura was surrounded by a haze of west sunlight coming through the windows behind her. "We can go upstairs to do this."

He stared. "I think you want to get rid of this, it's no good for you," he said.

"Okay. Well, it might be ditch anyway."

"Yeah, is there anywhere we can toss it?"

"There's a trash chute right out the door."

"Then it's as good as gone." He said, "Legally, it's not worth the risks. Let's bag it like garbage and toss it."

Laura handed Marcel a black bag from the pantry, understanding he wasn't turning her in, which was good. She had almost forgotten all about it. "I grew it in a field, so it's probably ditch."

He said, "I heard they poison fields, and marijuana absorbs toxins in the air. This is no good anyway; it's just too much...Wait. These are all just leaves, Laura, where are the buds?"

"I just got the leaves. That's what people smoke, right?"

"Actually, no." They both laughed.

They finished bagging it, and he tossed it down the chute in the hall, making sure no one saw.

Inside again, he looked around and followed her lead. Upstairs overlooking the kitchen and main room was an old desk with a bare top except for an old, rusted doorknob fixture, its black-enamel knob leaning into her book collection. He wondered, was she working further with magic? She sat at it with her box open. Marcel was slightly impressed, yet welcome, introductions aside. Admittedly, he was also looking for someone secure. He sat and felt his youth as he held his hands together and covered his mouth, now suspicious of her use of marijuana even though he had smoked before. "Is it just you here?" he asked.

"Yeah. I'll be here a while, but there's just no saving money now that I don't have a roommate. Jae had to go; he never paid rent at the studio. He and I fought quite a bit."

Marcel sat up. "You're lucky to be here." he said.

After loading the bowl of her pipe, she gave it to Marcel with a lighter. "You'll like this, it's gotten me through the week."

Marcel sparked the bowl and inhaled as his cheeks sucked inward and his eyebrows frustrated. It went back and forth until they were easing into a high. To Laura, it was as though he had been there at this spot before, and they shared each other's company in silence, a little unsure of themselves.

He said, "Doesn't it make the day feel longer?"

"Yeah," she said. They quietly laughed together.

He then smiled and appeared to have no tension as if he was present in a dream she was having. With the sunlight behind him, he was some side of heaven never shown, as if it were touching down for a moment. She was almost convinced it was real...

She paused to recall what they were saying. She had smoked with bad feelings before, and it only amplified her sensitivity to worse things... Time offered little opportunity to admire him as though he were a dream. "We're good?" she asked.

"Very."

She wanted to hug him then but glanced away and decided to lead him down the stairs. In silence, they left out the door, and she locked up.

In the hall, Marcel said he was glad he met her. She couldn't help but smile, but then she turned back to double-check the locks.

He could tell she was one to cry; it could be anything. "We should drive then," she said, smiling.

And she had the happiness of anyone. "Yeah. Okay, Laura," he said.

They crossed the street to her car and got in. As they sat for a moment, she looked at the mirrors and ignored the feeling she might've forgotten something. It felt right being in the car to go anywhere, so she paused for a deep breath. "Where should we go?" she asked. She was reminded of Jae, how things fell apart fast.

"I don't know," Marcel said, "I don't mind."

They buckled up. "Well, we won't get lost."

They were slowly leaving this area, then southbound on Thirteenth. "Down this road is the zoo on the, um, east side," she said. "We'll turn on Martha and take Interstate."

It was a bright early evening. The post office was like some folk-art canvas with animated people and trucks as she drove past, like something fit for a post card. She had her window open, and he was opening his.

"I like the sound of cars as they go by," she said. "Ever since the first time." It was a relief saying this and finally friending someone after this many months.

"You were high?"

"I think I was coming down," she said, nodding. He

appeared to be well ahead of her as an adult. Maybe in a few years, she'd catch up, despite the usual doubt. She came to a stoplight, then continued with traffic picking up speed to her side.

"You're not afraid of driving when you're high?"

"I like almost anything high," she said, glancing at him. "Except public gatherings."

Watching the road, he asked: "So, you loved those guys?"

"I don't think I know what love is really like," she managed to say with a shrug and a glance at him.

"I don't either." He sat back and wanted her to accept him in the same situation. They were both young.

"It's too complicated," she said. "I'm mostly happy."

"Same," he said.

Again, they were speechless. They reached the interstate, and Laura sped up to merge. Several cars loudly passed them. "You afraid of my driving?" she said as she looked at him.

"No." They both stared ahead.

"Do you know where the malls are?" she asked.

"I know a few."

"We'll go by one of them," she said.

After several minutes, Laura felt aware they hadn't been talking. He probably knew people to be more talkative. The lanes ahead were expansive and lit by sun. Westbound, as air blew through the open windows, a Jeep swerved in front of them without signaling, and a rush went through Laura's body.

Laura shut her window, Marcel shut his, and she turned the AC on. This would be a time to talk.

"You got any pets?" she asked.

"Nah," he said, shaking his head. "Not right now. You?"

"Well, we have Siva, our farm dog, but the apartment only allows cats." Laura readjusted.

"Siva's an interesting name."

"You know, I've got a lot of back pain, actually."

"I could show you a few stretches for your back sometime," he said.

"Oh, I don't know; I just have a mind that works at raising issues as much as trying to fix it. That, or dwelling on it until I forget. Even the little things."

"It's that weed, tellin' you." He hoped she'd understand eventually. "Back to pets. What was your first pet's name?" he said.

"Our first dog? You're going to think what the fuck; I shouldn't mention it."

"It's okay."

She hesitated. "We named him after the raccoons on the farm. He was a dalmatian we called Coon."

"Coon? Haha!"

Laura blushed. "I was playing upstairs one day, and I heard a gunshot. I knew instantly Dad shot him because Coon cried out before another shot. I was bawling. I remember now, I didn't talk with Dad much after that. I never knew the reason, to be honest." She was in a daze.

"Why'd he get shot?"

"Coon went after the last of the chickens."

"Wow. I can only imagine."

"You might think this is weird, but growing up, I always thought I'd be someone to help bridge the gap between black and white," Laura said. "I was crazy."

Much later, they were still subdued. "That's the mall. If you come this way, you just turn down there to get to it," she said. For whatever reason, Marcel hadn't spoken; he had mostly been watching the road. Then, Laura laughed, and Marcel joined, knowing they were high and appreciated it.

They arrived at the first stoplight on Dodge. Other than the air conditioner, the car was quiet.

"It's easy to get around with the streets numbered," he said. "I haven't been driving too much, though, just a lot of bus and walking. A friend bought me a bike."

"Yep. Easy town. I know a place you should see. It's a wilderness area everyone gets high at, by a river out in another town. Once you get out there, you'll see what Nebraska's like. Maybe you could see the farm."

"You like nature, I take it."

"Well, I'm studying a book on botany. It tells you how to create teas, oils, and uh, creams. For medicine--an herbal medicine book."

"Gotcha." He wanted to ask her something and couldn't. "You don't have many friends?" he said, which he had earlier intended to ask.

"I have friends. We just aren't involved."

"Cool." He looked out the window at buildings. The drive was longer than expected. He was focused on where his life brought him. Laura was someone just starting out, someone less aware of the world and more of herself.

"We're close to your neighborhood," she said.

They looked at each other again, he nodded, then they watched the road. She wished she could think of something. Hunched forward, her posture hurt, so she leaned back. Then, she looked around more and soon offered a cigarette. She opened her window and turned the air conditioner off. Then, they smoked as the sound of traffic surrounded them.

She said, "I hate being predictable."

"True, we do what's simplest," he said, nodding.

Laura paused. "But it's *too* simple."

"Do you think you'll remember today?" he asked.

"Of course. A lot happened."

"I will, too."

Laura began to worry. If she were to be involved with anyone, it would leave no time to herself, just as it had with Jae. It was all a distraction the last time. Truth was, she wasn't any happier alone. "Were you worried when they attacked the twin towers?" she said, as she looked at him.

"Girl, of course."

Laura continued, saying, "I couldn't believe it, and they knew about it before it even happened."

"Yeah, that's what I heard," he said.

"It's like there's no changing it," she said, "We just go on and on with everything until something like that. I don't see what the motive was."

He said, "Especially when it's that many people thinking they have to destroy something."

"Yeah. You know, I wouldn't know what to do. I think it's just people thinking they're worth more than each other, and the rest of us live as bystanders."

Laura was driving through a neighborhood and meeting stoplights, approaching downtown. "All those people on the upper floors," she continued. "That's really all I could think about."

"Girl, let's just be high."

Soon, saying nothing felt right for them. They had time ahead to get to know each other more. Then, they bumped fists, just as Jae and Laura used to.

No one was outside as they rode through the small Farnam neighborhood, which looked as though the houses were empty vacancies. Laura didn't have the peace of mind to appreciate it this moment. Somehow, it looked post-apocalyptic, or like abductions were occurring.

They arrived downtown, and she parked her car at the lofts.

"I wanna walk with you to your car," she said.

"What?" He smirked. "How'd you know I drove?"

"Well, I just assumed. Everyone out here needs a car."

"Okay, I don't mind, except you're not going to like my car. I'm waiting to afford a newer one."

They walked the streets downtown again, and it seemed an understated, everlasting day, silenced by the enormous mute in their ears from the weed. Marcel looked as though he knew the town well, as if he already knew Laura well. She was more at his side. She finally held his hand, and he held hers.

Moments later, they approached his car near the bar.

"I want you to have something," he said.

At first, Laura couldn't respond. She tried to recall what he had just said. Then, she could say anything.

She said, "Okay."

This felt right, maybe even the right step for him. She didn't have the confidence yet to make it right for him.

Marcel thumbed through his wallet until he pulled out a picture with a crease or bend on it. He handed it to her. "It's a photo of when I was young."

In a sort of blur, Laura said, "Are you sure?"

"Yeah, I want to see you again, Laura...sometime."

"You're saying that like this is the only picture you have of you."

"It is." They made eye contact then, and he smiled, just short of laughing. "Talk to you soon."

"All right." She watched him enter his car and head off with a wave. She had to look at the photo, and it simply said it all: Anything she never would've thought of him was in this picture. It was maybe a kindergarten class photo, and here he was looking away from the shot and smiling at a stranger, smiling about his mom and all the people he knew, proud and confident as if he believed he was no one else but himself already and he'd be like his dad.

Sure, she was high. She put the photo in her bag. Laura had never been more concerned about what to do, so she quickly felt her bag for holes.

She began her walk home while coming down, and tension came to her. Already she had forgotten about the photo, and the heat of the sun came from the west, the direction she walked.

For a moment in the shade, Laura wanted to remember this day, so she promptly picked up a black landscaping rock from the ground when she got closer to it. At home was a collection of rocks in a small, lidded basket, with the purpose of tracing back memories. She'd remember it all.

She came alongside an unmarked bar around the corner from her place. Looking through the door, she couldn't see in because it was too dark. She noticed her reflection. Of course, she couldn't decide if she'd have another drink or not, to check the place out, but the high followed by alcohol wouldn't feel right.

Around the corner, she came underneath some trees planted maybe five years prior. The sun was hidden behind a building, and she walked slowly, unsure of how the conversation had gone, or at least how he would've thought of it, except then she remembered him giving her the photo and the smile on his face when he did.

With her keys out, Laura opened the door to the lobby. Because it was Sunday, she didn't have to check her mail. She felt a chill with a vent somewhere pointed toward her. Again, in the elevator, she waited and took a deep breath.

The one thing Jae seemed to care about with Laura was her beginning to learn the world outside of school, and this was the same gesture Marcel had. This moment, it was welcome.

Laura shut the door behind her. Her phone had a message, so she dropped the bag from her shoulder into her hand and pushed the button.

It's just your mother. Hope you got home safely. Bye.

It was nearing eight. Laura picked up the phone, dialed, and waited.

"Hello?"

"It's me. I got home fine."

"Good. I was just waiting," Renae was sitting in bed with her laptop, tired, having shed the day's cheer. *Yeah.*

Well, have a good night. Thanks for calling. "Okay. Bye."

Laura felt awkward and hung up hesitantly.

At the television, Laura switched through channels to a reality show. Instead of watching, she left it on while looking for something to eat. She focused on her posture as she gathered a few things. At the sight of the bare table, she knew she'd almost completely forgotten about the weed they threw out.

Admittedly, she had a responsibility here, though she questioned whether she'd completely live up to it or not. Too often, people bothered her, various noises of strangers--who probably all went about life for themselves, not in the least in any right way.

She stood at the west window and stared out while believing the perplexity, believing Marcel was probably the only guy she'd care to know for a while. Of course, she couldn't entirely forget her past, but she had nothing to worry about.

❄ ❄ ❄

Individuation

Months back, Michael taped the remake of a horror classic. He and Dan started in the basement when Rico got them high and left them with some 'Kind Bud.' After Rico left, they were watching the movie upstairs. Michael now smoked a cigarette on the front steps with the sounds of children down the street. Traffic was in the distance, away from this area.

Days would be limited to what could be done at the job and to whatever he could do at home besides watching television. His interview the next day was near enough to the apartment he would walk. Of course, it had to be he couldn't drive at this time. This moment, he could do nothing. He finished the cigarette and returned inside.

"You missed some parts; they were talking," Dan said. He seemed annoyed.

"It's okay."

"I don't know." Dan had wanted to go home since they were done smoking in the basement. "I think I might leave soon. Got a few more things to pack."

"Okay. I'm going to the store anyway." Michael turned the movie off. "You wanna walk there with me?"

Dan was rubbing the back of his neck, thinking. "I guess I could. Are you going for cigarettes?"

"Yeah, I'm down to my last one."

Dan sneezed loudly. "I don't know, got about five left."

"Let's go then."

They went out the front, and Dan walked ahead while Michael locked the door, and the wind caught the storm door as he did. "I might try the lottery today," he said.

"Yeah? I've won nine dollars a few times, but otherwise, I don't know—it really doesn't work."

Michael caught up. "Okay, I've never tried it." He wondered, maybe friends had been a distraction? He'd been away from them all lately, and the demands of the day seemed more serious than they used to be. But moments like this made everything seem right: the town was small; they'd get around to places; they'd watch TV, play pool; they'd probably save up for a keg and have friends over, or drive country roads and listen to music. Dan would maybe share the room with his girlfriend, which would be all right--he had his own space.

They jaywalked the street separately to the opposite sidewalk corner, Dan being the more downtrodden.

"So, how's your mom?" Michael asked when they rejoined. They were walking north.

"I don't know; she's all right."

"Good. You think your girlfriend would pitch in if she moved in with you?"

"Maybe."

The neighborhood shifted from younger, lower class to

older, middle class as they crossed another street to where lawns were always stubbornly mowed (because everyone had ideas about their pesky neighbors watching them). Dan and Michael walked along the sunny side, and a reckless driver turned in front of them before they crossed another street. They walked as though still with days past, in the same demeanor, but as though both were abandoned.

Dan didn't say much, and this reminded Michael: people maybe hadn't known either of them well. They may have assumed Michael was different from others, and he had some odd times growing up, something he couldn't always look back on and be happy with. He couldn't see himself having a family. Dan wasn't a father type, either, and they made fortunate friends, in this respect.

Michael's parents were the only ones who visited him in the hospital, besides a few other family members. Sharing the details of why he had originally gone didn't seem right. Maybe they never understood.

Dan thought of the times they'd driven the country roads with music and drinking earlier with nothing much to say. He had some inclination Michael had forgotten all of it. It was as if he had no reason to be carrying on with his friend from high school, even when Michael could've thought the same.

The apartment was on Michael's mind, and it already wasn't worth the time, money, and commitment. But he was twenty-three; it should be easy living in a small town.

Here were homes with people who somehow always got by. He needed to do something, but he had nothing more to do than get a pack of cigarettes. Something needed to change. For one, Michael needed his license.

Dan was more headstrong as they made their way, walking faster. They crossed Military, and Michael started walking toward the gas station.

"They're cheaper at the drive-thru liquor," Dan said.

"Okay." Michael turned, appearing as though he'd been dancing there, worshiping God after God finally showed Michael the light, but the only light was the fuel station, alive with its people.

They arrived at the garage of the liquor store, where alcohol surrounded them. Michael was coming down; they knew the nutty alcoholics would be here soon.

"Hi, fellas," the salesperson said.

"Hi," Dan said, standing with her.

"What can I get you?"

"Uh. Could you get me some full-flavor smokes, I don't care what kind as long as it's under three dollars."

"Some ID?"

"I'm twenty-three."

"Need some ID." Dan managed to get his ID out. She said, "My nephew was born 1980." Dan said nothing. She got a pack and rang him up. "And you?"

"I'll try some of your imported smokes if you got any," Michael said.

"Your ID?" Michael accidentally slapped his ID on the counter. She stared again, then got a pack and rang him up. "Hot day out, isn't it?" she said.

"Yes." It was a lighter side of Michael while in public when he said the simplest things to strangers. Despite all self-doubt, he could always turn to the public.

She smiled.

"Thanks," he said.

She nodded and said, "You bet. Have a good one."

Dan and Michael returned outside and began packing their cigarettes before opening them. Both met times quitting, so they'd probably reach another time when it was pointless. They smoked, and the noise of traffic on Military, tires rolling fast over the pavement with ferocious echo, came from behind Dan as if he stood in a dangerous spot. Michael was relieved to have more cigarettes, even though his breathing was getting heavier. They could do anything now since the high still had them. "We should walk back," he said.

"Uh, I'm going home, though. Remember?"

"Oh, right. All right, I'll see you tomorrow."

"Yeah." Dan started walking.

Michael said, "Hey." Dan turned. "Once I get this job, I'll be all right."

"Okay, Mike. Later." Dan went his way then.

Michael checked for anyone driving by who may have looked at him. He walked around the liquor store and across a vast parking lot to the shade of the gas station, displaced because anyone else was driving, either on Military or anywhere.

In jail, he had a sense people knew him. The next morning when he was released, he walked the train tracks, contemplating this in a bright open day, for miles under the weight of the world and under a deep spell of curiosity and hopelessness.

Nothing today suggested his situation would improve. Maybe it was a mistake to live in an apartment, with the anxiety of living in a place with a questionable past, with a friend whose loyalty he didn't want to break, and therein was the reason nothing would change. Michael could be overwhelmed, alone or not.

As he smoked in the shade of the gas station, with cigarette butts rolling in the breeze and lifting plastic vapors in the summer heat, Michael realized he'd be doing community hours at some point. Winter would arrive soon enough, and he'd need his car to get to work. Even though the place was within walking distance, it meant he needed to cross a few active train tracks.

He stared for a moment at the traffic, and a relentless car entered the parking lot. Soon, Michael finished his cigarette and went inside. The wind from outside shut the door behind him like some crude act of gods almost catching his foot.

A busty, bellied woman said, "Can I help you?"

"Just a lottery ticket."

"You want a quick pick?" She had a country accent.

"Sure." After buying a ticket, he went to the back for a cup of coffee, took the last dollar from his pocket, and paid again. He sat at a table at the window, next to the sunflower seeds, candy, and soda. The coffee and a cigarette could alleviate the habit to worry, but too much would *create* worry.

An old friend from Chicago held the appearance and attitude of someone competent, clear-minded, assertive, and having no time for nonsense. There was the time with her at a bar north of downtown when he drank too much and stared at the base of the toilet with his vomit in front of him. He'd been liquored up at a bongo bar: fun, to say the least.

There could've been anyone now for him to talk with. Samantha, who he met at Heartland, was exactly the person to hang with him and meet up at places like San Francisco or Las Vegas, perhaps Los Angeles if they had the money. When he went to San Francisco to meet up with her, it was the first time he had done acid, and she didn't know until after. He drank tea and stayed up all night as though it was a permanent moment to be amazed by everything, laying down on a deck, fixated by the steady view of what was around him—the whole world where lions, crime, and all of profanity were at the same time, the reality of the present moment he had never realized before. Anything could have overwhelmed him into panic, as young as he was.

Michael took the tab by day, let it take effect while he was in a chair, and laid outside on the deck all night. He handled big thoughts well, and it was his nature at times to think big. Someone would tell him he always thought like his father, like anything was a new thing to talk about; or if it interested the person listening, it didn't always mean it interested him, to have to explain it. There was some crude monotony to talking he and his father couldn't figure out.

Michael would never do acid again because maybe it had a part to do with his recent psychosis. It all fell together rapidly and isolated him. He thought of Trish, a friend who had moved away from Fremont. She was actively getting into apartments around town, constantly moving. Perhaps money was trouble for everyone. He wished good things for her as he glanced out the window...

The coffee was a mistake, or it was the cigarette. Trish always smoked and had a large soda while driving. In no time, she had a kid with someone she left and got child support from, though they remained friends.

Michael leaned back. Out of wanting to think of something, he couldn't. Anything important would come naturally, but at this moment nothing interested him. People were meant to say meaningful things. Probably, he needed the coffee.

Outside a man was refueling, bound by errands, not thinking of anything significant, and otherwise unbothered. When Michael was younger, he looked forward to being an adult, and considering himself an adult, it demanded his attention to small matters. Its unending nature was unsettling.

Someone speaking at the counter reminded him of Michelle. Recently, he spoke with her for the first time since he got home from Chicago. Already, he'd been back a while. The sunlight coming in was bright on the table and warm to his arms. He took his phone from his pocket, stared at it, and dialed.

"Hello?"

Michelle was lying on a sofa with a cover coming undone; her baby was lying on her back on the carpet floor over a blanket.

"Michelle, it's Michael. What's new?" He suddenly felt monotone even though he cared to chat. He sometimes didn't want people to have any impression of him. Perhaps an uncaring voice came from attempting to be a grownup with people sometimes.

"Nothing." She was excited he called and thought he'd stop over.

"Is this a bad time?" Michael asked.

"No, Michael, I'm just watching a movie."

"Cool."

"What are *you* doing?" she asked.

"Drinking coffee at a gas station. I'm in Fremont." Her voice was the simplest reminder of good times.

"You should come over sometime. I keep telling my friends about you."

"I know, it's been a while," he said, smiling...

CHAPTER 4

Experience

T he alarm was going off when Laura woke up. She immediately got out of bed, showered, and dressed, then slowed her pace by cooking an omelet. The rumbling of a truck outside down below contrasted with the quiet in the apartment. She could vaguely remember dreaming something because it all felt lucid. Then, she finished, to stop thinking of Jae, who once taught her how to cook an omelet. She felt too unappreciative.

Time moved favorably. She smoked some, then washed her face, brushed her teeth, and put lotion on her hands. The high would just enter into the job. Her boss would be the only one working besides someone in and out...

After putting the dishes in the sink, Laura simply stood in the kitchen with no idea as to what changes should be made. Nothing was happening in her life at home. She checked her watch.

For whatever reason she wasn't in touch with the old crew, they still occupied her mind. Where she was now should bring some good changes. Perhaps they all had no one after school was done.

Weighted by her apartment and thoughts of Jae, she decided she'd make it in early for work. Her bag was already on her shoulder and she was locking the door behind her. After enough of the abuse, his torment came even during better times together and times like this. The constant aggression stifled her with all the blame he put on her for just about anything.

Laura couldn't deny it: Life was difficult for anyone, and if he'd continue to be angry with people, it'd even be difficult for him. She could never be sincere enough for him to be honest with her. One wrong move brought a fight.

Also, they were equals; she could someday have the same feelings about the world he had. Realizing this at the sight of him watching TV, she had cried her hardest at the futility, the innocence, and the child in his heart, which he kept to himself and didn't know how to give. She wanted to put in her best effort so he could open up more, and together they would know a bond between each other, if not for anyone else.

Nothing of the typical life came to them (the house, the car, the kids, the money, or whatever they want people to believe). Even at the best of times, they'd be in public, and he'd have to ask her if she met someone. It would mean she'd send him off to the streets because she was white, and in his mind, it was what she'd do. Still, she stood by him.

Laura walked Sixteenth Street. Since it was early, fewer cars were a whelming presence, with the rumbling of tires on the bricks as they passed.

Her immediate thoughts of Marcel suggested this friendship was only continuing. He was in the same town as if they were in a foreign place and the only Americans who knew each other...

Having been involved with someone who'd beaten her on one occasion, she'd forced herself into more privacy. At the time, Jae was the only person she knew; she hadn't spoken with anyone for a while, and the public posed something of the world she'd never belong to.

"You're a fucking stupid bitch!" he yelled. "I fucking need this money more than you!"

"Fine." She was caught off guard and calmly expected the worst again.

"No, Laura, it's 'cause you fucking want to fight!"

"How am I supposed to get through to you if all you give me is this shit?" she said.

"What?!"

"I don't deserve this from you." She was quiet.

"Look. All you need to know is that you're a dumbass bitch. That's all you're gonna be. Basically. And that is a white, dumbass bitch."

She said nothing.

He pushed her against the wall by her shoulders and slapped her. Then, she spit in his face... The next day, he threw buckets of hot water at her from the sink while she was in the shower before going to work.

At the time, she was given money by her parents, and he wanted her to split it between them. The first thing he would do with it was drink or go anywhere to be alone, maybe meet up with strangers when the two of them had made plans to move. After the fighting, she avoided him in the apartment but paid attention to his every move, which was what he wanted her to do since he kept getting up and walking around. This sort of behavior occurred much too frequently.

She had to go to the hospital where they took a picture of her face, but she didn't do anything about it. Those days, she belonged far from him. But she had already given him the money. "You know I'm sorry, bitch," he told her. They hugged on the walk back, and as always, he proved to be someone to trust some of the time.

Laura promptly kicked a rock up the sidewalk, or down, as she was more downhill and further downtown. The sun wasn't over the buildings yet.

After reading about spirituality, she was interested in caring more about her life, and in treating herself with more respect. It had always seemed important, yet she always held a sense of uselessness when time with anyone, or time with herself, was short. She looked at the ground again to find a rock. She continued walking and found just a regular white pebble, used for landscaping, and it would be the only one of its kind in her collection.

As Laura approached the store, aware again of what was around her, her boss stood outside with a cigarette. He wasn't exactly waiting for her but waiting for the day, as usual. "You're early!" he said.

"Yep. I guess I could smoke with you," she said calmly, stopping. She pulled out her smokes, and the pack wasn't too low yet. She almost laughed about her pack of cigarettes. "I met someone yesterday. We smoked at my place and drove around town."

"Really?"

"Yeah. It was something." She exhaled. They both knew they had nothing to say.

"You're high, aren't you?"

"A little," she said with a shrug. He was oppressed by his work, but happy. He had a family with a son who was older than Laura. Having fewer employees probably helped the business, and he didn't seem stuck in Omaha. It was easy for him to make conversation on the quiet days, so he fit right into the town. His son still lived with him and his wife, and they'd go to movies together. Even though Laura's parents would still do the same, it was an odd for someone else to. "It just helps to stop everything from moving so fast," she said.

"Yeah. Exactly," he said, smiling and nodding. "Some people do use that medicinally."

"I've got some if you ever need it," she said. He seemed to know something she didn't know.

"Yeah, I'll think about it," he assured her.

They didn't say anything more as they smoked.

She flicked her cigarette into the street. "Street sweepers will get it there."

"Better pick it up."

"Aw. They're cotton, biodegradable. Promise."

"All right," he said, looking her over with a subtle laugh. With what was shared, they had a bond to return to at work, but mostly he appreciated her honesty.

When she went in, Laura passed everything around her, then entered the office where she checked her watch again. This was a decent job for now, but it was nowhere nearly making her feel she'd always have one. Still, she had over five minutes. She'd just sit it out.

The television was on. As she sat, she thought of how the college or trade school commercials made jobs appear pointless as if only holding up the ideal about education keeping people going, but there was proof you could anyhow—yet still so pointlessly either way. It was always something taking money from people to do anything, so life was some kind of unreachable goal they couldn't stop but continue working toward. She thought of the students on TV and how they dreamed their way through, talking as though still in sleep to say how good the school was.

She didn't know it was the marijuana bringing her to think this. Her boss came in. "So, how's your book coming along, Laura?"

"Good. I'll outline this week."

"Tell me about it when you get further."

"I will." She thought she'd been loud.

"Really unique idea, I thought." He left, and she stayed in the office, alone with the television.

Maybe she could do something autobiographical. Maybe after some time with Marcel, she'd feel more settled down and less wrecked up.

Laura got up and punched in, then went to the cash register. "I've got boxes to unload, and I'll have you work on that," Jeff said.

"Got it."

Soon, she was unpacking boxes and pricing books. She could admit she missed school, but she was doing right by working as anyone else would. Soon enough, she'd have maybe two jobs and little time for anything. Maybe she'd even give up and live back on the farm.

Piano music played on the speakers as she entered another room, making the work private and steadfast. She contemplated books as she placed them up on a shelf near the first room when a customer came in, asking right away where to find books on the chakras.

"They're by me over here," Laura said.

The mildly robust woman said, "I almost didn't expect this place to have them."

"Yeah, we've got 'em."

"Okay, let's see." She walked to Laura, passing Jeff at the register and saying 'hello.'

"These are all the books we have on the chakras. And across here below the astrology section, we have books on rocks."

"What ever do I need those for?"

"Well, the rocks have energies that are absorbed through the hands and directed to the different chakras. You'll find some with those references, but some just have pictures and descriptions."

"Really?" The woman acted surprised.

Laura pulled out one of the books on rocks. "I actually have this one at home, and it's a good one. It relates the rocks to the chakras for you."

"Wonderful! I'll buy it."

"And there is a book on the chakras here I have that talks of archetypes related to each one."

"When did you get involved with this?"

"Well, I study astrology mostly, but with the books on meditation, they often refer to the chakras."

"That's how I got into it, yes," she said, enthused. "I know a lot of it now is becoming popular, but that's certainly news to me about the rocks!"

"It works. You just become mindful of your thoughts as they ease. You use your left palm, someone had told me."

"It is interesting, isn't it?"

Jeff came into the room. "Laura, I've got coffee whenever you're ready for some," he said.

"Thanks," Laura said, and she went back to work.

"Would you like some coffee, ma'am?"

"Oh, no. Thanks." The woman knelt at the books with the rocks. She thumbed through another one. "I'm so lucky you were here," she said. "But now I don't know what my husband will say."

"Yeah." Laura smiled, watching her. It felt as though she were shopping with the woman because the place was small and quiet. She also reminded Laura of a distant relative. Laura then had the slightest memory of a nursery as a kid. The woman, well into her sixties or seventies, had a tattoo of a rose on her chest.

"Laura, could you help this man?"

"What is it?" as she entered the first room.

"I need books on Paris," a man said.

"Oh, those are all in the basement, I'll show you."

Laura and this customer went downstairs to a travel section. She quickly looked for Paris alphabetically. "Paris. Right here. Let me know if you need more help."

"It's simple, just going on a trip with my wife." Boastful was his way of saying this.

"Oh, you'll like Paris, I went once." She turned to go upstairs. It was honest resentment toward his approach to her.

"I hear they don't like Americans, so I figure I'll see it for myself, maybe make fun of 'em if they don't speak English." He had a mischievous smile saying this and seemed he could laugh and expect her to also.

"Okay." So, she smiled. He seemed typical.

Laura left to go upstairs. She'd never involve herself with someone like him because it would only amount to wasted time. He may have been a jerk early on and somehow maintained it even though it was hardly sustainable. His wife would divorce him, or the sex was good, and she was one of those.

By the time she reached the top of the stairs, she wondered if she'd only evolved from people she didn't like. Maybe it was why she rarely spoke because it divided her attention. Piano music was a paradox of people who didn't give mind to these things. Again, she was alone.

With several copies of a book, she rearranged a shelf and remembered the coffee upon finishing. Thinking of the woman she had helped, Laura filled a small cup in the office and drank it quickly. In the front room, the man was buying a few books. "Thanks, again," he said.

"Sure."

"What's your name?"

"I'm Laura."

"Nice meeting you." He nodded. She received it as she would've with any stranger, and at least trusted him since he seemed mindful again of a wife.

"Okay. This is the place for books, so come again," she said.

Jeff smiled at Laura, but she didn't notice.

Two hours had passed, and she was working at the register. During the last hour, several customers came and left, and the two had traded places. It was now less busy, and Laura was waiting with a novel. "Go ahead and take your break," Jeff said.

"Okay."

Soon, Laura was outside on a bench where she lit up. As she smoked, she looked over her shoulder and squinted her eyes at the sun, then returned to the view of a building across the street. Something was changing. She felt unsure of herself, sitting alone, shaking her foot.

She inhaled the warm air and smoke and tapped the ash from her cigarette. Thoughts returned to her book as she looked at the ground. She was visualizing the murder, and they would be standing still, facing each other before he would shoot her. It would cause her to fall on her back, and her vision would blur while she'd be silent in a panic.

Laura looked across the street again. The man wanted money, but the woman had nothing. He would leave out the back of the building to an alley. But he'd shoot a cop at some point.

Laura had her legs crossed and kicked her upper leg. It had been a while since graduating from high school. She was twenty-four now. At the time, she had plans of meeting new people, and she was passing the time as though she were at the graduation, still with the word "BORED" on her graduation cap in bold, black electric tape.

Her break was soon over; she wished she could stay outside. At the cash register, she opened her book again, aware she'd die someday, and it maybe wouldn't matter to anyone as she once thought. She needed her friends, and she wanted more to set her straight. After all of her affections and everything behind her, she was afraid it was all in vain.

"You okay?" Jeff said.

"Yeah, just thinking."

❋ ❋ ❋

Confidence

Earlier, Michael woke before the alarm went off, and he stayed on the mattress for about five minutes, calmly looking around before getting up. There was less in the refrigerator to manage with, so he skipped eating. Then, he prepared the bath because the shower wasn't working. In the tub, he knew Dan would move in today.

After fixing up in the bathroom, Michael got dressed into what he prepared the night before, then rapidly smoked a cigarette out front, confronted with the peculiar noise from trains nearby. Once back inside, he was confused but ready to head off. He paced to the bedroom to double-check the lights, then went through the kitchen, stepped out the back door, and locked it. Since clouds had covered the sky overnight, it was cool outside.

He had his sleeves rolled up casually. In his bag, he held a book on Buddhism, a journal he printed out, a book of worldly wisdom, a house design he was working on, and an MP3 player with headphones and a car attachment. He also had a picture of his grandmother among miscellaneous items, including pennies, besides dirt and debris.

Thoughts returned of his grandmother housed in assisted living while his grandfather was in the nursing home. They were in their late eighties. Elsa always had an active mind, toward religion mostly, with straightforward conversation, which never failed with Michael and his cousins. She could be quite convincing, and she carried humor like an extra card, but whenever it was time for him to leave, she'd say "Okay, kiddo," and they would hug. As Michael only knew her as such, and she only had black-and-white photos of her younger days, she was meant to be a grandmother in her lifetime. Grandchildren were all a source of longevity for them, and they'd remain a significant influence.

Michael would have to visit. Being without a car meant he'd go with his mom or dad. Elsa warned him about 'smoking dope.' While he suspected people in the family knew about the drugs, he doubted she ever did.

Everywhere around him were similar duplexes, and here he was, stuck in Nebraska again. However TV depicted people, he'd see the locals reliably habituated in as if TV had all the answers. It only meant together they belonged to shallow water. Once, he swore never to wear jeans, so he had a collection of trousers.

Michael passed through the neighborhood and came to a small basketball court with a picnic table, bordered by a field of wet grass and weeds. As he walked into the field, he looked ahead toward the trains. At his left were the backs of more housing where wild trees had grown, and ahead the sky and field surrounded him, making him feel insignificant. This always came as a feeling he rejected.

As he walked, he again remembered Trish because he met her at this job a while back. They were the fewest of people to meet each other the way they did, for him to give mention, jokingly, to cellophane, and they even got into some trouble at the place for smoking out in the parking lot. He remembered the scene in the office: since they were high, they didn't want to laugh, but sure enough, being reprimanded brought out the giggles.

The railway was closer. He made his way to it and took a moment to look around because maybe someone wouldn't want him walking near the tracks. He crossed an old rail and looked around at the parked cars before going around the facility toward more tracks. A train was stopped, and he had to climb over it.

Michael presently walked over the gravel and shoved his bag further around his back to grab the ladder with both hands. He shuffled between the two cars to the other side and jumped back down onto the rocks. He had somewhat fallen forward, so he quickly got himself up again. Ahead over a field were some houses, and to his right was a road with a dead end near the tracks. As he walked toward it, he watched his feet.

Fremont was somehow harshly separate from him; he was much more alone than he had been through school. Things weren't steady anymore, but he wasn't depending on the support of his parents any longer.

For him to be thinking so much, maybe he needed

medication. Something had isolated him, though he'd befriend almost anyone. Adapting with this was difficult because it often came with pessimism about people whose behaviors seemed below him, though his opinions were changing: it was necessary not to think this.

With silent despair, he came past a broken fence line and onto the pavement: he needed this job. Had he forgotten anything?

The path was at an angle to another street, and he briefly came to the intersection with cars passing violently through toward the same building, as if being revisited by strangers of a town where everyone had a like mind to each other: they were free to notice Michael and think less of him than what he thought of them, which in turn made him think less of them.

He crossed and went up the length of street, passing more homes set apart from the rest of town, to an apartment complex, to gravel, and a paved parking lot wrapping around the back of the place. Many cars had sped past.

Michael was still coming out of his time in Chicago when he started respecting people more. Despite whatever flaws they had, Michael held a lot of trust. He noticed more and more people of Fremont his age were short of having respect for people who deserved it, often having more respect for those who didn't. This was far more of a challenge than he expected.

He was in good time, so he sat in the open smoke shelter and pulled out another cigarette. Despite these ideas about people, it was easy to let go of. No one greeted him. Then a girl spoke up. "Do you work here?" she had asked.

"Not yet; I'm in for an interview today."

"You're not going to like it." She looked down. "I'm about ready to quit and find another job," she said, shaking her head.

"You should come back and let me know if you find one better."

"Yeah. Right?" she said, smiling, rolling her eyes.

He said, "I remember everyone smokes here."

"Yep. Same shit every day," she continued.

Michael didn't say anything more, and he leaned forward with his elbows on his knees to rest his back. His bag was at his side, and he smoked until he was halfway through. "I'm Michael, by the way."

She finished her cigarette and stood up. "Well, see ya later. I'm heading in."

"All right."

Michael continued smoking. Another person came to him. "Can I get one of your cigarettes, man? I'm out."

"Sure." Michael pulled one out, staring at it, then met eyes with the guy who was younger than him.

"Cool. Thanks, man."

The only life here was the smoke rising from the cigarettes and the motion of hands, the boast of having work and the feeling of being so above, yet so below. A person could hear it in their voices.

Michael finished his cigarette at the waste bin. He put the butt in a container and walked over the lawn around the front to open the door impatiently, where the cool air met him, along with the noise of people and ringing phones. He approached the woman at the front desk. "I'm here to see Cara."

"I'll let her know you're here. What's your name?"

"Michael Brown."

He sat when she left, and the noise of the place returned to him. Everyone was selling phone service, and it demanded focus always. It'd be easy to think about other things while reading over the script if he was careless. With nothing more to do, he sat with a lot of anxiety because most people had an advantage over him going into jobs, and maybe he would miss this opportunity.

He worried he was inadequate but also felt, had he gotten the job, he had an advantage over some people. This made him feel guilty.

Immediately, Cara appeared. "Michael! You made it."

"Yes." He smiled but couldn't let go of the guilt.

"Come right over to my desk and we'll talk."

"Okay." He followed her, and they sat.

"First, I'm going to give you a card with my number in case you need to call me."

"Okay." He was still anxious but took the card. It made him a little more at ease.

"Great. Now I need you to look over this script and read it to me." He took the paper and read it aloud:

"Hi, my name is [Michael]. I'm calling on behalf of Heartland Tele-Services. We're offering a low, seven-cent long-distance calling rate for all your long-distance calls, and it's only five dollars a month. It even includes online billing. I can help you with these savings today, so let's get you started."

He spoke well. "Great," Cara said. "Now, I know you'd be a rehire. Tell me what's been going on with you."

"I was in Chicago, attempting school and working."

"Uh-huh."

"And I had debt, so I moved back here."

"How was Chicago?" She had an honest smile.

He nodded. "It's a great place. I liked it, it was good." Now he had enthusiasm.

"So, tell me why you want to work again for First Marketing."

"I'm just within walking distance from here," as he pointed behind him, "So it's convenient. I'm also used to the work. I was a recruiter in Chicago besides the last time I was here." He was speaking too low.

"Yes, I noticed that on your application."

"I don't know, I just think it's easy, and I'd do well," he said a little louder.

"Okay," she said, smiling. "If you have any questions, you have my number. Our training starts tomorrow, so you're welcome to start at eight tomorrow morning if that works for you," she said, animating with a smile and the most encouraging eyes.

"Okay, I'll be here," he said with a smile.

"It was nice talking with you, Michael."

"Great." He held his smile when they shook hands.

He left the building to return to the smoke shelter and sat for another cigarette. Things were finally working out. What luck! Still, Fremont bothered him. He used to have a passion for Heartland, and the thrill of meeting new people still lingered some.

His focus would be to get his car back before winter, but if he were early before trains, he'd make it in time for work. He anticipated staying with the job.

Michael stood up fast and dizzy. With the cigarette, he started walking a considerable distance past houses and old sheds, a workplace with old metal, and finally the gas station where he checked his ticket. Cars violently passed Michael as if they couldn't slow down for him. It was a long walk, but having work made it easier.

Nothing from the lotto. Something gave him the idea to use his coins to match the odds on the numbers for the next drawing, and with nothing more from the station, he started walking back to the train tracks. This was the outskirts of town where, during the day, the sun overwhelmed the grass and pavement, and at night, the moon overwhelmed the wild. He walked slower than before, watching his step, noticing empty packs of cigarettes, including a full one someone had driven over. He took it to salvage what he could, but then he tossed it because it was a cheap brand, not worth the trouble.

Again, cars passed loudly, always picking up speed from the intersection at the gas station, so they accelerated past. It was long and slow, but he made his way across the tracks and back to the basketball court, where he sat at the picnic table. He went through the bag and took out his coins, some paper, and a pencil. As he tested the numbers, he remembered some gang members he smoked pot with, in an alley in Chicago.

Patiently, he tested all the available numbers and even came up with a combination, after a while. Nothing bothered him. Indeed, he intended to win the lottery, and he was convinced he could. He could do plenty with money. Thoughts of the hospital seemed finally behind him.

When he returned home, he expected Dan to arrive soon. They wouldn't drink but maybe finish the movie. He went to the sofa downstairs and opened his bag. The day was still cool.

In an effort to fight boredom and go with his hopes in the lottery, he took out the journal he wrote before his psychosis, and began reading...

I tend to hold back from actively keeping relations with people in whatever ways needed to be a positive influence for myself and others. This is due to being more introverted, thoughtful, and affected, versus active and involved. It doesn't provide any refining, volunteering myself to anything currently isn't an option, and I'm at a more isolated than independent point in life while nothing really functions to an end. I tend to draw further into the unknown, though people and places are restricted to what I directly know. At times, I can feel halted by the idea that too many notions are put on me from a heavy, negative past, and these blocks are easily neglected though present with people. I haven't seriously confronted these aspects because I feel that my personality is workable, and I don't know what it is about me that is incompatible. While I may be predictable or sometimes dull, it may be an appropriate time to separate until I can prove to be otherwise.

He began smoking and continued.

Recent introspection away from people, unrelating attitudes, and aspirations have built a plateau of unfulfilled wants. I believe through high school, I had anticipated a more open path, and living with restrictions and inexperience propels much of my emotional stature apart from the crowd. Though I know some experiences may have been lost, I don't regret abandoning original steps. Day by day accepting this, living with debt and without opportunity to work and advance, is neither upward nor downward but still a challenge. Too many people in this battle allows me to feel no more deserving than the next person. Most of my emotions are jostled by these outcomes, being less on a network of confidants. It is easier to take things for granted if opportunity arose, but any one outcome isn't going to set a real solution at large. Life as a success even appears to be a superficial gain.

Now, I've come to an intermission of sorts. It's a feeling that nothing has been lost, less is to gain, and opportunity isn't available without money to support it. My creative ability is one outlet for supporting myself, and avoiding the living situation as an issue may be an option to relieve isolation and open up to potential friendships. Music, movies, television, and games all have become less fun; I'm easily bored, and I think my interests lean more into the adult world.

With people, I don't put forth my negativity. It isn't something I feel people want to work around. I'm open to talking with anyone, but I can undermine myself by confronting some of what others may sense in me. I may under-credit people. I don't know enough, and I haven't adapted to overcome some of the blocks, but it has always appeared to me that everyone is secluded to a reality apart from a common one. I could recognize trying to win over in a conversation rather than accepting everything as it is, weaving around for answers, and it can make for superficial ties. Above all, I don't make conflict; I tend to reasons and solutions.

Currently, I feel as though everything I'm doing isn't what I want to do, but I settle to restrictions in the day-to-day. With others, it's difficult not to put myself in the forefront when making conversation. It's difficult when replacing self with trivial matters revolving around me. "What's going on?" and that's all there is about us; it's rarely a situation where both people feel they're making common ground. Nothing exciting ever happens, and when time is worth sharing, social habits can set that block of not really having anything important to say.

It's a common feeling if I believe my situation is common, but most of the time, it just feels like me. What outside of our experience would allow us to adapt outside of ourselves and allow change? Most people seem happy. What I have is a dead-end feeling, and it's a greater discomfort being among so many people I don't know and people I do know who altogether don't speak their mind. It makes matters look like they're just coming and going, chances are being missed, time is lost, and everyone around cannot change it for the next person. Anything to break the routine and work against the mundane is something worth achieving.

So far said, I'm met with the limited potential and freedom I have while living in a town with no car, no public transportation, weather trouble, and no job to depend on. How I say this sounds like I'm living it to a mundane. I live to the least of needs, which include petty stuff like cigarettes and coffee. Everything moves fast. A day is won slow and then passes into a duration of days lost. I'm not one to defend my capabilities and myself, and therefore, I am easily left to the vast majority of people who'd just say "whatever." At the same time, everything appears so easy for some, and so far surpassed and gained by others, considering the short amount of time we have to make anything for ourselves.

So far, this information would set an undefined path involving my attitude. It would also bring me into the unexpected, being less prepared. While it may be a giving-up on really creating a success I thought possible, I could have the attitude things should have worked out: schooling, relationships, and work. While either active attitude makes sense, I don't know what the solution is.

Lack of experience doesn't open doors toward any real experience at all. I realize I sometimes lack any real guidance or common sense; it's something I can accept, and I don't regret the person I've become through detours. In this way, I was giving up before really starting on any course outside of my education, which would say life and education aren't as related as they could be. It's up to us to make the connection.

It's unfortunate people with real capabilities are not involved for financial reasons or lack of inspiration and drive. Real advancement is not about fitting into any conformed occupation but identifying and working around real problems and eliminating them, working toward solutions within a dormant system. We need serious adjustments in our society for us to advance. A united way within community and nation would well advance solutions abroad.

Michael was finished with his cigarette but lit another one, and he stood up with heavy nervousness. He had accomplished nothing, and he missed his usual sense of balance, which came easy before. This moment, he wasn't comprehending what he wrote. At the time, it had all made sense....

CHAPTER 5

Instruction

T his afternoon when she arrived home, Laura took a recipe from Country Living for a tomato and Camembert tart. She quickly prepped the kitchen and somehow put it all together with ease; when she had it in the oven, she anxiously went to the window and began smoking.

A little into the cooking, she switched the television on simply to listen for the weather. It was on a sitcom, so she went through the rest of the channels until she got to the weather. She sat near the ashtray, sporting the expectation this would be a day to catch up with someone, and Rebecca was also in Omaha.

Rebecca had carried on with her youth, and Laura had always thought less would change with her, though she probably had her fair share of changes. Maybe Laura herself had not changed relatively much.

Thoughts returned to Aunt Margaret, who Laura lived with while back on the farm for a brief time. Laura cooked for both of them and helped her to bed. It was throughout most of the day the assaulting news about terrorism would blast into the living room. God knew Margaret could handle it, but Laura didn't.

Laura sometimes had the idea Margaret was a witch, simply

because people talked less and less with Laura, just as they had with Margaret. It was always about making sandwiches. Thoughts of quicksand, plus the word 'witch' kind of tripped her up.

Laura could've been concerned about being alone as much. On the bright side, she got Siva around then, and things were looking up.

At the window again, she recalled mornings waking up to the radio. At a sharp click, she heard loud commentary, commercials, or a pathetic ditty to entertain local elders, but only into further sleep at their chairs, just as it did Margaret before Laura would enter the kitchen to turn the unwelcome noise off.

Laura normally had no conflicts with people, though being agreeable all of the time made it painfully difficult to talk about anything meaningful. This caused Laura to wander off toward other people.

Jerome stayed in Omaha for a short time and moved back to New York. He was kind, considerate, and open-minded, unlike anyone she had ever met. She could never see into his thoughts, though she tried. When they were involved mostly as friends, Laura had doubts about being in a relationship for the first time. They had separated after he somewhat abandoned her to move to New York alone. He'd have phone calls and act like she wasn't in the room with him before he was moving.

Laura questioned what her adulthood would be. She could be a wanderer with nothing to say.

She finished the cigarette and turned down the volume. Fortunately, the TV didn't dominate the space, and she could easily ignore it. It was now back to the sitcom with its aggressive commercials.

Laura's cat, Pursy, came down the steps and meowed with her mouth shut as she got to the floor. Laura grabbed one of the toys, dropped it to the floor, and Pursy began rolling with it. "You're too easy," Laura said. She was almost speaking of herself.

Laura checked the time and raced upstairs to her desk with her bag, took out the cards, and shuffled them. Laying them out in sequence, she looked them over.

She was beginning to understand it.

Despite her fears, she kept grounded, and her surroundings formed out of maintaining what she wanted. Worries made her timid, yet she acted complacent. Her optimism was maybe false because she could think negatively, and it led to her fears....

Overall, she was happy and unaware of the things bothering her. They came and went. The more she was dominant in mind, the more things made sense, despite the fears...

She mostly ignored the fears ruining her despite any optimism. Out of being timid, she had no control over whatever came inevitably. She liked making sense because it helped her to know more, but the more she was happy knowing it, the more it worried her because they were consistent with her fears. She wondered now what she was ever afraid of.

Laura returned downstairs and prepared her meal. She ate alone and imagined Marcel doing the same. She had cards out to read if she wanted to...

Tomatoes, basil, olive oil, and thyme all made it flavorful, if not healthy, and she was done. With the rest of it in the refrigerator, after taking off a piece of cheese from a cut end, she decided to save half for Marcel, and the rest for later.

With a cigarette, she threw herself on the sofa, and above her were the knots in the wood ceiling again. She needed Rebecca's number, so she grabbed the phone and called over to Rebecca's parents. It rang, and finally her dad answered.

"Hello?"

"Hi, Wade. Do you have Rebecca's number?"

"Yeah, give me a second, would you?"

"Okay."

A moment later, he gave her the number, and they hung up. She had written it on a notepad by her phone. Pursy was done playing with the toy and sat next to Laura. They shared a glance, and Pursy blinked her eyes, seemingly approving of the call. One of the commercials on local education came on and went into another commercial about tampons: *It fits. Period.*

Laura laughed and rushed upstairs. Soon, like a fiend, she smoked, a high came to her, and she put everything away, leaving a loaded pipe in her desk for later.

Alone upstairs, apart from the television below, Laura sensed the quiet of the apartment, undisturbed and ready for her. She could go over her astrology notes and birth chart at the computer, but it would bring too many ideas at once.

Laura then decided laundry needed to be done before calling Rebecca, so she turned the TV off. Somehow, with all the smoking, errands weren't a challenge, yet.

From her bedroom, she grabbed some laundry and took her bag with her. Older kids were in the hall, laughing like dorks. They probably wanted to meet someone to smoke, and Laura's neighbor may just as well have been ignoring them.

Laura walked further from them and around the corner to the elevator. It was better not to know certain people.

Laura leaned against the elevator wall and took a deep breath. Questions always distanced her further, but understanding never eluded her. She could admit people weren't like her, and she was often content with this. She was in the basement when the door opened....

It was a white load, and none of the machines were running. She moved slowly. New York had been attacked and most of the population probably lived paranoid of future attacks. Anything could happen with local extremists making bombs for the subways or apartment complexes. People would be doing laundry or watching television.

She took her empty basket with the detergent and waited for the elevator. The new skyscraper in town overlooked the river to Iowa. Before she knew it, she was almost at her apartment, and the kids had left the hall. She heard yelling through another neighbor's door again.

Laura threw the basket into her dark bedroom and shut the door so the cat wouldn't get in. She walked the length of the apartment back to the living room where the light shined. Here was the sixties living room set from Margaret's basement. Luckily, it wasn't floral-patterned.

Still high, she looked around the room upstairs again before sneaking a few more hits in from the pipe. The flame sparked toward her eye before it diminished, and she relit it in a myopic focus, having no patience to smoke but feeling it enough she had the patience for whatever else.

Her computer was on, so she sat for a moment. A picture of a Persian rug was posted up as the background, and there was a daily journal. Other files pertained to her book, and several were about her astrological influences. She wanted to create her own personal deck at one time. She opened a program and went over some of the astrology from her birth chart: *You prefer constant, stable, exclusive relationships. Restless with routine...always have obstacles.*

Impatient, Laura shut down the computer and went to her books, glanced over them, and continued to the stairs. She took the phone and sat on the floor with her back to the wall, dialed Rebecca's number, and waited. Anything they could say would be predictable, but it was an opportunity to speak to one another after a long break. She couldn't remember the last time.

This is Rebecca. Leave me a message.

Laura was abruptly saddened by the sound of Rebecca's voice. She couldn't relate to always being so happy. Somehow, these days, Rebecca was living in a reality where people were happy.

Great.

Laura was in a paradox. The apartment had the charm of an empty holding cell. Here in a daze, Laura had to leave a message. What could she say? Her mind was blank. How much time had passed? She hung up.

Laura got up and put the phone back on the table. Then, she turned the television on to more news, so she sat and turned up the volume.

Ignoring the TV, she thought of Rebecca. They had long been best friends from a young age, but Rebecca was carefree, humorous, and freely spoke what was on her mind, yet maybe not always from experience. Rebecca in her own right was a genius of sorts, how she'd keep score during beauty pageants on TV, always chose Raph when playing Ninja Turtles on the NES, or made appropriate selection of a cliche to the situation at hand, often jokingly. Rebecca sparked a sort of relevance to Nebraska many overlooked.

Perhaps they both took for granted they could handle things on their own from their early judgment. Above all, they had been eager to get into the real world, once they had to.

Laura tried calling Rebecca once more, returning to the floor against the wall again because the television didn't grab her attention. It rang.

"Hello?"

"Uh...Rebecca, it's Laura."

"Did you just try calling me?"

"Yes." Laura shied as if she was interrupting someone she didn't know.

Rebecca had been pacing. "What's up? I haven't talked to you since high school!"

"I know. I'm in Omaha now. We should get together and do something since it's been this long."

"Yep, I'm in Omaha, too. I taught kids in school this last year. Rebecca is a teacher now," she said of herself. "Bet you never thought that was going to happen, huh?" Rebecca had wanted to tell Laura about this and expected Laura to be excited also.

Laura was unprepared for this, intending to be a better influence than she used to be. "It's up to you." Then, trying to direct the conversation, she said, "I haven't had many people over in a while." Laura was scratching her forehead.

"Well, I'm getting ready for school. It's starting up again already. This summer went way too fast."

Laura was under the impression she was supposed to already know what was new with Rebecca, who clearly had no time for self-esteem issues. Good that she made her way as a teacher.

Laura said, "Still, you'll like the place; I could read your tarot." Laura remained calm in her high.

"Really? Aren't you afraid of that stuff?"

"No, not really."

"Well, get a hold of me later this week, and we'll do something."

"Okay. You want my number?"

Rebecca was then panicking for a paper and pen. "Yes. Hold on…Okay, give it to me." She was excited and smiling.

"It's eighty-seven, twenty-five."

"Cool." Rebecca was surprised Laura called, as if Laura hadn't cared to call because she had other friends. There was too much front, as if they both could talk to strangers in the same manner, so they needed to meet sometime.

"I'll talk to you later," Laura said. She hung up and got choked up because throughout the call, it seemed she had already lost touch with someone she believed had been her truest friend. Little help would come from the people she'd known in her youth, no matter their importance to her.

Confused when Laura hung up, Rebecca expected more, since Laura had reached her after all this time; she didn't know what to make of it. Something about Laura suggested she was trying to be more connected or didn't have friends at all. Then,

Rebecca decided it was just a drug thing, not as bad as the last time. Here, Rebecca was with a friend and having a few drinks at home.

"What was that all about?" Rebecca's friend said.

"I think she's been alone for way too long. I'll call her sometime."

Laura looked around as if to reawaken a little disoriented where she sat at the wall. Pursy soon ran toward Laura, then slowly approached, tail perked.

Laura rested her chin on her fist with her knees up, until she was too frustrated. When she got up, she cried aloud, looking to the door as if the door was some gateway from being tucked away in a loft, which itself should promise some peace of mind, though it now seemed a public property more than her own home, an often heavy idea taking from her all backbone. Where else did she belong? What was she working for but to become homeless despite all her effort?

Though she felt the high, she went upstairs to smoke. If she continued to feel like this about her relationships and the apartment, it could derail her.

Laura often had a mentality she could do anything. Maybe she'd even talk more openly with Rebecca, who was probably sometimes faced with it, too. The world hustled everyone to death.

Laura tried smoking from the pipe, but instead violently choked and coughed. Finally, she went for a glass of water.

While downstairs, she put on a song and filled the room with the volume. A cigarette from her bag and the view outside the window was all she needed, to stop and forget. Maybe she'd eventually understand what kept her from talking; it had been like this for too long.

The song put various people into perspective for her, but it was also a welcome estrangement; she wasn't into what everyone else was in, nor had she ever been, really. It was necessary to go it alone.

* * *

Michael sat smoking at the kitchen table. Maybe journaling would help map his way out of this. His eyes caught a walker outside as the haze of smoke filled the room. For once, he had his Guinness cap on from the basement. Dan soon arrived outside with the truck, and it didn't faze Michael. This moment, he wanted to maintain his privacy, but if he were to leave the table, he'd surely lose this sense. So, he took a deep breath and continued smoking.

* * *

With the music off, Laura sat with the volume of the TV down to near mute. Then, she turned it off altogether and stayed on the sofa. She didn't give her ideas any further thought, because it would only set a time she was separated from her friends and had to face things alone. However, something about marijuana brought her to always think of the same troubles. So, it was simple being alarmed about anything the deeper she got into something like this.

Somewhere in the bag was Marcel's number, so she took the bag to the table and emptied it. She grabbed the phone and steadily dialed and redialed with a growing headache. Downstairs, the laundry waited. Though this wasn't a simple task, everything was placed back in her bag as she called Marcel.

Hello? "Marcel?" *Yes. This Laura?* "Yeah."

"I was just thinking about you," he said.

"Really?" Despite previous emotions, she smiled.

"Sup, girl?" Marcel asked.

"I wanted to know if you'd go to Fremont with me."

"Sure. When?"

"Well, I've got laundry to finish, but I'll call you." *All right, bye.* "Bye."

Laura rushed to the elevator, then to the laundry room, and put the clothes in the dryer. Immediately, she thought of New York again. She had hurried herself and needed to slow down. True, she wasn't a kid anymore, but she felt like one this moment. In the elevator, it had all passed her. Although she got the laundry in the dryer, she barely saw herself in the basement. She walked with a stride through her apartment and was back at the table, where she wondered blankly about Michelle, a friend from Blair who had a baby now.

To break free from everything, Laura watched television for about a half hour before getting her laundry. She phoned Marcel when she returned.

"Yes...Yeah, what's the address? Okay, I'll be there soon."

❊ ❊ ❊

Amplification

Dan had arrived to move in; even though Michael didn't want to leave the kitchen table earlier, he helped until they finished. Afterward, in the suffocating warmth and staleness of the living room, they made plans to leave for West Point. Dan was on the sofa, and Michael stood near the TV because he had just turned it off.

Dan said, "So when was the last time you saw Meghan?" He felt in a position to say something, though he knew of nothing more than this.

"Oh, I went with her to the bar downtown, but no one was there. We bought a six-pack and drove the country roads in her boyfriend's truck. A while back."

Dan was confused. "I don't know. I haven't seen her

really since high school."

"She hasn't changed. Well, some."

"I kind of thought that."

"Yep." Michael sat.

After they took hits from the pipe, smoke surrounded them. They would leave soon. "Man, I'm high," Dan said with a laugh.

"I know, right?" Michael had taken the phrase from someone he used to know, so he remembered him. He thought of the job. "I had my interview today. I've got work now."

"I don't know how you can stand it."

"Pays well."

"I guess." Dan thought Michael was gay then as he had thought from time to time. It made him feel somehow more mature, or with a stronger male identity. It also stopped him from talking further because he'd prefer to hang with someone more like himself. Michael was sometimes someone to laugh with either way. He probably wasn't gay--whatever.

"We better go," Michael said. "You okay to drive?"

"Yeah." Dan was relaxed but stood up when Michael did. The room was quiet. Michael took his bag before they went out the back door to the truck. They both got in and shut their doors at the exact same time like they were on a mission, so they laughed.

"Isn't that fucked up how we always shut our doors at the same time?"

"Yeah," Dan said with a smirk.

They were out of the driveway and slowly turning onto another street. Soon enough, they arrived at Dan's house, parked the truck, and got in an old, beat-up sedan. Dan said he'd tell his mom where they were going, so Michael waited in the car and thought of the times in West Point when they used to get high.

As they drove out of Fremont, they smoked. The noise

of the muffler got to Michael, and he remembered the hospital. Fremont was dull and flat and overrun with commercialism, like any town, as if each town maintained a Vegas Strip. Still, he liked downtown with its older buildings, antiques, and coffee.

Michael was on probation, he had to cross train tracks to work, and he'd have to give a urine sample soon.

Dan had been away from West Point, too. It would be the same, but the two of them were of age for drinking now. He missed the time because he felt more of an adult as a kid and now more stuck in his youth as an adult. It was likewise for Michael.

"Fremont sucks," Michael said. "You need to see Chicago. I'd still be there if I didn't have all these bills to pay up."

"That fucking sucks."

"Tell me about it. Fremont is the same shit," Michael said. "People have money out of nowhere."

Dan said, "You could work as a plumber or some shit. Makes me wanna drink."

Michael grinned, even though it wasn't funny. "Hey, you know Trish moved out of town?"

"Oh, really?"

"Yeah, she just up and left without talking to me. I couldn't find her in the new phone book." Michael saw himself back to being a kid suddenly. He got this from Meghan. (Anything to cheer Dan up).

"That sucks."

"Everything sucks," Michael reiterated.

Dan laughed.

Michael said, "All there ever is to do is watch the fucking TV and buy shit."

"God." Dan was impressed by the idea everyone had altogether reached eternal boredom.

Michael hooked up the music and less came to bother them. Fields surrounded them as Dan drove the highway, and

Michael couldn't get himself to sit still. He was aware of his bills at home, of living in Fremont, of the probation, and situations he wasn't confronting. He wanted to stay with the job, but they often fired people if sales weren't being made.

"I hope I can stay with this job," he said over the music.

"Yeah. I don't know--you won't see me working back there. I hate talking to people over the phone like that. Really, it's *stupid*." Dan's high was intense as though he were cold and shivering in December.

Hanging with Dan like this, Michael didn't know what it was. Better to be with friends, when outside of any friendship, the world was otherwise meaningless. He stood out in school, but it didn't matter now. Like many people, he was faced with bills, and he didn't anticipate any of it when he had expected an easy road.

"The world is strange. You know how everything moves fast?" Michael said. "It's like there's no time for anything. My grandparents are almost there, but I don't think they're bothered by death."

"Yeah, old people are strange, though," Dan said.

Michael said, "There are people in the nursing home who don't stop cussing."

"Yeah, but you really don't have to worry about that. Not yet anyway." Dan scratched his neck.

"Like, I think they can't stop thinking about everything they hate before they die," Michael said.

"Yeah," Dan said, smiling through another boring situation in the works. "They're like, 'just kill me!'"

The music was loud, so Michael turned it down. He leaned back in his seat and watched a field pass. He wanted to say something, but it hurt to think. He made the mistake of lighting up another cigarette because it only sharpened his headache. "Man, I'm fucked up right now," he said.

"Sucks." Dan was back to his usual self. "Do you know if gas is cheaper in Scribner?" he said.

"Usually."

"All right."

Before long, they made it to Scribner's gas station. Michael went in to get his numbers played in the lottery and returned to the car. They peeled out onto the highway again.

A light rain was coming down. Michael focused on the road ahead as it passed underneath him. He was still buzzed enough to be amused by it. They were otherwise surrounded by the usual scene of grassy ditch, cars in motion, and fields, moving fast until finally arriving in West Point.

When they reached the house, Michael went up to the porch, knocked, and waited. She shortly was out the door. "Hey, dude," she said with a smile. "What's up?" They had been coming and going from this freshly painted, old white house many times before.

Meghan got in the back, behind Dan. She was still smiling. "Dan, I haven't seen *you* in a long time!"

"Yeah." Dan appeared both stiffened and mentally relaxed.

"Ready to get drunk?" Michael said to Meghan.

"Fuck yeah," she said, smirking.

"What bar?" Michael asked Dan.

"I don't know. Whichever."

"Right." Michael sat up.

They were shortly downtown and turning onto Main Street. "Without a car, we'd be screwed," Michael said.

"Fuck yeah," Meghan said.

Soon, they parked, got out, and crossed the street in a disordered mess, when someone almost ran into Meghan with their car, its tires screeching to a halt. Meghan swore at the woman.

Classic rock played, and people off work were already at the tables. A few were at the bar. Meghan was the last one in and looked around. In a town like this, it was one place animated inside.

The three of them sat at the bar with Michael in the middle. "What can I get you all?" asked the bartender.

"Just a beer."

"Same here."

"Me, too." Dan and Michael lit up cigarettes after the first swigs. "Dude, I don't know how you can smoke that shit," Meghan said. "It's fucking sick."

"I'll buy you a pack to get you started, honey," said a man.

"Whatever," Meghan said mostly to herself.

"It isn't worth the money, I know," Michael said.

"Yeah, that's what my mom says, and she keeps buying the shit."

Dan was silent; his focus wandered to the television as the news came on. He remembered the cat kids had mutilated and killed, and he didn't think well of them. He took a drink.

Michael laughed. "Meghan, do you remember in sixth grade when you told that girl she beat the bedpost at night?" he said.

"What? How'd you remember that?"

"I don't know."

Then it came to her. "Trudy Pass Gas." They laughed, and Dan almost choked on his beer. Meghan then said, "Hey, dude, we were tripping on 'shrooms after you called, and a cop searched us."

"No shit?"

"Yeah, since we didn't have anything on us, we were looking at each other and laughing. You should have seen us. We could not stop laughing, and the cop really got embarrassed. We kept telling him we had nothing."

"I bet," Michael said with a smile. It was as though together they always went against the law. "Where were you?"

"Wilderness."

Michael tried picturing it. "With who?"

"Roger, Jon...some other dude."

"That had to be funny." They drank a while without talking, and he thought to ask her kiddingly: "You love me, Meghan?"

"As a friend, I guess. Yeah."

"Sometimes I wonder. You're not the type of person who loves anyone." He said this with a bright grin.

"Sure I am," she said in her humor, smiling, then took another drink.

It rained outside as the three of them left the bar. Other people outside were finishing errands as they drove or walked past.

Momentarily, Michael felt anxious. "Recovery seems long in the hospital," he said. "You just take things slow. When everything moves so fast, you have to catch up with it, and drugs don't help. Like, sometimes all I feel is paranoia when I smoke pot. Other times it's okay."

"I get paranoid sometimes, it's normal," she said. "You must have been messed up to want to kill yourself."

"Yeah, kind of."

Later, as they rode out, Michael commented on the rain. Meghan said, "We can get high at my house before you guys leave."

"You sure?" Michael asked.

"Yeah, it's okay."

Soon, they were in Meghan's kitchen when she turned the light on. "Hold on; gotta get the good shit." She was imitating an old granny again.

"All right," Michael said. He sat at the table. "You buzzed?"

"Yeah," Dan said with a sigh.

Meghan came down the steep stairway. She skipped a step and was nearly falling onto Michael's backside. Everyone in her family had a trip and fall down these narrow stairs once or twice, or more. She sat with a baggie and pipe and started managing it. Her attitude shifted to plainly say: "I got hooked up with this from one of the Mexicans in town. I asked 'mota?' just playing with him, and he had the shit on him."

Michael gave a subtle laugh.

"A lot of people are racist. More now that Hispanics are moving in," Dan said as he sat.

"I have no time for bullshit from some people," Meghan said.

"Yeah," Michael said.

She handed him the pipe. "Whatever. Your start."

Michael took a strong hit. "That's pretty skunky," he said. He handed it to Dan.

"I don't know," Dan said. "Everyone here talks happy." He spoke through his boredom.

"Hey, are you going to baby-sit that?" Meghan said to Dan since she knew her mom would be home from work in an hour. So, the rounds went until the bowl was cashed. "What's up, space cadets?" Meghan asked. It was her most relaxed smile as she raised her eyebrows.

Dan said with a grin, "God, I have to drive in the rain now."

Meghan stared at Dan. "Sucks to be you." She wanted to be alone in the house and freshen the air. She'd take a bath stoned and watch TV before her mom got back. At this idea, she laughed.

Dan assumed she was laughing at him and figured she hadn't changed much. Her humor was endless. At best, she had concern for a situation, but it wouldn't be up to her to help the matter, other than directing focus to other things.

"I'm watching Simpsons tonight, for sure," she said.

Michael was thinking. "Don't you get the feeling we'll never change?" he asked Meghan.

"Why do you have to always be serious? You'll change," she said, throwing her hand in the air.

"I don't know. Life's boring when we're not high."

She mimicked an old granny again, saying, "That's 'cause

you're *hooked on the shit.*"

"And there's nothing to do," Michael added.

"Yep." They sat with each other without talking and glanced at one another with lingering and fading smiles. Meghan rolled her eyes a few times. They were sometimes about to laugh in their high, but they dreaded not having anything to say. After a few minutes, "You guys can go if you want."

"You wanna go, Dan?"

"Sure."

"A'right, Meghan," Michael said as he stood up. "You'll call me sometime?"

"Yeah. Sure, dude."

The two left to the rain outside. "Bye." She shut the door behind them.

CHAPTER 6

Consideration

L aura was out of her building and into her car in a hurry. It was raining lightly, the sun still shining through. While driving, she grew impatient with the road and its stoplights but made it to Marcel's street. As expected, it was a quiet, more secluded neighborhood with plenty of old trees lifting her curiosity and patience as she drove through it.

She came to Marcel's street, where he was waiting outside. He got in, and said, "I'm feeling good about this."

"I am, too." They rode off. Laura took another street toward Dodge, headed west at the light, and they hadn't spoken. Then, Marcel made a comment.

"What?" Laura asked.

"My day was good," he repeated as he looked at her.

"Good. You worked?" She spoke slowly, gathering ideas about him, and wondering if he really was the friend she'd been looking for all this time.

"Yes, I work every day but the weekend." It was obvious he didn't like working this frequently.

"Good shift; same with me, mostly," she said. She almost couldn't get herself to speak up more.

"Maybe we'll hang out weekends?" he said before they shared a glance.

"Sure, maybe." She stopped to think. "I called an old friend today. It's been a while since I last saw her."

"How was it?"

"I don't know. We were best friends growing up, but I think it's my fault we aren't so much these days, like I should've been the one talking. It's like my closest friend and I haven't had a friendship grow since grade school."

"I wouldn't worry about it. Maybe there isn't much you have in common."

Laura could see he was the kid in the picture. When the picture was taken, family was more important than television. She said, "Mom thinks I'm too young to worry, too. She said if she didn't have a problem, I shouldn't. My only choice is to accept that there's just nothing new going on."

Marcel looked ahead. "We don't have all the right answers. You also need to slow down."

"Yeah, life is fast."

"I mean your driving. You never know if they're gonna slow down ahead."

"Yeah, it's okay." She watched the road. "I think as kids we were used to talking all the time, and we enter into adulthood with a lot of questions. I'm alone a lot now, and I always get anxious and have to do something."

"Yeah, I see what you're saying, you're practically still a kid," he said, glancing at her.

After a moment, Laura leaned back in her seat. She wondered if what she could say could ever matter. She could have saved the trip for a later time since it was raining out.

He was watching the road, then looked at her. She said, "We could read cards all day if you wanted to, and get high."

"You must really be into that." Some moments, she seemed to always know where she was going and could visualize what would bring her closer to adulthood. Being an adult appealed to him, but it was rare to find.

Most of his ties soon broke up after school. Laura would

now be one of the few friends he had. It wasn't by necessity but came to him anyway. He remembered just a day earlier meeting her at the bar, and it was as though he already knew her much longer.

She said, "Do you think there's always someone out there for everyone?"

Immediately, he looked away at the road, at whatever she could be staring at. "Don't know," he said.

They were shortly at a stoplight. "Do you want anything before we leave town?"

"Nope, I'm good, Laura."

"Alright," she said, trying to calm herself.

They got past the intersection and were up a hill. The road widened and traffic dispersed. Her book came to mind. If she were to get a second job, it would take away the time she had for writing. Wanting more out of the conversation, Laura realized it would just be forgotten. Without direction to face the world, meaning was for her to find on her own. Maybe it was the same for Marcel.

"Do you ever watch that show with the funeral house and someone dying in every episode?" Laura said.

"Yeah, it's a good one."

"Yeah, I like it." She wanted to say more. She sped up with the rest of the traffic. He wasn't saying anything.

She said, "We have serious inhibitions."

"We'll get past that. We're just getting to know each other."

"I mean people generally."

"But we do grow up. People just need to be happy. I think I've been through it. Just take it easy."

The comment nearly passed Laura as she focused on the road. "What do you remember of me at the bar?" she asked.

"I remember you were happy. Friendly. Honest."

"I've never been too outspoken," she said.

"You don't have to be shy with me. We're cool."

"Yeah." They were on the outskirts of town. She adjusted

herself and could finally breathe. "Maybe you're right. I was anxious leaving town with all the traffic; now I'm okay. You notice?"

"Some. But I think you're right, you're different from a lot of people."

"You think so?"

"Trust me."

They were out of Omaha with less traffic. Marcel had likely grown up with a broader understanding of people. She could drive as far as her house and show him where she grew up, but driving to Fremont was enough. Laura opened her water, drank some, and set it down. "You haven't been out this far yet?" she said.

"Uh. No. I haven't. Honestly, I'm nervous, too." He gave a chuckle. "But I'll be a'right."

She turned northbound where the road narrowed, went over a viaduct past a town, to a four-lane, divided highway, and it would be about a twenty-minute drive further. She picked up speed.

Marcel was quiet, then said, "You're very smart."

"I don't know, my school was just average, full of smart-asses," she said.

He laughed to himself. "What did you do on the farm?" he asked.

"Walked beans and pulled weeds."

"Sounds like work."

"I drove tractors as a kid. Can you believe it?"

He smiled. "I could see that."

"Kids can do a lot."

Marcel looked up at the road. For whatever reason, Laura was even more distant now than at the bar. "If you could change anything in your life, what would it be?"

"That's a hard question. I don't know."

"You don't have to answer it, I just don't know what to ask," he said, smiling.

"I would change my attitude first, and the relationship I have with my mom. I care about her, but I guess I got distracted. We're not as close as we could be."

"What's her name?"

"Renae."

"What's your last name?"

"Schneider. What's yours?"

"Johnson."

Laura smiled. Marcel thought she was smiling about him, so he smiled.

Finally, a weaving road outside of Fremont brought them to a stop sign. They went past houses, then through a commercial area, and past more housing before they were at another stoplight with plenty of traffic. This was Bell Street. "What town is this again?" Marcel asked.

"Fremont."

"Is it a boring town?"

"There just are no jobs here. It has its places."

He had to wonder. "This is where the place is?"

"Yeah. It's by the river. Good thing it's not raining too hard," Laura said, looking up at the sky out her window. She seemed quiet, appearing to be waiting.

"Yeah, it's only sprinkling, really," he said, double-checking out his window. Marcel wondered what was on her mind.

"You like rain?" she asked.

"Yes. It rains a lot in Chicago, and we walk outside more than people do here. Every place has a sidewalk." Some of these people surely were racist; it was extreme to know this, and to be here with her.

She said, "I bet it's nice."

"Are there black people here?" he asked quietly.

"Some, yeah. It's mostly all right out here. Cheaper."

She knew nothing to say but maybe suggest going to

Chicago with him sometime.

Soon, they passed a small park and approached another stoplight. The windshield wipers were on low. Some parts of the town were charming.

Always believing it would make her too much of what everyone else was, Laura avoided relationships until getting out of school. She was emotionally unprepared.

"Too bad I didn't bring some bud," she later said.

He was a little restless, both at the town and the mention of weed. "You could have *big* thoughts. Stay away from it."

"I'll be careful."

"You need to be. It really causes problems for some people. You don't want the trouble."

They crossed Broad Street. It placed them at a part of a square where young people drove on weekends to meet up with each other and drink. These kids weren't aware of the mistakes they made because many were together in the same shallow shit, doing the same thing. Their only example of what life was like was each other.

Laura drove past more houses where trees loomed over the street. "There isn't much to do in this town," Laura said.

"I can see that. Omaha isn't permanent for me."

"Why did you come?"

"I met some people who said it was cheaper; I see them once in a while, but otherwise, I don't know too many people." There was a pause. "Are you attracted to me?" he asked.

She hesitated, thinking this would reveal something about her, as though she were manipulating the situation to be with him. She'd be just some white girl. She was attracted to him. "Yeah, I am."

He laughed. "I thought you were, at the bar."

"You might think this is weird, but the only two guys I've been with were black." She was serious.

"Oh, for real?"

"Yeah," she said with a shrug. Maybe it was too much to

say. She turned south onto Ridge Road. "We're almost there." She was almost too quiet to hear. She looked back at the road, seemingly unsure of herself, though mostly happy. Maybe some people here were racist. "Since your mom had a stroke, is it hard for her to talk?"

"I don't think so," he denied.

She pulled into the site. "Okay, this is the place." She drove further in.

"Looks nice," he said, thinking of his mom.

They parked and shut their windows. "You ready?"

"Yep," he said, opening his door.

She got out, locked her doors, and walked ahead of Marcel to where the trails began. It was cool outside for summer. Laura stood at a tree. "You can eat these...have you ever tried them?" she asked.

"No."

"Try one. The darker ones are ripe."

He pulled one and tasted it. "They're good," he said and picked a few more.

"Yeah. They're in a book I have about botany."

"Yeah, you told me about that. What are they?"

"Mulberries."

She couldn't help but smile. They went into the trails and walked side by side further in. "We need more places like this."

"I agree," Marcel said, smiling because he could easily bring her out to Chicago. They could go to the parks or Lincoln Park Zoo.

Birds could have been in the trees, but they weren't saying anything. Other than some cars passing on the road beyond the trees, it was quiet here. Rain was lightly coming down, and the sound was above them on the tops of the trees surrounding them. They walked further to where the trail branched off.

"This way goes to the river," she said.

"Okay." He looked ahead, ready to settle with her friendship much longer than he had originally thought. She seemed unique to this place, despite the ignorance and haphazard hustle of everyone. There were things she didn't know.

Laura had been here many times previously, to smoke with her friends back when it was all carefree. It was one of the few places to get away from town, whenever they'd visit Fremont. They approached the river.

"This is wider than I expected," he said. "Wow."

"You see the cliff side?"

"Yeah, it's a nice place to get away and think." This moment, they were staring at the slow-moving water. Marcel picked up a rock and threw it a distance up and into it. The trees were more open, letting more rain around them. "I'm thinking I'm glad we met," he said.

"Oh, same here." she continued staring at the river but smiled. She thought she could have brought something to smoke. Then, she remembered her cigarettes and pulled them out. "You want one?"

"Aww, sure."

They each took a cigarette, lit up, and exhaled. She could tell how much more grown he acted. She was nervous, saying, "What are your future plans?"

"I'll stay in nursing."

"You want to afford a house?"

"Someday."

"Do you want a family?"

He received this as he would've from anyone like her, though it was quite obviously her alone saying this, and no one else ever had. "My family is taking care of my kid, but not really. No."

"Neither do I."

Laura was overwhelmed by not having much to say.

"Was your summer quiet?" she asked.

"Yeah, very quiet. You?"

"I was alone most of the time." She nodded.

"Okay. Welcome to adulthood."

"Right?" She laughed. With the sound of the river, they continued smoking. Laura noticed rain on her cigarette. "I hope this trip didn't bore you."

"No," he said enthused, "We should come here again sometime when it's not raining. I don't know—we'll pull up some lawn chairs next time."

They smiled and smoked some more. "There's fishing at the lakes."

"Oh, they got lakes here? That would be all right."

They finished their cigarettes at about the same time. Marcel would probably someday head back to Chicago where his family was, and it meant she'd be losing contact with someone again. "I feel like I've known you," she said. It just wasn't enough to find someone like him and not express it.

Marcel hugged Laura, and it came as a shock. At first, she didn't feel right. She had her hands around him and held him tighter. He was one of the fewest of people she knew. She barely knew her family anymore. Laura could trust him.

"What's *wrong?*" he asked.

They stood to each other, and she rubbed her eyes. "I don't know. Maybe no one cares." She refocused. "I can't remember the last time anyone hugged me."

"Okay." He kept his arm around her, and they faced the river. Just then, it started raining down on them harder, and thunder was approaching.

"Shit, we gotta go back," she said, unaware anymore of their time as it was. She led him through the trails, and they hurried to the car, both getting in at once. When she closed her door, Marcel put his hand on her leg. The rain covered the windshield thoroughly. She looked at him, and together they kissed gently. A moment later they drew back and looked at each other, speechless.

Then, as a kid would, she hugged him.

* * *

Discovery

This night, thunder drummed through the sky over Fremont, and rain filled the street outside. Normally, Dan worked nights but had the night off. He and Michael were in the living room, watching free cable from the last tenants. "What a storm," Michael commented. The windows were open to the sound.

"Yeah. I think I'm going to bed," Dan said.

"Alright."

Dan walked across the light of the TV, the only light in the room, casting shadows. His steps scuffed across the linoleum floor as he left through the darkened kitchen to his home in the basement.

To fight off a headache, Michael lit up a cigarette. He flipped through channels, landing on offensive comedy, knowing how seldom he ever laughed. Whenever he did, it was with uncertainty about his future.

The thunder moved through the sky over the apartment, and a car drove wetly past with its lights on. With windows open, the lightning showed through.

He was no stranger to the conflict of meeting the demands of adulthood, but it seemed there was some other place he should be. The apartment wouldn't work out if he continued to think this. On the other hand, with free cable, he almost didn't care.

He smoked and exhaled toward the TV in front of him. His headache persisted, so he sat up, thinking it was more back trouble.

Meghan had been in the wilderness tripping on mushrooms. He imagined them being searched and laughing, so apart from what was happening on the TV, he grinned.

The show was in the middle of explaining something he didn't follow, so he flipped through the channels again, landing on a movie, which seemed quickly scripted, maybe even unrehearsed. However, he didn't have commercials to throw his attention in countless directions.

Dropping acid was maybe responsible for his trip to the hospital. Then, there was nothing he could do about it. Could've been much worse, anyhow....

Not long after the hospital, he had been on a skiing trip to Colorado with his family. Instead of skiing, he studied one of his house designs.

At the thought of it, Michael got up for some lamplight and sat with the drafts already out of his bag. Part of his study covered the perceptions of each of the zodiac animals, and he attributed one to each room. During his mania, he had envisioned the rat as being curious of its surroundings. His imagination with the house helped him during his hospitalization to focus less on complicated issues. It was an imaginative world, and he had the space to do it and be alone, despite a heavy past, fearful of strangers, friends, and even family from the beginning.

On the TV, some guys fell to the snow, and it struck him like a lucid vision, reminding him of skiing. "Fuck you!" a man shouted on the TV, shooting.

Michael set his prints to the side and quietly left through the kitchen to the pool table in the basement. He was aware of Dan in the next room, so he used the light from the stairway to get the bud. Back upstairs in the living room, another car's headlights passed the window. He thought he should avoid television, but it would be okay without voices.

He sat with the box open on the table, took out the bag and pipe, then leaned back and pulled a lighter from his pocket. He moved the table closer to the light of the TV and sorted seeds out, packed the bowl, and held the pipe to his mouth.

"Go to hell!" the man shouted.

Drawing his attention away from the TV, he took in a few hits. On the TV, the guy shot from behind a tree at a few other men positioned behind a large boulder. It was a movie in the mountains. Michael lit the weed again, looking at it as it burned. He was quickly high and drew attention back at the drawings under the lamplight.

A car drove past, and Michael watched its light. Then, the noise of the TV intensified, so he grabbed the remote and turned it down. He switched the channel to the news. Somehow, controlling the situation in his high gave him immediate pain in the back of his head. He sat up to adjust his back from side to side.

The news was discussing a heightened terror alert due to the coming month of September, entering the room as though it deserved to be the only channel watched. More commentary followed with another dull anchorman, so Michael became disinterested and looked at his drawings again. He left the news as it was.

After impatiently thumbing through the pages, he came to the window and waited in slight paranoia for cars. None came, so he looked back at the darkened room with the light of the TV. Now was not a time to recover where he was and plan for work the next day. He lost all focus and tried to think.

He had plenty of coffee earlier.

Michael sat again for a moment before switching back to comedy, which didn't come pleasantly because the words were articulately rude. He had the idea they were, in some instances, talking of him, so he leaned back, trying to ignore it and regain his high. He was reminded of the job.

Anxiety held him this moment to the worry over money. He had to breathe.

Michael then switched back to the movie because he could mindlessly follow it, but it was loud in its credits with rock music now. The comedy channel was still loud, so he ended up flipping through the channels before listening to a few words of commercials and finally landing on a show with a house being built. It was also just finishing up.

He then kept the channel running to have a cigarette, so he got up and lit one with the flame in front of his eyes, full of hypnotic motion, as he was aware of the noise from the TV and the rain outside once more. He cracked his neck, then stepped over to the window again, to have some distance from the TV even though he wanted it on.

Oddly enough, he got his focus back, but the words coming through the TV distracted any sense of privacy. He had to listen to it in a stare, which held him at the window. It wasn't simple to think of anything, and his thoughts weren't clear right away. It was something about Meghan again. He and Meghan both were all right, but maybe some changes were ahead.

It was wrong staying up late, he'd be up for the experience, whatever it was. He forgot about his cigarette.

Michael refocused. The TV caught his attention before the street outside did. It was late, and it would be rare to see a car in the storm. Anyone could be coming home late, but if there were cars, they probably had no other business driving here.

Michael wanted the type of relationship to maybe knock him out of the routine, out of the unbearable mundane, and back to his senses. Much of his attraction came from desiring a real connection with someone.

Men were too often incompetent and rude; they came from egotism and believed only the obvious. They were sometimes sex-driven, interested only until they would land as family men. Once arrived at this, they would become fixated by the sports and liquor other men gave their souls to. Finally, they'd become detached from the women who no longer attracted them, to slump to their added weight and maybe have an affair. Or simply put, they were aimless: competitively aimless.

Michael was fortunate to come across what he knew,

or who he knew. He felt extreme this moment but started laughing a little anyway, before stopping himself.

These thoughts remained with him, and he returned to smoking. He breathed more to focus on his high. In all fairness, most women were equally misguided...

The television still distracted him, so he turned it off and waited in darkness at the window with the lamp and the lit cigarette. He smoked a ring for the first time ever, standing there.

Had his friends displaced him? Ideas and flashbacks related to this quickly passed Michael's attention. It was his choice to leave for Chicago when things fell apart back home. He was sometimes overwhelmed by his insecurities, and his behavior showed he took influence from the people he knew. When one approach didn't work, there were other ways to talk with people, but it didn't hold up.

He laughed silently again. The usual attitude he carried was also marked by shame. It left many things unsaid out of fear.

Michael could be someone adults had compassion for because his boundaries kept him less open. He did what he knew was best. With a certain amount of paranoia, he was targeting a fear of people he always had, but it wasn't necessary or even typical of him. He considered it as something he could grow from, but he was defensive of a behavior that wasn't like him.

He then looked at the blank TV and was ready for it since he no longer had a headache. It was more houses being built. "Fuck this," he whispered. Normally, these people were so complacent, it just didn't match his reality. He scratched his forehead with a look of concern.

Michael then flipped back to the news, waited a while, and let it roll past. There was mention of the war, and he stared. If these people were like him at all, they wouldn't have war.

He went to another movie, and it was unbelievably fake

and suited a time when people dressed up in extreme attire with vacant expressions, speaking simple lines with back-and-forth talking and pausing. He was following it anyhow and smoked until the cigarette burned at the filter, then lit up another one. A boring romance was in the works with the woman needing the man. Then, the man accused her of being with another man and wanted nothing to do with her. Michael could've sworn they wore polyester in the seventies, even though it was set in the thirties.

Michael finally turned the TV off.

Here in the darkness of the living room, he scratched his forehead again, he thought about the job. Since he had one, there was nothing to worry over--except maybe the headache that came and went.

His friends were all met at the right time, but he wanted something else; if not for himself, he wanted to be more for them someday.

No doubt, there was a world beyond Nebraska. He wanted to face real issues, and he thought knowing someone through an actual relationship would be right. And for anyone else to be true to him, it depended on how true he was to them. Face to face, he respected just about anyone.

He didn't intend to have recurring effects with the acid, but it was possible. In his slouch, he didn't care. He just smoked. Perhaps one day it would show he did care.

The high wasn't relaxing as usual but intense. He could have a long, tiresome day ahead if he couldn't get sleep. Then his mind was suddenly blank when he thought of his grandmother. It was as though he could someday forget too much because he simply had no thoughts of her at this moment. He owed it to her not to forget.

Michael turned the television back on, and it snapped before it lit up the room again. A car passed slowly, and he could hear it over the low volume of the TV.

Finally getting tired, Michael gazed outside. His mind accelerated the last time with TV, so with drugs, maybe he really did fuck up. A few minutes into the program, he dreaded Fremont. Why he had to be living in this town was beyond him because it seemed meaningless. These places offered nothing to the youth.

It was all a mess, the whole world. People would rather watch a movie, play games, drive around polluting the planet, or smoke something. And yet, no one could do a thing without money. Life was some crude arcade machine sucking quarters by the dollar. The youth around here also seemed uninspired and contagiously narcissistic. Whatever did inspire them had nothing to do with them personally. Maybe they'd forget their grandmothers in favor of a grandmother in a movie.

He was watching the same romance, and she was moving away with her kids. The man was left to himself, and the movie would follow her as she got her life together. Still smoking, Michael decided to step out; it was only thundering now.

Outside, he turned the porch light on, adding this duplex to the neighborhood already lit up outside, and he shut the door behind him. He sat at the top of the steps, adjusted his back, and waited--as if throughout his whole life, he had never once spoken to anyone, and with all he could say, he still hadn't.

He hoped to slow down. It was three, maybe four weeks before he was let out....

Finally, he started to calm himself because the interview went fine. If the job didn't work out and he couldn't get another one, everything could reoccur, putting him in a complicated cycle and throwing him to wanting more than he'd have.

Then, the only road he had was a dead end. He could work at Heartland and take the paychecks, but it wouldn't precede a bigger job. Eventually, he'd switch jobs, but at this rate, it would have to be a place within biking distance. He was reminded of having to constantly talk on the phone, too aware of how much he didn't like working there.

He thought of Trish again and looked around. He took another drag from his cigarette and exhaled, suspecting he might never see her again. With the look on his face, no one would've suspected these thoughts were coming from him. He was somehow left alone to this. Maybe he'd handle it, but the coffee was too much.

It was suddenly urgent to look Trish up in another phonebook. Maybe Omaha?

Michael flicked the cigarette to the sidewalk while it burned, and he stood to go inside. Therein, he noticed how quiet the room actually was. With or without him, this room existed. Returning hesitantly to the sofa, he wondered how he'd get up in the morning. He'd just go to bed at nine the next day to rest up. It would slow everything down, and he'd have more patience, at least the patience he had before this wretched night.

Aggravated by his thoughts, Michael wanted the paycheck already, to have gone to the bank and deposited it, just to be closer to something better. He would've played the lottery and bought smokes. He'd have coffee in the morning.

Of course, he'd prefer feeling secure with people when he talked as seriously as he did. He wanted things to change, yet he couldn't adapt to this.

The TV was happy and adverse, so he decided to finally try and get rest. With the lamp and TV off, everything was quiet, as if he was the only one late to bed.

The refrigerator made noises. It had started when he turned the TV off, but he noticed it now.

Voices rose from below the kitchen. They were the same as in the other apartment, and they continued as he went to the bedroom.

Michael quickly lay in bed with his clothes on. Maybe he

was in trouble like no one knew. Again, everything about him earlier was wrong.

He set his alarm. In response to the idea this was only the start and would get worse, perhaps even tonight, they yelled louder, and he couldn't recall the marijuana or the coffee.

Still, they yelled some more.

This was a wild fear he'd ignored but somehow felt he'd have to confront again. When the noise finally fell silent, he lay on his side with his eyes wide open to the dark. Whatever he thought wasn't intended to go against the voices but went further in a manner of protecting himself. In itself, this went against the voices, so they kept him up for an hour before he fell asleep a lonesome, ridiculed, overgrown child.

CHAPTER 7

L aura switched her alarm off, took a shower before getting dressed, and prepared. She thought of Marcel with some doubt because she hadn't exactly moved on from the last situation. With a pleasant rest behind her, she could see the memory of it all. After finishing her cereal, she was out the door to work, leaving the bowl on the table for Pursy to find.

❊ ❊ ❊

Trust

Michael woke tired to the sound of the alarm, which had been on for about five minutes already, so he now sat alert. The voices were gone. He had to keep quiet or occupied. Unworried, he took a bath and prepared. His shirt was rolled up casually and tight again, and he threw his bag over his shoulder...

Through the grassy field, he thought only of the job. His pants and shoes were now wet. With sleep, his body regained itself overnight and less would bother him this day. He made it across the barren train tracks with a line parked further west. As he walked across, he checked both ways for coming trains, but none were arriving.

Michael breathed and felt as though he had held it in

for too long. The rain had cleared the air. Beginning his walk on the pavement, the road looked long past the intersection. He was afraid of being unprepared for the job and under some scrutiny by whoever surrounded him.

This road also made him uneasy about being within the openness of the world. It would be obvious to some he was walking there, but to them, he was just another stranger and an outsider to Fremont. As he walked further, cars continued rushing by. He walked a narrow slope on the side of the road, so one side of his body stepped lower than the other, probably appearing like a drunkard, and would be the only other person walking here anymore.

For as long as he could remember, he had the impression kids his age were ignorant, so he saw it necessary to find meaning beyond what most knew. Anymore, their lives were complete if they had cigarettes, drinks, and cars. There was just something else, something more he wanted to understand.

He got to the smoke shelter, sat, leaned back, and smoked. He was early for the day with no one outside. For a moment, he stared at the employee entrance. Cigarette butts littered the grass.

The morning was lit through clouds, and the breeze continued. To keep himself occupied, he rummaged through his bag, then changed his mind. Instead, he gazed at the parking lot; someone had parked and was now walking through the smoke shelter. Their eyes met. "Hello," she said.

"Hi."

When she went in, he wondered why he felt this agitated about her saying nothing more. Traffic was distant and in the background. Somehow, there were people totally cool with everything.

Halfway through the smoke, he wished to be in school in Chicago again and remembered some of the friends there. Drinking and drugs had taken him away from his studies.

After falling out of the situation, he found little purpose in staying.

He had curiosity for something under the surface, both before and after the voices, believing he could do more than what a simple job like this asked for. It was like asking a grown kid to play in a child's sandbox while the adults did their own thing.

But it was a job. Michael finished and went inside.

Therein, the place hadn't changed much from a few years back. Computers hummed at the pods, and no one was at work yet. "You here for training?" Elena asked.

"Yes."

"You can wait there or in the break room. You know where the training room is, right?"

"Yeah, they're just next to each other, right?" He pointed.

"Yep," she said, nodding with a bright smile.

He came to the fountain and took a drink...

In the break room, coffee was on already, and Michael filled a cup and sipped. He checked the vending machines of sugar and salt but didn't want any of it, so he left for the training room—too early for people, but if he had had to wait for a train, he would've been late for his first day. The coffee cleared his throat and tasted ordinary but strong.

He faced the room at the table furthest from the door, much more awake than he expected from the few sips of coffee. With nothing else but his journal and a few books, he took out his floor plans again, looking first at the breakfast area which would be an adobe brown, next to the dark turquoise kitchen. The conservatory had a glass roof and a card catalog of plants, stone outer walls, a brick interior wall up to the exterior of the floor above, and plants. He envisioned its floor to be like a slitted deck, allowing light to pass through to the theater below.

✳ ✳ ✳

Laura made it to work. Jeff was waiting inside the office, startled when she came in. "I don't need you today, Laura, but I promise this will be the only time. I tried calling, but I think you were already on your way."

"Okay," she said. "Well, have a good one."

"Thanks."

She left.

* * *

Michael still sipped from his coffee, alone in the training room. There was a new marker board, the white walls, and a phone was set up for demonstration. The room surrounding him was somewhat unsettling. It was sparse and plain, part of a less interesting memory. Although, it did seem energetic.

Again, he studied his floor plans; an indoor, underground garden would have boulders, cobblestones, and a black-and-white theater. It would have a mirrored wall and beamed ceiling with plentiful lighting. It would have a large aquarium and link to the basement of a separate house fashioned like a barn....

He checked his watch. Still, about fifteen minutes would be a while before anyone came in. The next day, if he got up on time, he'd walk the viaduct to work. He was somehow happy to be alone with time ahead of the schedule but feared the voices could return. His mood then brightened sharply, so he took the coffee outside to have another cigarette before people arrived.

Quickly, he left the building just outside the door, where he lit up. He kicked at the back of his foot as he puffed and looked down at his coffee. Maybe it would be safe just to watch what was around him again.

More people were coming in. "Hi," someone said.

"Hello."

Clouds rolled in overhead from the west, then a car

pulled into the parking lot. Besides the breeze, quiet stood when the car parked and disengaged. Something drew him into the smoke shelter. "You new here?" a girl asked him.

"Sort of. I worked here before."

"Oh. It's a boring job if you ask me. What's your name?" she asked.

"Michael. I'm across the train tracks and walked."

"That's cool. I have to actually drive to work."

"Figures."

"Yeah." They were at the end, it seemed. "My name's Angela."

"Nice to meet you," he said, nodding.

"You, too."

Michael checked his cigarette and flicked its ash off. He leaned back on a post and looked the girl over, as she wasn't paying attention to him. Another guy was making small chat with her.

"I'm heading in now. See you later," she said with a smile.

"Yeah."

Maybe she was attractive. However, believed he should remain a trustworthy friend who only had respect for women.

There was a sort of laziness to all this smoking. He could be doing something productive, but what? Had he quit smoking, he'd still be sitting in the break room, looking over his drafts. He let go of the cigarette and returned inside.

In the main room, Michael felt the same uplifted mood as the first time working here. It would be a quick day, demanding less of him. Maybe it was the high ceilings. Of course, with a tight, repetitive script, and after so many hours, the work would drag him down by the afternoon. At least, this had been his last experience.

An older woman followed him into the room, and he looked back at her.

"I'm Nancy."

"Okay, I'm Michael."

"Where is everybody?" Her voice was hoarse.

"Not here yet."

"Oh, I'm going out for a smoke, kid."

With her hands full, Nancy waddled out with a cigarette already in her mouth. It would stick to her lips, and her lips would peel off a little.

Later, a few people entered the room together; the rest came just in time for it to start as the trainer prepared. She had graduated with Michael.

They started with scripts and information about the company. Later, they would have a quiz, and anything below eighty percent failed.

❊ ❊ ❊

Enchantment

Laura arrived home and didn't think twice: she went straight to the pipe because she had good feelings about it. Upstairs in her office area, which overlooked the main room and kitchen, she shuffled the cards between hits and laid them out. She barely looked at them before finishing the bowl. The cards would represent what her day would be.

The seven of spades represented futility as it was upside down. Maybe it was meant to be trust or a combination of the two. At least, in the relationship quadrant, truth would come, but she had emotional disappointment cycle all of the cards and route much of the reading. Her creative mind would lack, possibly, but she had virtue and passion at play. It was possible whatever virtue would bring disappointment....

She craved going back to Fremont, away from the busyness in Omaha. The drive out would calm her, as it always did. She reloaded the pipe, fastened the lid, and put it in her bag for the trip. Out the door, she didn't forget she'd be met with disappointment.

Much later, Laura drove out of Omaha again, thinking of Marcel who was at work. Anything too close or clingy, they could end up hating each other. People typically didn't talk openly around here, and it wasn't enough just to love someone without really opening up. She was good at holding herself back because taking steps forward wasn't easier.

Road construction wasn't overwhelming traffic with detours yet. Trees would disappear here.

Her mother appeared happy in all things. Renae had grown up with a steadfast belief in God, and it seemed consistent with what it had been when Laura was younger. Growing up, her life was probably simpler. She wasn't aware of much more than what she knew of family and friends who were all from small towns and had a decent upbringing. She wasn't far from her younger days and could feel vulnerable to change, possibly. But she was an amazing mother in every way.

It could've been Renae was afraid of getting older. She was still teaching kindergarten, and they were all growing up and passing through her class by the year, so there *was* a matter of getting older. She met changes with ease, but really, she stayed the same. She must've wanted to know something different, or something more.

Laura turned to another highway, northbound. With her window open, she felt the high from earlier. Hunched forward, she had to lean back. When she did, energy went up her back, and she became fully high and aware of her surroundings, bracing the wheel as if she'd yell out 'oh my god.'

Thoughts returned to the job, but she was on track. Then, she thought of Marcel, and it was enough just to feel good and smile for once.

* * *

At Heartland Tele-Services, the group went through the

routine. Michael passed the quiz, so he went outside to reward himself with a smoke.

"You made it through training?" a girl asked him.

"Yeah." He nodded and lit his cigarette.

"I'm Sarah, by the way."

"I'm Michael. I caught your name earlier."

"Cool." She liked him. "My mom was going to kill me if I didn't get this job. She wants me out of the house, and this place just fired a bunch of people a month ago."

"Really?" he asked.

"Yeah, one of my friends was here. I came up from Missouri."

"Fremont isn't great, but we've got the lakes. It has its places."

"Yeah, I like it here. Do you have a girlfriend?"

He shook his head. "No, I'm not interested in relationships. It's always been like that for me. I'm better off alone."

"Not true. Everyone needs someone," she said. "I'm not kidding. You could go crazy."

"I could go crazy in a relationship, too."

"True. But you'll find someone. What, do you go for guys?"

"No." He had a certain lack of confidence.

"And you don't want a relationship?"

"Nope."

"Someday, you're gonna need someone. We could hang out sometime. I've got a guy, though. I promise I won't play matchmaker." Michael didn't know what to say, and they met a pause. She laughed. "Do you smoke?"

"Yes."

"Yeah, we'll hang out sometime," she said with a laugh.

"Okay, cool."

Their break was over. Her hair had blown lightly in the breeze, and she had to arrange it back with her hand. They returned through the glass door.

* * *

Laura breathlessly parked, then walked through the cool breeze before entering the east doors of the local super store on this day off work. Many people animated the place. Somehow, Laura was a part of it, but she didn't want to be. She was hungry for oranges, bananas, yogurt, and maybe peanut butter.

Laura had less holding her back today. She quietly walked through a vacant aisle. If she were truly content, maybe she would've stayed in Omaha with whatever she could do alone and at home.

She walked swiftly to the back for whipped yogurt, and a spoon from another aisle. After gathering the food items, she walked through the clothing area to where the movies were. A few actors and actresses crossed her mind before she was coming down, finding herself browsing, though not so much browsing as much as staring, and contemplating through a troubled focus.

The usual, everyday reminder of what used to be, music had awakened her to the time, represented by everything, so she suddenly came out of the fog like a cloud had finally lifted around her. She could relate to other people who called Nebraska home. There were people like her, maybe even here at the store.

At the cash register, the cost was negligible, and she returned to her car. She used hand sanitizer, took out some yogurt, and ate slowly, before peeling an orange. The radio station played R&B. All her windows were down to the cool weather. As she ate, she looked around to see anyone outside, but there was just an older woman in her blue work apron, who smoked a cigarette and stared into the abyss of the sky from her beat-up van with her mouth agape like she was hallucinating.

Laura was relieved and leaned back; she had remembered to feed Pursy....

Owning a home was dramatically out of reach; she'd have no choice but to keep up with the constant expense of an apartment. It wasn't her to be bound by anything. Further on, she could see herself running away from it all, as she was now, in a parking lot on a day she didn't have to work.

The fear of being homeless had sometimes been on her mind before she started cooking for herself. She'd expected adulthood would be much less challenging. As long as she could keep her car, she was fine. Maybe she wouldn't find a second job, and it would happen.

In countless ways, the world was new to her. She still had a sense of abandonment within the public.

Laura almost choked at her memory of it all. It had once been a real emotional connection with Jae before he was forced to leave. Here, an uncommon loneliness reminded her, and the landscape of fields ahead added to it. This was likely how he felt when he left.

Traffic across the field was either slowing toward the intersection or speeding away from it. People everywhere always drove.

Why she had to think about the smallest of issues, she didn't know. Maybe it would change if she gave it more time. Perhaps God talked to people through thoughts or had once tried showing her how to understand even though she'd ignore whatever message there was to it all. On the one hand, she had no control over her thoughts; maybe they weren't her own.

It was probably nothing but an attempt to know more. She couldn't pay mind to it now; if it was uncomfortable, it wasn't worth going into.

As she watched traffic in the distance, she fantasized about Chicago. People around here always approached her as if meeting for the first time. If they didn't understand her as far as she took herself with them, it was a loss. Considering TV, people lacked not just the emotional reality but self-guidance; they were just distracted. Further distraction was even driven by music. Maybe it was different in Chicago. For now, she was in an insecure world.

Somehow, Laura had already been acquainted with the complexity of various issues, so approaching it now seemed simple. She could nonchalantly blow a bubble with gum if she had some, but an undermining fear would follow, because she couldn't deny sometime in the future she may be without money and a home.

* * *

After a few more hours, training finished. "Do you need a ride?" Sarah asked as people walked by them where they stood together.

"Sure," Michael said quietly and nodded.

Sarah and Michael got in her car, and he complimented her about it since it was well-kept.

"Thanks," she had said. They drove out of the parking lot. "You're gonna have to tell me where it is."

"You just take the first right over the viaduct. Cuming Street."

"Okay." She actively watched traffic, and they didn't talk. Instead, she had the radio on and smoked out her window. Michael watched the street pass by, which he would've walked to get home. Up the road was a line of traffic leaving work. Moments later, they came to the stop light near the gas station where he had previously bought a lotto ticket. He was aware of the radio and the sound of the blinkers at the intersection, and his back hurt as they came over the viaduct.

"That's the street."

"Wow, I almost would've missed it. Okay." She turned sharply over some loose gravel, and they came to the end of the road where it broke off. "Now where?"

"Over there," he said over the radio.

"I see it," she said. She swiftly switched the radio to CD. "I hate commercials. They fucking yell at you."

"I know." They were shortly at his place. "It's this one." They stopped at the duplex, and it appeared heavily afflicted or cursed.

"Hey, see you tomorrow," she said when Michael was walking towards it.

"Yep. Thanks a lot, Sarah." he smiled brightly, yet concerned.

After she waved and smiled, she drove off.

Just as Michael was approaching the front door, he discovered he was missing his keys...Dan's car was gone.

"Hmm."

Michael went around to the back to check the other door. He then sat on the step and prepared for a cigarette. Wherever Dan was, he wouldn't take long.

Alone again, he let his legs out in front of him and leaned back on the door. The neighbor's basset hound barked at him for five long minutes before giving up. Michael was calm, but soon enough came aggravation.

Overwhelmed with a dire lack of options, only to see how people might commonly feel without money, he wondered if there was anyone else worried so much. If he were to stay in Fremont, he wouldn't change much from this level of boredom. *Whatever.*

He cracked his neck.

Michael glanced at where the dog had been barking as though tempted to provoke it. He placed the cigarette butt at his feet before lighting another one, then watched the street and listened for cars. An attitude he deserved more brought the realization it wasn't in reach.

Between puffs, Michael reflectively focused his eyes,

expecting the voices to return as if they were listening to him. It disrupted his focus.

When he'd overdosed, he had the feeling of falling asleep. After he had taken the pills and alcohol and it was taking effect, he wanted to change his mind while the emergency crew surrounded him in the vacant room, asking him questions when he couldn't say anything. He now glanced up at the sun as though someone was there. The last remaining roommate had found him.

Thoughts returned to Meghan, and he decided the constant thinking didn't change his situation. What could he say? The future was unknown. If he were to lose this job, he'd end up walking for miles in Fremont just looking for more work. With probation, maybe no one would hire him.

Just then, Dan pulled into the driveway.

* * *

Laura decided whatever concerns about money and the future were needless worries. Thinking only gave rise to more than what it was at this point. To stop worrying, she drove off. Again, there was no solution for either herself or for others to talk more openly.

She turned the radio off and let the cool air rush through her car. Everything around her was alive. Simply, she was another driver in Fremont's never-ending traffic, significant at one of the busier intersections where she stopped. She remembered someone from grade school who was once a good friend. She had switched schools before they were both in high school, and they never shared classes. When they were young, his laugh always made her smile.

Later, she drove through a neighborhood with old trees reaching over the street. The houses had time behind them. Raising a family always seemed daunting. Of course, there was no beginning to it.

Finally, she arrived downtown and parked across the street from the courthouse, where it stood large with purpose. In her amusement, standing at the entrance of an antique store, no thoughts came to her. The welcoming atmosphere held her there for a moment, as if she entered reality, a world she knew nothing about previously.

"Hello," a woman said calmly as she came out of the office. People like her made it easy to admire Nebraska.

"Hi," Laura said, smiling. Laura glanced around the front room as she made her way toward the back. In the main room, Laura first noticed a large buffet and hutch, painted black. She went to it with its height reaching about eight feet and imagined black-and-white photos on its shelves. Maybe someday she'd want something like it. And near to her was a heavy, marble-top, iron table. She glided her hand across its surface and further inspected what surrounded her. Here, also, was the newer furniture from reclaimed wood, done in traditional country fashion, all matching with the same stain. This was one of the fewest places for shopping unique and genuine items in the area. Almost everyone else just sold particle board.

She walked slowly through the store, noticing oak pedestal tables, an old piano, and some iron garden furniture...the authentic period items could someday be expensive.

Old things often brought ideas of being born following a time of hardship. Most people these days always wanted more than what ever was, but she believed she had enough sentiment not to go too far into it.

A couple browsed the store with their son. Laura briefly gazed at them but couldn't tell what was said. The mother's encouragement surely gave brevity to what he believed in her.

On her way out, Laura glanced at the fabrics. "Bye," she said in a hurry as she went for the door.

"Take care."

Temps were still cool with a breeze, unlike the usual August day. What was she thinking? After all, she had no money for spending. She crossed the street, then soon left in her car and passed by the courthouse and jail. Several minutes later, she was at Ridge Road, then parking near the river again.

Laura ducked into the path and watched her step. At this time, no one was walking the trails. In her curiosity, it seemed if she were homeless, she could eat from nature.

She went to where the trails branched off and looked around. The marijuana wasn't what she needed, but she had planned for it...

...After Laura finished the bowl and put her pipe in the bag, she walked under the trees toward the river, where she was met with young pheasants being led across the trail by their mother. Here was a lone pheasant frightened enough of Laura, it walked back to where they had come from, away from its mother and on the path to the river.

Further in, Laura sneezed and felt the high. Then, she enjoyed being under the trees, repressed enough she wouldn't smile. She could deny being weak with people, and afraid of others sometimes, afraid of not knowing what the future would be, and of never being understood. Laura was still alarmed by the briefly frightened young pheasant since she had just led some defenseless baby bird astray.

A few minutes at the river, after the pheasant went back securely to where the others had gone, it came to Laura that much of the book was unclear. She should have worked on it, instead of wandering around, but she needed a sense of freedom away from Omaha.

Overwhelmed, she looked at the ground to refocus. She took a few deep breaths before letting troublesome ideas pass. The wild sound of birds surrounded her then and there. When she first looked into Marcel's eyes, he seemed to have already known her.

Then, aware of the wilderness, its birds, and the river, Laura simply belonged here. Everything was a calm reminder of where she'd been. The old trees reminded her of times younger when they existed. Life surrounded her.

But the river was different this time. Alone again, she had to think of why she came, after being here just a day ago. Maybe it was just a moment to herself, somewhere familiar. Whenever she'd want to think of the day with Marcel, she could just be here, because even though she could barely get a foothold anymore, he seemed to be the start of something else.

Was she forgetting everything? Oftentimes, she came here to recover her steps, but she couldn't recall much other than a few times with friends.

She couldn't hear the cars crossing the bridge in the distance. The mute motion and life behind them and all of Fremont gave her a sense of coming changes. She could remember seeing him in her apartment when they first got high with the sunlight behind him. She would've preferred having him here again since the weather was right. She had been clinging to so many memories.

Then, Laura could only see herself as someone too often alone, which could outlast her time with him. Maybe Marcel could be a friend, but what else could it be? All this time, she wanted a deeper understanding, and most guys didn't seem to want it themselves. He could give up on her to be with someone else, just as Jerome did.

Overwhelmed, Laura lost her train of thought. She came to the usual idea her friends could do nothing for her, and happiness with people seemed to be long over. Maybe none of what she felt for them had been mutual. If they cared, they would see what she was seeing and know what? Not to leave each other behind?

There was no turning back to what had been. A pain in her throat came to her; she remembered this thought from the few years spent with Jae, and she had no solution for being completely separated from everyone.

Laura walked back. She'd remember being here with these thoughts. Maybe it was the start of something. In the car, she felt incredibly pained with the high. She looked around as though she were waiting for something to happen, like a storm or a cop pulling in. The trees around her would be an invitation where they stood, much like the trees on the farm.

Without another thought, she turned on the car, and the radio blasted on. Laura jolted back, screamed "Oh, my god!" and quickly turned it down until it clicked off. After a moment passed, since she was high, the trees had her attention as though she were dreaming about them.

She left slowly with her seat more forward to help her posture, and she soon passed the lakes and trees of Ridge Road before turning onto Military. Again, she was another driver with nothing in mind but what surrounded her. She was passing everything, or it was passing her; it was hard to tell.

Just then, she reminded herself of the picture Marcel gave her. Last she knew, it was in her bag. As she waited for the light to change, she searched her bag for the photo. Then, she left town, ready for a cigarette because she couldn't find it. She lit up with little patience to get home. Why she had to be anxious without marijuana came as a concern. She was more at ease with the road, but she wondered if more interaction with people would even help.

She wondered, what was with the tarot reading?

She ignored much of what came to her when she was in Omaha. Finally, she arrived at her apartment, and she had a message on the answering machine. *Laura, please call when you get the chance.* It was Renae and sounded like bad news.

Laura dialed and waited. "Hello?"

"It's just me. What's wrong?"

"Your aunt just called." Renae's words only hinted at what could've happened. "Grandma passed away earlier today." She spoke softly, then hoarsely. "I know you're busy, but I needed to call and tell you." She was waiting for a reply. Maybe

Laura would cry with her.

"I'm sorry, Mom." This made Laura feel like a child, and she spoke like one.

"I know you loved her."

"Yeah."

"Will you call sometime?"

"I will, Mom." They hung up. Laura sat at the table, and stared at the blank TV. She didn't know what to do or think about this.

CHAPTER 8

Awareness

L aura still stared at the blank TV, wondering about her grandmother who had passed. With nothing to do, she went for the remote and turned on the TV to watch anything if it meant she wouldn't have to think.

When she was a kid, Laura sometimes played in a park and walked back to her grandmother's a few blocks from it. For whatever reason, her parents let Laura be alone in places at a young age. Maybe it was moments like this when Laura would better feel a sense of security among people.

The show was all hype, and Laura felt the undercurrent of an unmistakable fear. Everyone was working or dying, but they didn't do much else. Even with people, she'd feel alone, and possibly no one in her family had been more alone than her grandmother.

The idea people didn't open up was often the same issue coming from the television, which blared its commercials now. With the apartment, Laura had first appreciated more happening, but lately, it was as though she had no time for it. Her plants needed water again.

Later, she took out the tart, cut out a portion onto a plate, and sat with it on the sofa. The rest belonged to Marcel. Her grandmother always sat alone, facing relentless boredom.

When she finished eating, Laura filled a pitcher at the kitchen sink and began watering her plants. It more or less seemed the deceased were happier to be through with it all, and giving water to her plants was a sort of contribution to life, lending mindfulness to be thankful in rare moments. Renae was probably still crying.

Again, Laura sat at the TV, wondering if it could offer anything. Flipping through the channels, her eyes teared up at the thought of her own mother's funeral.

A movie was on with a couple deciding whether to move in with each other. The woman worried because her daughter was always out of the house, and she wanted her daughter back home. As Laura listened to the television, she prepared coffee and waited in the kitchen. She glanced at the TV when it approached the issue of the man wanting to live further away, which meant they would leave the daughter behind. They argued with each other because the man thought the daughter should already be taking care of herself, and the woman didn't agree.

The coffee percolated faster when it was almost done, and Laura watched as the mom was out looking for the daughter at a friend's house. Laura filled a cup and sat with the TV going into an advertisement for a fast-food place. She sipped from her coffee, then set it aside. The phone reminded her of Rebecca.

The time was around three, and the movie returned with the mother at a house. She knocked and waited, but no one responded. Then, she went to her car while calling someone. *Yeah, I can't find her. Well, I don't know where else she could be. All right. All right, I'm going home.*

The daughter stood outside a building downtown, smoking with her friends and talking about her situation looking for a job. The mother returned home at night.

Laura breathed. With days quickly passing, she had little opportunity to make decisions to any effect. The apartment situation wasn't about to change, but a crude end to her past was the unknown future starting here, after her involvement with Jae. She'd be honest if she wasn't happy—if it meant people would better understand--yet with people, she *could* be happy. She couldn't blame Jae, and she didn't want to.

She needed a cigarette badly.

No one seemed to understand each other. Her friends would say they knew her, but it was as though she'd been left to herself with nothing but the task of reconstructing the past in her mind, as if that was intended.

Again, Laura breathed; it was all the same thing with no real answers. Television was just a distraction. She had nothing more to do than sit in an apartment and become restlessly alone. Maybe it would all come back in a new sense when she got older, but for now, she had to get past the usual behavior of everyone.

Laura would have to talk to Dawn. She would call her. Now was the right time, so she took the phone, dialed, and waited...

"Hello?"

"Hey."

"Laura! What's new?" Dawn Caplowe was on her cell phone at a grocery store.

"We need to talk sometime. Are you off work?"

"I've been working nights, and I have to get ready soon. How about tomorrow?" Dawn said.

"What time? I have all day off." *I'll be there in the afternoon. Just wait for me.* "Okay." Laura was calm.

"See you then, Laura."

"Bye." Dawn would get her away from this. She'd assume everything was okay, and maybe it was.

Laura switched the channel to a music video. Rap was popular. She continued watching, adversely, implications to sex and money.

Laura switched back to the movie, but she didn't follow it. She drank her coffee and ignored the dialogue as she looked at the apartment around her. She needed to do something, so she took her bag and turned off the TV. As she went downstairs, she wondered if she would make it a short drive, but it would waste gas. In her tiredness, she wanted to think nothing. Somewhere in all this thinking was something she didn't want to know. Whatever had been on her mind, it wouldn't follow her out.

Around the corner, she came to the club she had noticed before and decided to go in. At a poster of a nude man, she found it to be a gay bar, and even though this was one scene she didn't belong to, she was already inside and wouldn't mind staying for a drink. The decor here was dark but had good lighting: suitable for professional people. There was also a nice, shaded enclosure outside behind the place.

A girl noticed Laura as she sat across the bar, and after finishing with a few people, she approached Laura. "Who are you?" as she sat.

"I'm just here for a drink. I'm not gay."

"Oh. You mind if I sit with you?"

Laura shook her head.

"What can I *get* you?" asked the bartender.

Laura often wondered why people weren't more like herself. She gave him a smirk. "Just a beer," she said.

"Another beer for you?" he punctually asked the girl.

"Yeah. So what's your name?"

"Laura."

They got their beers over napkins, and each took a drink. "You seem different, like real quiet." The girl didn't smile. She seemed too drunk to be happy with whatever had been on her mind.

"Well, I read too much into people."

"I'm Jess." They shook hands. Then, each took a drink. "Some people you just don't want to talk to." Laura nodded. "Oh, I'm sorry, do you wanna chat or not?" Jess had clearly been drinking. Her attitude was shifting.

"I don't mind," Laura said.

Jess sat back with her beer in hand.

Laura drank, not knowing what to say. "It's difficult to make conversation. Because I always expect to have more to say than what I get out."

Jess grinned and laughed. "You probably think too much," she said.

Glad to hear it, Laura slouched then. "I've been told that. It sort of goes in circles for me."

"Sooner or later, we talk. Drink up!" Laura didn't reply but nodded her head. It did not occur to her that Jess would be a lasting friend because Laura wasn't prepared to make an invitation to anyone here. "Do you have a boyfriend?" Jess asked.

"I met someone a few days ago," Laura said.

"Good for you. I get along with guys." Jess acted as though the conversation was going somewhere. "I hate some girls, though," she said. Laura nodded, looking at her beer. "Some of 'em don't give a shit about anyone. They think they're so important, but their game is real fuckin' cheap," Jess said. "You know most girls would walk right over you?"

Laura looked at her. "I'm on the right track."

Jess took a drink. She had long hair tied back. She said, "You know what I told this one bitch?" Laura shook her head. "I told her if she kept talking about me, it would be all she ever thought about. All the way to the grave."

Laura gave the slightest laugh behind a grin.

"She's probably talking about me right now." Yes, Jess had been drinking. "She has a mouth that doesn't shut up. I told her, 'The more you talk shit about other people, who the hell cares about *you*?'" Jess was jealous of what Laura appeared to be. Either Laura knew a lot or nothing at all.

Laura nodded. "Do you smoke?"

"Sure."

"I mean pot. I've got some. I just live next door."

Jess smiled. "Sure, let's have a cigarette and finish this beer first." They both lit up. "I moved here with my girl. We're happy. She's my best friend, but we almost can't live with each other."

"Oh," Laura said.

They said nothing more through the rest of the smoke, and Laura wanted to see Marcel again soon. They finished and left.

"It's just around the corner," Laura said outside. They came to the building and Laura was unlocking the front.

"Wow, this building? You're lucky."

Laura said nothing. Soon, they were inside the apartment.

"Wow. I like it," Jess said. "I never noticed this place before. I wouldn't expect an old place to look this good on the inside."

"Thanks. Hold on." Laura got her supply box and brought it to the table, and the two quietly sat together.

Jess coughed. "Nice pipe."

"It's alright, I guess."

Laura packed the pipe and gave it to Jess, and Jess smoked without hesitation. Laura skipped. "You don't want a hit?" Jess asked.

"I'll just take one." Laura took the pipe and smoked.

After she smoked a third time, Jess stood up anxiously. "Fuck, I have to leave. This shit feels wrong to me right now."

"You're paranoid?" Laura asked.

"I don't know, girl, it feels like I've got a freakin' brain tumor or something."

"Okay."

"Fuck." Jess rubbed the back of her head. "There is a limit to this shit." She got up, and they went to the door. "I'll see ya."

"Okay," Laura said, concerned about her own health. Jess left.

The high slightly came to Laura when she was in the kitchen, enough to change her focus, and everything was more than what she wanted to think about. But it was all there. She started clumsily rearranging things on the counter and decided she'd hold off on the smoke because she needed to get clean.

While focused on her breathing, the high didn't come on too heavy. Pursy was at Laura's feet for once today, so Laura felt momentarily cheery. Coffee was still on, so she poured another cup and returned to the sofa, where she turned the television on. None of what she'd been thinking came to her. Then, she remembered her grandmother had died and could think nothing of it.

* * *

Expression

Wednesday? It was another day, and Michael walked again to his job at Heartland. His composure suggested he was living by good choices, though he felt arrogant enough to boast about the job and having a place. It was a shame to only be smoking and drinking, but he often shared what humbled him, too.

It was enough to have someone like Dan around. In his own words, Dan said it was right to move in, to smoke up, drink, watch movies--whatever, in order to live it up, apart from doing nothing.

Michael drew his attention away from the road. He felt it all through his walk: life would come slow, and he'd continue to endure minor, persisting conflicts. Chicago respected its diversity, but the people he met were a little above the simple interactions of Fremont, to say the least. The city was more than what he had ever been exposed to. It was easier then because he felt more accepted, but he'd had enough obstacles to go home.

He presently balanced himself between wanting either to go back to Chicago and live around people he wanted to be more like or stay with the people he'd be closer in like mind to.

He'd sometimes mention Chicago, and it was nothing to them. True enough, Fremont was friendly, but too much on the surface and looking for something better. Enough time away from people who cared, and he'd hate himself.

He arrived at the smoke shelter again and sat to rest his legs. Of course, he was smoking, and the pack was almost out.

Leaning back on the bench, he realized he honestly didn't want to kill himself. But he had to make this situation work, and there were the endless bills at the last apartment. The whole situation was meaningless. He never belonged to Fremont. No one knew his mind, not his friends, not even his parents. They weren't aware of what he had become. He'd someday die; not just die but die here, and he'd've accomplished nothing.

But it didn't matter. They accepted him. Of course, he barely ever said much.

The nicotine came easy but penetrable, and a headache returned. For now, he couldn't reach another time in Chicago, and his attempts there were useless. He'd have no money. But here, he'd obsess; he'd lose friends, continue to have voices, and his family wouldn't know what to do but keep him in the hospital, where he'd be trapped in a head with these stupid suspicions. He'd have to say something about the voices if they were to happen again because honesty was the only way.

He'd be on the phone today, and the headache would stay with him. He threw the cigarette to the ground, stepped on it, and the headache worsened at the thought of it.

Inside with sufficient time to himself again, he heard the same hum of computers ready for work, and the monitors were lit up with screen savers from Windows '95.

In the break room, someone had made fresh coffee. Michael took a cup to the training room where no one was. As he sat, he placed the coffee on the table and took his papers out.

People started arriving and didn't notice Michael. For once, it was a comfort being around people. After everyone settled and waited, a manager came in. He said, "Okay, folks, I'm sorry to tell you this, but we just lost the client we had you working for. So--I have to let you all go this time." No one said anything but started getting up to leave. "We will consider you all another time. I'm sorry."

"Fuck," someone said.

Michael was the last to get up, and he shared a glance with his old classmate before he slowly exited the building to an inevitable cigarette in the smoke shelter where everyone else went.

"Well, this sucks," someone said and gave no surprise.

"Yeah, it's tough finding work in this town," Michael added.

"Hey, man, can I get one of your cigarettes?" An older guy stood to Michael. Michael took one out and gave it to him.

Michael's license needed reinstatement. Months had gone by without one, and he'd done nothing to get it back. He could only think he needed to do something, but at the moment, he could do nothing.

Of the group, Michael was the least worried, because his house design was still on his mind. He wondered what he'd been thinking earlier, and whether it was important. He focused on the group around him, but they paid him no mind. He felt concerned for his well-being.

He gave up on the cigarette and the time with the group outside, so he walked through the parking lot to the road and finished his coffee later into the walk. It was awkward being on foot in this area, but he'd get a forty-ounce beer at the gas station and take the long way home over the viaduct to walk off the stress.

More often than not, he enjoyed working, but being good at the job didn't promise employment. He had worked at an import store in Chicago. Maybe the apartment was a mistake.

Instead of letting it bother him, Michael was ready to go through a list of the jobs closest. It would still be a considerable bike ride. Though he needed money sooner, talking on the phone every day would've only come to annoy him.

Here on the road, he recalled the class he graduated with. They were probably all more comfortable with themselves, and far more into the conventional extras to engage their minds with.

He was like a beacon on the road, though not the beacon of distress his grandmother would be on a road like this if she ever needed to walk. He neared the gas station and finally went in.

Michael knew what beer he would get, and he browsed nothing more. Along with the beer, he bought another lottery ticket—even though he lost again. A poster of a woman appeared as though she were smiling at him, but what was she smiling about? Apparently, she knew something he didn't, and for her to know him as her photo suggested? What was he even thinking?

Outside, he felt exposed, and aware of people. The voices could return in the air from whatever direction made him vulnerable. His pants started sagging. Again, he felt pain in his neck and suspected it was from the car wreck with Roger, Meghan, and Ron...

Already, he was walking up the viaduct with its chain-link fencing. He noticed several moving trains, so he would've had to wait after all. Just then, his presence frightened a few pigeons into the air, and he stood for a moment to finish his coffee.

At the bottom of the viaduct, he headed east on his street, passing tree after tree on the same old sidewalk from years ago, with its jumps and cracks. He kept watching his steps and the houses.

This was the bottom after aspiring for much more than the cigarettes, the alcohol, the weed, and the walks around this town could ever be as if there was nowhere to go and no end to the walk. His boots needed to be replaced after wearing them since Chicago.

He arrived at the apartment, and Dan's car was gone. Michael would have to cook something for lunch, and some chicken would be good enough.

Upon entering the apartment alone, the kitchen held a stigma, as if strangers had been here, and as if someone was watching him. Then came a bubbling noise that rose from the floor underneath and all through the refrigerator. Worried, Michael needed to pay mind to something else, or it would get worse. His senses were too keen for him to move.

Then, he could only speculate the outcome of a noisy refrigerator, so he paced back and forth, hoping it would stop, until he left the kitchen for the living room, where he came to the sofa with his beer. Although he wanted to lay down, he positioned himself to the waiting television. With the remote, the TV came on as loud static. He drank a small amount of beer to start out, only because he thought it might help.

He took a few more swigs and held the bottle at his side as a show announced the news on celebrities. It wouldn't be today to start looking for work.

A fast, fleeting, unproductive day was well ahead as he watched a game show. Maybe it was enough for everyone just to know each other this simply. The people on TV were an outburst of cheer before going into a commercial, the same paradox: there was no difference between people in life and TV in this estrangement.

Dan arrived, and Michael was in the position to explain he was out of work. Dan entered the back door and went for the basement, but with the TV on, he probably knew Michael was home.

Michael lost his train of thought. Here, he needed a job but was stuck watching TV instead. Soon, he heard every step as Dan came slowly up the stairs. As he looked toward the kitchen, expecting Dan's usual expression of boredom, asking Michael if he wanted to smoke, Michael wanted out of this situation living here.

"You wanna smoke?" Dan said.

At this, Dan was the one friend Michael had these days, maybe someone he'd never tell about the voices. He endured them for months the last time, but crossing past it with anyone was difficult. Dropping acid had probably done significant damage. Ten months off and on with meth probably did a lot more. Michael was a friend, just like anyone, but one they'd leave in a hospital if they could do nothing.

"I guess we could. Yeah," Michael said.

"You're drinking," Dan said. Here was Michael, sitting at the television, watching a game show and drinking in the morning.

"Yeah."

"You lose your job?"

"Yeah, man...I was there, but they lost the client we were going to work for." Here, Michael was supposed to handle the apartment. Not wanting to take charge for the moment, he said, "I have to get a different job."

"Fuck," Dan said long, leaning against the wall.

"Yeah, I know." Michael turned the TV off.

"Fucking right, we'll smoke." Dan then came over and sat. "Your hit," he said, encouraging Michael into the next job. Michael held the hit.

"Tomorrow or Friday I'll go to the unemployment office. I doubt they have any openings, though." He finished exhaling. "They didn't the last time."

Dan blocked the comment, smoking. After a moment, he said, "I don't know...I might quit my job and look for something after you find work." He handed the pipe back.

Michael took another hit, almost feeling the first one. As he exhaled, he said, "You want a glass for some of this beer?" He didn't know what else to say but handed the pipe back.

"Nah, I'm straight." Dan smoked, happy for once, and proud.

Michael felt the high and focused on his books below the TV. "I've got those books if you're bored during the day."

Michael considered what could've been an offense may just as well be an attitude.

"Yeah." Dan coughed and handed the pipe over. He clearly wasn't interested in books. It was either just another stupid thing to him or something he admired and didn't do.

Michael smoked. The refrigerator began making noises again. He said, "Do you hear that shit?"

"Yeah, the fridge is annoying."

"It's really getting to me." Michael handed the pipe back. Dan took his hit and handed it back. Michael was high and responded slower, saying, "You know what I was thinking today?"

"No...What?"

"Hold on." Michael smoked. He was about to forget. He said, "I don't know, you're right, it's like everyone's a fake." Feeling his high, he said, "I don't see what they're happy about, either."

Dan smoked, then handed the pipe back. "I don't know— You shouldn't think about it too much."

Michael set the pipe aside. "You high?"

"Fuck yeah."

"You sure you don't want a drink? I can pour you some."

"Nah."

"I'll put it in the fridge." Michael went to the fridge and Dan was already up to go downstairs. "You don't wanna stay up here now that we're buzzed?"

"I don't know, I guess I could."

They followed each other to the sofa and waited.

Michael said, "Nothing to do but get high in this town." Dan didn't reply. "It seems permanent."

"Yeah," looking away from Michael, ready to laugh. Now Michael seemed to know nothing. Dan said, "We just watch TV and smoke up."

"TV is probably the reason no one talks." Michael said through his high.

Well, Meghan had too much influence on him. Michael knew stuff, but Meghan was too much to him. Dan said, "Yeah. I don't know." He began laughing. "Not all people are like that."

Michael had already given some thought to this, and he said, "That's because they're all just oblivious to the fact that a lot of people don't have money. I know it. It never fazed me before."

"Yeah."

Michael looked at a car passing the window, and they waited, only to feel the high. "I get so fed up."

"You got that straight. Geez," Dan said with a grin, looking away again.

"I know, it's easier just to let boredom take the place of everything and make excuses for it."

"This place really does suck," Dan said.

"Yeah, something's rotten when we need money to live. We're in fucking deep shit," Michael said, rubbing his eye. He threw his hand up, "I mean, look how close we are to being homeless."

CHAPTER 9

Revelation

Wednesday.

Laura was met with a morning with another day off, expecting Dawn later. She prepared water and food for Pursy, cleaned the litter box, and took the trash out. Back up the stairway to her floor, she stopped to watch traffic on Leavenworth through the old warehouse window.

The book would start with their youth, then a point when they were either in a job or looking for one, and this would start the fall of events. Since she wanted to relate to it, she'd base one character on her mom.

Back in the apartment, she watched television and tried calling Marcel, who didn't answer. Then, she remembered the photo she couldn't find earlier and spent some time looking for it. She needed coffee for another cigarette, so she prepared some. TV would be a distraction, so she turned it off.

She wore the same jeans and tank top from Sunday, with sandals. As she stood in the kitchen, she recalled a few memories of Rebecca, then stared at the floor, wondering where she could've misplaced Marcel's photo.

She hastily filled a cup with coffee, dripping some as she went to the table to light up a smoke. Her cousins were also now something of a distant memory, but whenever Laura saw them, it usually helped Laura refocus her thoughts about the family. New kids were coming into the picture, and since Laura wasn't a kid anymore, she wasn't much of a part of it.

It was difficult for Laura to try getting across when she had always kept to herself. Her family may have thought less about her than they did about their own friends. She'd been out of school for a few years, and she'd continue getting older, which meant she'd only be further separated from them...

Laura could see it now: she'd be thinking about Marcel's photo all day. It may have been in the car, and she may have lost it between the car and the apartment, or between the bar and the apartment? She couldn't believe this was happening.

After putting the cigarette out, Laura took the coffee up to her desk. The first three chapters of her book alternated between the woman and man as children. Both were good kids and brought their inspiration home to their families. Laura had two printouts of rough outlines to get a feel for what to add to the plot.

The girl would be brought up closer than the boy as his family dealt with more stress and less time for him. He'd become isolated from friends he didn't relate to any longer, and he'd fight with his younger sister.

On the other hand, the girl interacted with a few sisters as the youngest. She would go to church and talk about her beliefs at home. Both would be growing up in the sixties.

The boy wouldn't be exposed to crime but would adapt himself to being guarded and reclusive because less was socially available for him. At least, it was what Laura thought as she wrote an notes about the parents' relationships with their children. He'd maybe pick up on racism, so less would stop the shooting.

His mother would be preoccupied with friends who made fun of him. He'd always be interrupted. He wouldn't be shy and would reject the emotional distress from not having anyone to talk to. He would hate the world while the girl would have an honest love for it all.

Laura was prepared to read for both characters when she laid out the first nine cards. The girl would often fantasize about finding love for the first time. She would also wonder about a life granted to her by God with her decisions, but she'd have an ordinary life. She would consider her religion important, but she may or may not have matured with it.

The woman would have a dog, one source of happiness, and she wouldn't have any children. She'd be living with her husband, and he'd be in the book from time to time. Laura decided she would first be working on a commercial, singing with a small group, which would later show her as having less in common with the other singers.

Also, she'd have no permanent job, so her husband would be supporting the two in either an inherited house or an apartment. She would be singled out because her sisters would've moved away, and she'd have few friends to meet with her for coffee.

She needed an emotion. It wasn't just happiness, but it would be something privately challenging her. Maybe she'd be at a loss for words and would say anything for the sake of saying something: desperation. Her approach to people in public would always be with good intentions, though often worried over whether she was being undervalued. She'd stay with the outlook she normally had as a matter of protecting herself.

The guy who would kill her at the end would see her as being crude and white because it would show she was uncomfortable late at night with him there.

Laura wrote and filled in spaces with the cards in front of her. She'd come back to the spread, but already she was visualizing the woman as her own mom in different circumstances.

She laid out the next cards. The man would have grown intolerant of other people, and he'd have a habit of hating anyone in public and wanting more than what he had. He would've never been in love and later wouldn't even attempt to even seek it because it was phony. His hatred would be a source of pride; he'd think he was right about people, time and time again.

He'd often lose jobs. Of course, it would meet him at a time he was losing his job, and he'd already have a kid from a relationship outside of the ones he was in with a few women who came and went. He and the mom would meet up and fight. His son would be like him, with the same playfulness and curiosities as a kid, but he wouldn't know his father. The kid could be a subplot, where the reader revisits him in private moments when he'd be thinking about his dad, or when he'd play with a friend and his mother would appear and surprise the reader about the kid being the son.

Laura wrote and copied the cards to the outline for later reference. The man wouldn't have many ties, nor would he have a singular friend. He would've had a hard time in school. As mentioned, his intolerance made him proud, because it was his only 'strength.' All of it would dictate where he was when he'd shoot the woman. He'd need money, and the woman would have nothing. He'd believe in a government conspiracy since he had no job.

The latter part of it would take place in the eighties, and the woman would die afraid. Against the pain of the bullet, it would only make her hurt more. The story would end with him getting away.

Laura went to the table downstairs with her coffee. She turned the TV on, lit up a cigarette, and exhaled.

The greatest danger the man had was his own thoughts. He'd enter places to work with little hope of keeping a decent job, and he would often barely land one. He'd be on foot and become aggravated by small things while always running short on money and time.

The TV went into a commercial, so Laura turned it off and took the ashtray upstairs. What she had in mind so far was good, but she didn't have everything down on paper. She began jotting terms down matching her thoughts, holding her place at times before scribbling a few words to each idea.

She returned to the woman, but nothing came to her. The girl would sing in church, matching her singing for the one-time job later on. Laura couldn't decide what the commercial would be. Maybe a theme park because Laura knew of one in Des Moines with a ditty. It would be easiest, so she jotted it down. The news would come on in the evening about a murder.

Each chapter from this outline would contribute about ten pages toward each of the characters as it went back and forth. Laura didn't mean for it to clash two different cultures, but it sometimes happened anyhow. She'd develop the man's hatred and simplify the woman's view as something related to their youth. Laura didn't believe people evolved far beyond their youth, or at least it wasn't what she was exposed to.

Dawn would show up later. It seemed a long day ahead of Laura, but the week was already quickly passing. She could smoke and get more out of her, so she took her supply and emptied portions of it toward the pipe.

She held the first hit before letting it go, and she thought it was enough before she took another one, which made her cough and tear up. She then leaned back to correct her posture, finished the pipe, and absorbed everything around her with an added conscience to her writing. Soon, though, she decided she spent enough time on the book.

Already, she was overwhelmed. The book may not work.

She descended the stairs slowly and thought of her mother. Then, she let it pass before she made her way out the door without double-checking her apartment. Pursy took up the living room.

Laura made her way outside, walking the same street as before. Breaking free from the apartment made the book seem more possible. Though it wasn't her original intention, maybe it was Jae in her book. He never would've expected her to be a writer or anything more than what she was with him: constantly shut down and belittled. And yet, as he'd always say, she was 'ordinary' and didn't talk enough.

Jae and Laura both thought the other betrayed their their kindness, their remarks often like spiteful strangers disrupting each other. Without getting to know each other first as friends, getting along came as a challenge. She had always expected people would change, and she would've changed with them. Then she met Jae, and it broke off all her ties.

Laura kept walking in long strides with her sandals, a matter of authority over him as though he were doing the same now, to keep up with the time lost.

She didn't have time for anyone outside. They wouldn't have come out of the same dealings she did, so she remained a silent presence amid everyone as she meandered past them and walked briskly. Laura could cower to some out of fear of what they may have thought. Jae despised white people, but she picked up on this view herself, even before knowing him. Everyone together was out of line. Then, Laura smiled as she imagined Rebecca carrying along with the same ideas, humorously impatient among the various people.

Laura crossed a street and came to Retro Recycling. In the basement, filled with tapestries and black light posters in front, she went to the girl at the cash register. "I need a few of your baggies for incense."

"Got them right here," she said and handed Laura three.

"Thanks."

"Yep."

Laura stood at the incense, contemplated over several of them, then filled each of the bags with ten sticks. She started browsing through clothes...

Rebecca had led Laura on when they were young. For Laura

to have been disassociated from everyone could've been from her own habit of being secretive with the family or anyone she needed a stronger relationship with.

It was true she once experimented with meth and let it go to her benefit because the potency was much worse these days. It gave her momentum in caring more (or less) about the people she knew, as she was getting ready to leave high school. It was the wrong drug to try, and she was happy it didn't continue. For her to do it probably meant a lot of people were doing it.

As she rummaged, she came across a shirt with a soda logo. She changed into it in the dressing booth and bought it with the incense before browsing furniture. Some of it could work, but it would sell before she'd come back. She just didn't have the money. Of course, she still hadn't deposited her paycheck.

Fitting into the new shirt was a strange feeling, mostly because it hugged her breasts, but red wasn't a color she typically wore.

This reminded her of Dawn. What Laura could expect from her was something less usual, something far more agreeable than the everyday thing going on lately. She still felt the high and considered a few pieces in her apartment. Then, gazing at a mirror, she could see herself as a stranger to not only herself but to anyone, like some oddity as everyone in public generally was. She looked totally baked.

She continued browsing the store to a song from the sixties because she wanted to hear all of it.

❊ ❊ ❊

Empowerment

Michael went for the phone as it echoed through the

kitchen.

"Hello?...I'm okay. I lost my job...Yeah?...Thank you!... Yeah. You're coming to pick me up? I'm ready. I just need the title...Yep, see ya." He hung up. "I'm leaving to get my car back," he said to Dan.

"Yeah?" Man. They could go to Omaha, to the store that sold pipes. Michael always drove people around Omaha.

"Yup," Michael said.

Dan nodded and was already headed for the basement, high as ever.

Michael went into his bedroom for the title, returned to the sofa, and looked at the blank TV. Thoughts of an old friend reminded him everything would be fine. He was fortunate to be alive, after everything, and driving soon. Boredom was deep shit, but with the car, it could all change; he could go to Omaha, maybe even get work there.

Having no patience for waiting, Michael sat worried, shaking his foot. Again, he was stuck in Fremont, and it was far easier back when he was a kid, to appreciate everything. He used to go to the movies, even graduated, and saw Chicago. He'd known so many people. Now, he was faced with the petty loathing he grew up with.

He had the urgent need for it all: the money, the car...decent furniture. He wasn't exactly set to be an adult, but it was what he was after. If it could only fall into place at this moment, he'd get on with his life! Knowing what he had in the living room, he would never move this furniture again.

Usually, he didn't have this many thoughts while high, so something was wrong. Maybe the beer. Coffee sometimes got him excited.

His mother arrived; Michael was outside and shut the door behind him, ready for driving to add up as another responsibility he wasn't prepared for without the job. He got in the car.

"Hello," his mom said. "You're ready?"

"Yeah." They drove off and were moving swiftly.

"So. How's Dan?"

"He's fine. His girlfriend in Lincoln might move in, but we haven't really discussed it. I'm just worried about getting a job now."

"I know...You ready to be driving?"

"Can't wait," he said, looking at her. He didn't know what it was like for her getting older, but she had a few friends in town. Her sister-in-law lived here, and they got together frequently. "How are things with you?"

"Fine."

"Good. I don't know--I might look for work in Omaha."

It was a fading thought as he watched the road. At least he had some help to start over. Not often, he felt jealous of other people making it, but frustration in high school went well into the years he was in now. It was easier now to accept he didn't need school.

"You know I saw Meghan?"

"Yeah? What's she up to?" She assumed all types of drugs.

"We drank and talked. It was fine," Michael said, thoroughly mindless about Meghan this moment, and they waited to say more.

His mother yawned with her hand in front of her mouth as though she were crying, and said, "I'm tired today. The week has been so boring."

"Watching TV?"

"No. Driving everywhere. Bought groceries twice, went to Omaha a few times, and never sat down."

He said, "I hate how much time it takes to drive everywhere."

"I know, and look at how many people are driving. It never ends," she said long and tired.

They arrived downtown.

"Well, we're here," she said, parking in the lot as though

Michael were still a child who needed to know where they were.

"Yeah," he said brightly, taking a breath.

Walking across Park Avenue, Michael watched for traffic, and recognized, for once, the courthouse bearing a significance with its bulk and height and dominance. Here, he had been jailed before.

He took a number and felt as though he didn't belong to Fremont at all. The public was fidgety and didn't give a damn, unlike his mother, who stood with him and smiled as they waited. Maybe it was he who was fidgety. Surely, he didn't give a damn, or he did. Just, maybe not now.

Finally, they were being helped. His mom laid out the situation for the woman, when it announced itself, and he was the incompetent kid who couldn't take care of himself yet. His headache returned.

They managed with the items he brought before he and his mom left the room. "That was easy," his mom said.

"Yeah." Michael then went to the examiner's office. He took the tests and passed before they returned to the treasurer's office for the license.

"Do you want to have lunch anywhere?" his mom asked when they were outside.

"Yeah." His headache remained. Ideas were already coming to him about where he could work, which stopped him from saying anything more because he could see past the excitement.

She couldn't deny he'd been in a hospital. Something *was* wrong, and surely *nothing* was wrong. He'd someday pull through because he had a strong youth to back him up. But Fremont didn't have much to offer these kids.

"Should we just get hamburgers?" she asked.

"Sure."

They rode up the street and soon parked at Runza, where the buildings behind the restaurant stood somewhat tall in old brick. Traffic was noticeably busy here on Military. They went through the west entrance.

Michael ordered first; his mom ordered a salad. They soon sat with their food near the bright sunlight. Across the street were more buildings, which outlasted people and would continue to do so.

His mom daydreamed. She wanted to talk. Here, she was in the position to say something. "Nice day out," she said.

"Yeah." Country radio played. "It's a good day for driving," he said.

"You be careful."

"I'll be fine."

"Some people really don't know how to drive here. Man," she said.

Michael smiled. "Trish was a wild driver."

"Where is Trish?"

"Don't know. Her whole family up and left. I could check Omaha's phonebook sometime."

"Did *she* do drugs?"

"We all did," he said with his mouth full.

"Michael. Why do you do it?"

"Calms the nerves." They ate more.

"It amazes me you can even get away with it. Are you doing them now?"

"Not always."

Now she was serious. "Michael, I don't want you to end up in the hospital again."

"I'm okay," he said, remembering the voices.

"Please give it up," she said.

"How's Deanne?"

"She's doing okay." She wanted to lay it all out for him with her hands in explanation. "We were in Omaha the other day, and someone nearly rear-ended us. I was watching my rear view mirror, and right before he was about to hit us, he swerved to the left of the car and raced past. Couldn't believe it. Didn't even have time to brace for it."

"Wow."

Michael's love for his mom was kept to himself, though sometimes obvious. Little did he know, she worried about him privately, not sharing any of it with Michael's father. She wanted to sort through it as days passed by, but it was always coming apart with words he had said to her. He didn't have a strong perspective outside of himself.

They calmly ate the rest of their food and left.

This day, she didn't feel important to him. It was somehow difficult to understand he remained the same kid she had brought up, after his friends took so much time away. Raising these kids was a happy time, but at some point, she and others had lost their reach. The idea took over, and they didn't talk.

They arrived at their home, a place he had known to be ordinary. The house wasn't much of a home to him; he was always leaving it. He simply missed West Point. "Thanks for helping me with the car, Mom," he said.

"Sure. Don't you wanna come inside now that you have the day off?" She had a look of concern.

"No, I'm going home."

"You know this is home. Not for a little while?"

"I'll be fine," he said, as he started putting plates on his car.

"Be careful; will you?"

"I am."

"With the drugs, too. That hospital is expensive," she said, pointing her finger. She had no way of telling him.

"Okay."

With the plates finally on the car, Michael drove off and

waved. She waved back from the kitchen window.

Maybe he always controlled too much of the conversation. Whatever role he took up was severely distanced from everyone else. Smoking pot or drinking beer only felt right, and he was on his own. He remembered the beer as he left the neighborhood. At some point, it would have to stop.

Michael expected more from adulthood: everyone having common ground. Whatever way of being so meant it wouldn't remain what it had been. Maybe what he'd been wasn't so bad.

He listened to the radio, but he was suddenly oblivious to everything as though it had all went mute.

Michael arrived at the apartment, threw his keys on the table, and a rattling fridge was his welcome home when he got his beer and went to the sofa. A court show was on. He took a large swig of the beer, hoping to reach a good buzz. It'd be easier to watch television, he'd have less hatred.

After his attempt at Chicago, school, the hospital, and now restless in wanting change to occur of itself, the only thing he could do was further sort through hopeless ideas. Most of the old friends were out of the picture. There was Dan, but they together manifested the boredom they shared. Michael drank to his thoughts....

Reaching a buzz, thoughts began to fade. Glancing around the room, he knew he wouldn't keep the apartment up. Outside the window was the neighborhood; its people all had stable jobs.

He wouldn't find work anywhere, or it wouldn't come when it needed to. The whole public would come to annoy him here, but he tried to relax anyhow.

CHAPTER 10

Affection

D awn arrived. Not knowing what to expect from the visit, Laura opened the door. For once, her friend appeared like an unmistakable salvation after too much time alone. Laura recalled various times driving around Omaha late at night together. Sometimes, the only thing fortifying were actual memories. At the sight of her, Dawn was maybe preoccupied, but still salvation.

"Hey," Dawn said. "You think I could use the computer to look a few things up sometime? Internet is slow at my place."

"Sure, but let's smoke. I've got some bud."

Dawn paused and stared at Laura, her hair a tangled mess, and a heavy shoulder bag weighed down on her. "You should think about quitting." She then smiled. "I guess I wouldn't mind."

In the main room, Dawn glanced around to see if anything had changed as Laura reached over the cupboard for her supply. Dawn had quit almost a year ago. "You think you'll smoke all that?" she asked, with silence in the room.

"I only bought a half; I'll give you some, you don't need to pay me." Laura said.

"I'll gladly give you twenty-five for the rest."

"You'd probably just throw it away," Laura said. It

seemed Laura had isolated herself in the apartment for months without speaking to anyone. "Do you know what day it is?" Dawn said.

"Wednesday," Laura said.

"Day of the month?"

Laura had to count from Sunday. "The thirteenth? Fourteenth. Temperance."

"No, it's the thirteenth. You're still reading tarot?"

"Yeah, I'm using it for the book, just a regular deck of cards," Laura said.

Laura sat at the table with her coffee, and Dawn joined her. With nothing to say, they could say anything. Dawn said, "What's it about?"

Laura had to adjust herself. She said, "It follows two people. The guy kills the woman, and it starts with their childhood." Laura felt like a kid explaining it to a parent.

"Do you have a title?"

"Right now, it's 'City Limits.' I have a lot of circumstances in mind, and I'm doing the outline today. Worked on it earlier." Laura could see herself somewhere between Rebecca and Dawn, learning from both while holding on to two different pasts, one she no longer belonged to and the other she somehow didn't match up with. "If I can write, you probably can," Laura said.

Laura's behavior amused Dawn. At this moment, Laura needed encouragement, and before they'd say anything, they would say nothing.

"I just met a guy from Chicago," Laura said.

"Oh. Black?" Dawn asked as she regained her posture in the awkward dining chair.

Laura didn't want to admit it. It didn't always seem Dawn would agree with the guys Laura knew. She shrugged. "Yeah. But totally unexpected."

"Is he going to be like the last guy?"

Suddenly, Laura couldn't tell if he would be. What if he could be? She felt herself descending into the same apprehension from before. "I don't think so."

Dawn said, "You weren't exactly the same after that. You were afraid of voodoo at one time, then the fights with Jae. You remember, don't you? Relationships aren't right for everyone."

Pain surged in Laura's upper back, a reminder of how hard it had been with Jae as he got her to cook at the times she couldn't feel comfortable. Maybe the food wasn't good enough. Or he'd suspect she spent her day at someone else's place. Watching his every movement after he first kept her awake in his angry jealousy was exactly how she felt now.

Laura said, "Yeah, but I hope Jae's okay." Somehow it always seemed he needed her. Laura drank more of her coffee. "Should I put on some music?"

"Sure. Do you have any more coffee?" Dawn asked as Laura went for the sound system.

"No, I don't." Laura set aside a CD case as the first song played, and she returned to the table. "But I could make some."

"It's okay, I have caffeine pills, I'll just use one of those. You know–I'm actually planning a trip to Chicago," Dawn said. She messed around the bag for her caffeine pills and took one.

Laura thought, could she go with Dawn? "When?"

"October, maybe. I can't decide if I'd rather stick around here, but I requested time off to visit a school, talk to people, hang out." Dawn only knew it wasn't right to mention after what college had been for Laura. To be in this position with her, she just wanted to be supportive.

Laura said, "I'd maybe go with Marcel sometime."

"Marcel is his name?" They met another glance. Laura kept looking down.

"Yes."

They were silent, and Laura reached for her coffee. She

looked at Dawn, wondering what she felt, and how she got through it. "What were we doing the last time?" she asked.

Dawn nodded. Laura was okay. "Shopping, before you were going to California. You kept running away from him."

"Oh, yeah." Laura thought, another reminder.

"How was it?"

When Laura sat up to correct her posture, it was as though she had awakened from sleep. "That's months ago. I saw downtown, slept outside a skyscraper, and left the next morning." Finally, it seemed she had regained herself.

Dawn grinned. "Was it nice?"

"All I thought about was earthquakes and a huge building falling on me. But it was good. I just walked around, mostly downtown."

Dawn thought. "We'll go sometime. It'll be better if we go together."

"Yeah. I talked to Rebecca. She's getting ready for another year of teaching," Laura said, taking sides. "I was upset that all anyone ever does is BS. It all amounts to just catching up on what's new. It's nothing," she added, shaking her head.

After a moment, Dawn said, "You're probably doubting yourself."

"I feel I should have more to say, and it's nothing," Laura coughed loudly. "We're nothing like the movies."

"No. Do you think I BS?"

"It's different with you. I haven't seen Rebecca for a few years. We should be thrilled to finally talk after so long. With you, I see you all the time. But I grew up with Rebecca. I think she's distracted. It's like we don't know each other at all."

"Well, I don't talk with many people lately, so I just– I don't know. Everything is going fast. I'd rather just sit at a computer and work."

"Same here," Laura said.

"What did you and Marcel talk about?" Dawn had more often been polite and patient, and Laura was sometimes tracking the effort to be like her.

Laura had to think with the distraction of the weed about her trip to California. "I can't remember. I mentioned the last two guys. He knows they were black. We just talked."

Dawn said, "You know what I was thinking today? People around here don't care to learn. I mean, the more I learn, the more I understand...the more I understand, it's easier to relate. For a long time, I was a little dull."

Laura nodded, but the idea left her. Her mind was blank, and then it came back to her. "That's what I feel. I'm just normal. A waste of time," Laura said. "I wish I could read more, but my back hurts."

"Well, you're not boring."

"I don't know, I just got to a time when I was like 'What else is there?' Everything was falling apart. My aunt was old, and I couldn't live there anymore. And no one talked. I left everything behind." Laura thought for a moment. "Sometimes all we think about is ourselves," she said.

"Yeah. Don't worry." Dawn said.

Laura nodded. "You want a cigarette instead?"

"Oh, sure. Let's take it up to the roof!"

They each took a cigarette. "You still quitting?" Laura asked.

"Yeah. But I still bum a few when I drink."

They were out the door, and Laura left the top lock open. She said, "What about you, have you met a guy?"

"No. I just want a guy as a friend these days, especially after the gamble you took. I can't live with them. I just stay home. Whatever, you know?"

Laura breathed. She said, "I think I have your attitude sometimes. So, I'm outlining, and I did tarot readings on it. So far, the guy is going to be out of a job and fights with his ex about child support. He'll be short of money, and frustrated. The woman loves her husband and has temporary jobs. I base her on my mom: innocent, youthful. It's good what I have visualized. Like it makes sense as something unusual, or not so much fantasy."

They were up the stairs and soon came out to the roof to a glorious sky.

"So, there's a party in Fremont tonight."

"Oh. Where in Fremont?" Laura was hesitant to go anywhere after being in Fremont twice in one week already, and at the farm. They both lit up.

"It's at a place being rented tonight off Military. I know where it is. My brother's going to be there."

"Okay, so it's younger people? I can drive," Laura said. "Or Marcel can. Why on a Wednesday?"

They came to the half-wall overlooking the west.

"Don't know. But it's at nine tonight."

"I work tomorrow."

"Well, I can't go alone."

"You want me to call Marcel?"

"Sure," Dawn said standing straight, considering now as the time; she began to sway toward the door.

Laura thought. "He's at work, I'll call him later."

"Okay," Dawn said. "You know something?"

"What?"

"We're in this world, and we don't know what we're supposed to do."

"I think a lot of people are in that," Laura said.

"Everyone just works," Dawn said. "It's like we need to feel secure, but we don't get security working just any job."

Laura shook her head. "Just don't worry about it. We just do what makes sense."

"I'm trying, but you're right. We bullshit."

"I know." They finished their cigarettes. "You wanna get high?" Laura said.

"Not really."

"It'll relax your nerves. Trust me."

Back in the apartment, Laura had her supply at the table. Soon, the pipe was ready, and Laura handed it to Dawn. Dawn took a hit and blew it out in the same speed, almost choosing to pass up on the high.

"Here," she said, as she handed the pipe over like she was guilty of something. Laura held the pipe to her face. The pipe whistled as she lit it and inhaled. They gazed at each other after Laura took her hit. Laura handed it back. Dawn followed with another hit and handed it over again. She rested her arms on the table and held her head. "I think I have to go, and I don't want to be high right now."

"Okay. Hold on." Laura took her hit and put the pipe away. "Give me a hug before you leave."

"Sure." So, they stood and hugged.

❊ ❊ ❊

Structure

Watching television and finishing the rest of his beer, Michael felt the pressure of getting back to work and keeping up with the apartment. He had the car, but he wanted to live somewhere away from Fremont. In Omaha, he'd still need his car. He contemplated this slowly while sitting slumped. Maybe he'd sell the car just to make the move, and this meant he could look for work in Omaha, on foot? Crazy.

Michael was often too serious, not often approaching times with anyone to know they cared. He didn't understand how people remained so happy when he obviously wasn't these days.

Impatient, he got up and checked the fridge to nibble on something. With little to even bite, he needed to go to the store. Groceries should be easy, but he used to hear voices there, during his psychosis.

He couldn't remember what he and his mother talked about. At the TV, frustration hit once more. His mom was on his case about the weed, and he'd mentioned Trish. She mentioned a wreck she was almost in. He could've discussed something relative to whatever common ground they still had. He was then in a predicament with Dan, smoking pot, and it wasn't the same.

Ideas of the hospital returned to him. Then, the intensity of the commercials narrowed his focus, and shortly, the TV returned to a court-themed reality show. With the remote out of sight, he watched it anyhow.

Michael took a cigarette and lit up. His head hurt from the back to the top as he held it up in his slouch. Wanting coffee again, Michael could see the lack of control he had over his addictions. He went and stood his ground in the kitchen for a moment to take a few breaths and slow his thoughts.

Of course, he had once taken an overdose of pills, and this could be the aftermath since he had pulled the IV from his arm and left the first hospital too soon. The psychiatric doctor had suggested it might be schizophrenia and put Michael on an inhibitor. He was off all medication now.

Michael could hear Dan's TV, and the place was thick with smoke. They could go to the river and get high, or they could drive the country roads. He almost decided to look over the material in his bag, then went to the sofa. He aligned his back with several pops, then sat straight.

The apartment could use a touch. The kitchen had been swept, and a pile of dirt, bits of plastic, and a bottle cap altogether waited for the trash. It had something of a permanent spot on the linoleum, if only because he'd never have patience enough to keep ahead.

He smoked and exhaled back at the TV as annoying complaints went back and forth as if they talked with their noses plugged. Michael laughed.

In a short time, he forgot what he laughed about when it went into commercial, and contemptuously, he smoked. He hated the commercials and anticipated nothing worth seeing in them. They were meant for people with money, who mowed their lawns every day in the summer and surrounded him during his psychosis. As if he'd end up in the hospital again, he cowardly laughed at himself. Cutting the laugh short, he rubbed his head and raised his eyebrows in an expression of resistance, away from the TV, as though he were his own father, knowing what he was doing was wrong—he should leave.

He had time for his cigarette still, so he stayed with the television and smoked. The cigarette had all the ingredients for an unbalanced mind, and he wanted to cut back as he watched it burn in a private, restless moment with the noise from the TV. Being here, he was already in the habit of constantly smoking.

It seemed if he were sitting in the house with no television, he'd simply sit and drink to whatever adversity he faced without a job. All he'd have done this day was pace around and accomplish nothing. Without the weed and without Dan, he'd simply be alone to these impeding thoughts.

Michael finished the cigarette and was out the front door with a connection to earlier times when he felt the same way, before the psychosis, happy for once, as though he might see his way out of this. He got in the car and drove.

This part of town other people his age found themselves in surrounded him with his lingering adolescence. Most adults of Fremont went about their day with responsibilities to their kids, and even they couldn't let go of the weekend drinking. It was the one thing people did here since there was nothing else. They'd look down on someone like Michael because he wasn't much of a drinker.

He drove First Street, where older drinkers watched television and dealt with their kids who were drunk and had their own kids in the same house. They were all watching TV and smoking cigarettes. Being in his car wasn't private like it once was. Here on this street, he was in the same hell they were in, though he didn't have kids and he wasn't ever angry.

At the grocery store, he took an application at the service desk, then brought a cart from the entryway. He quickly passed the pharmacy and its aisles, to the produce section. Maybe he needed medication.

He was surrounded not only by products but by everyone behind the products. The people harvesting this lettuce, the person behind the machine which packaged the cheese... The last time he went about shopping with this, he had no choice but to battle his own aggression.

Shopping alone again, it was as though his friends and family had left him behind. He didn't have the time now to prove he was still the person they had known. As though they needed to know they were important to him, he wanted out of the store to be free to talk with anyone and maybe share a smoke.

Going through the aisle of drinks, he found the green tea he drank when he tripped acid and stared at them before taking one. He grabbed a few cheap cereals and went to the coffee. It could almost help his mornings. Mindful of a small diet he kept to, the coffee could throw him off again, but he held onto it. He cracked his neck and stood straight. Again, a headache was coming on strong.

Today was slow for him. He was mindful of people and of himself, somewhat comfortable in public but nowhere near to feeling secure about money. Some of the people were only examples of how difficult it was to make a living, others an example of how oblivious people could be, and others were happily raising a family. What he said to Dan was right: this was right around the corner from homelessness.

At least, the wonder he had about the world was sometimes in the right direction, but seeing it was fair for him to have a difficult life? Life should be easier for people.

Sausages, pasta, and sauce were essential. Also, he needed to stock up on frozen vegetables and soups. He went through again, grabbed a few extra things, and stopped at the magazines. He browsed through one on interiors.

He soon led his cart to the register with the cigarettes. He took a pack of menthols even though he knew they would be the most toxic.

Michael gathered nothing significant from the person working the register and realized he had a problem, where he was in this town, in finding anyone. It didn't come urgently to him. He wanted to forget everything on his mind lately because there was no getting around it.

Once outside, Michael parked the cart next to a bench and decided to smoke. He sat and opened the pack. Cars demanded attention past the parking lot, he contemplated the business going on inside the places across the street while he smoked, and he needed someone. Everyone was a stranger to him, and life was too complicated to be alone through any illness.

Focusing on a woman driving away from the liquor store, he thought of a movie until the car was out of view. Everything was too fast for Michael, and he couldn't change anything apparent from before. His head hurt. Weed wasn't the same, smoking this frequently.

Most people didn't seem to feel alone as they entered the store or their cars. And there were the people who seemed aggravated by every step in their walk. Together, these people were the same ones who'd possibly see him homeless on this exact bench. This is how they would be, just like any other day.

CHAPTER 11

Intention

Alone again, Laura sat at the table and finished the pipe. She slowly made her way upstairs where the cards were still out. Since she had noted them, she put them away, soon unaware the task had been done. She traced over her steps as she scratched her forehead, then gazed at the Art Deco design of a woman walking a greyhound; the deck was given to her by her mother, though it wasn't intended for 'reading.' This moment, she wanted to create more art.

With the papers at hand, it made sense the woman wasn't far different from when she was a child, appreciating the world in the same light. This would show in her relationship with a friend she would frequently have coffee with.

Laura wrote. She wanted the woman to be singing at church as a child, matching the time the reader would meet her as an adult singing for a commercial. Her friend would also be at church when they were both young.

With these ideas, Laura sat back, then remembered herself stuck without words to say to her friends and family, strangers...Marcel. Maybe the verbal attacks still bothered her. Talking to Jae or even trusting him was difficult after he first fought her. After all of it, Laura found herself venturing away from her life on the farm because no one gave her attention, no matter who she turned to.

The world was endless. People were everywhere, and only Laura knew her mind. It was a wonder how people got where they were when she was bound to go about life on her own. She had to do something different, something allowing her the freedom everyone else seemed to have.

Back then, she tried to admire the world as it led her curiosity outside of her normal realm, to be away, maybe watch movies on a portable DVD player. The places she found herself gave her an expansive sense of the world, which wasn't like before, and the forthcoming unsteadiness was at her side to return to even with people. Getting away from everyone wasn't normal.

When she was still with Margaret, who had more help at the house, Laura would be away all day when the week was over, browsing stores and leaving to unpredictable places hidden away on less-traveled streets. She'd drive randomly until she found herself behind the mall, near the wildlife outside of Fremont, the wilderness several times, the lakes, a neglected park in Omaha and driving along streets there, once a place near to the airport, off a highway she had no reason to travel. She had a tendency to return to these places because the thoughts were, if not always pleasant, at least new.

She remembered her graduation, a time she sat silently with all the friends she wouldn't see again. It was easy then for her to say school meant nothing, but in reality, these people influenced her daily. They were her foundation.

It was all too much to think about. Maybe she'd been wrong. Maybe the world would come to overwhelm her, as it was now, as she sat at the papers she intended to work with.

She needed something else to do. Laura leaned back again, and the high was too much.

After regaining herself, she focused on her outline, adding events. Soon, she would just start at it and write. Obviously, she could base the woman on her mom and the man on Jae. But they had different faces.

The week was throwing her off the routine, as she had been off work for two days now, getting high and watching television. It was more time away than what she needed.

Laura studied and let go of the worry now, as the weed was actually a comfort, but the hesitancy she found in her conversations called for her to smoke more to relax, further throwing her off. If she had it, it would be a temptation when nothing else could occupy her time.

Jae wasn't someone who'd always share a respect for other people. Perhaps with her, he felt too ordinary. They drank often as they had little else to do outside of their schooling. Both Laura and Jae had studied outside of high school and quit, so they were in the same predicament. He wanted to catch up with everyone else and somehow grew angrier, hating her at times for her weak intentions and her cluelessness.

Practically meeting on the street, she immediately invited him into the studio she was living in. They were supposed to split the rent, and he never paid his share.

Trying to control the situation with him was wrong. But she could see a lot about him just from the stories he shared, enough to stay with him and endure the unpredictable fighting and bitterness. Perhaps also, he saw much in her, enough to overcome the frustration. Getting things accomplished was crucial.

It had to be the marijuana for her to think about this when she didn't want to. He insisted on eating out at places where he'd argue with her in public, and they'd often leave abruptly over nothing. She had people more in mind as they were missed, and she had no choice but to let go of them. After the split, she worried he would never change.

Laura lifted her pen, contemplating what she could add.

* * *

Jae was also involved with someone new, feeling always too mindful of what she wanted of him or what he thought she wanted. She never matched up to what Laura was. The girl obviously didn't like Jae because her respect for him was minimal compared to how much he found Laura had actually cared. The new girl's wit was too bitchy, and it came sharp with dishonesty. Jae was in the position to feel under her in the same place Laura felt with him.

He thought of Laura often. He was in Omaha and knew Laura was around. Today he was alone. He thumbed through the phone book. He and Laura could do something; it would bring more time as friends if nothing else. So, he dialed and waited.

Hello? "Laura?"

"Yes."

"What's up? This is Jae."

"Why are you calling me?"

"I know you won't believe me, but I changed *a lot.*"

After a moment, "I don't know what to say. How are you?" She was high and nervous, staring at the wall.

"I'm with a girl, but she's nothing like you. I really miss you."

"You miss me?" *Yes, a lot. I can't stand it with this girl because she smart, but she is straight up using me.*

Laura wanted him to not rush into anything. "I'm sorry, I'm seeing someone."

"That's cool. I just want to tell you I'm really sorry. It was all a mistake." *Yes, it was.* "Tell me we can meet up one of these days."

"Well, I'm busy lately. You know I was just thinking about you? I thought you still hated me."

"Please, I want to meet with you somewhere."

"Let me call you. I have to think about it. Everything's moving too fast for me right now." *Promise me.* She thought. "I promise I'll call you."

"Laura, you don't know how happy that makes me feel. This girl has got me strung up."

"Sorry to hear." She lit a smoke after standing up. They met a pause. She took the time to sit down on the floor at the wall. *Hello?* he said.

"Yes, I'm here."

"I promise it won't be like the last time. You don't know how sorry I am." She never initiated conversation. All his hopes were being tested now because she wasn't talking. It reminded him of what it had been.

"We'll see each other then."

"Call me." *I promise.* "I miss you, girl," he said, smiling.

"Okay, Jae, later."

"Bye."

Laura, sitting on the floor again with the phone, had too many people to catch up with. It wasn't a decision to be with either Marcel or Jae. It was suddenly a commitment to juggle both while she was high.

Laura went to her papers and looked over the man's half. He could have the polarity of trying to be nice with no respect in return. He'd carry the gun for protection at first, and he would have less choice than to shoot the woman, out of fear.

Maybe he needed to shoot her in a place she was working part-time. She would be alone; the boss would be away, giving the man more opportunity to fight with her at first, and she wouldn't know what to do.

Isolated, he would pass judgment on people as though they were in the place of mind he found himself in, further adapting him with a criminal mind. He wouldn't trust anyone. He'd have to be abusing cocaine, or crack, and his family would have no idea what he was doing or how unstable he became.

Laura thought of her mom. The character would be shy with customers and try to be sincere as best she could. The story would have to follow what she was afraid of. Maybe she had a secret fear of black people. She would be alone in some of the chapters to think to herself.

Maybe she used public transportation and would be waiting at times before work or after shopping. She would feel inadequate compared to other women, and maybe she would have gained weight. She wouldn't be jealous of women with children, but she would've wanted children herself, though it was too late.

❋ ❋ ❋

Consolidation

Michael was almost set to leave for Omaha as he paced around the kitchen to maintain his space. Noises were coming from the fridge again, and he didn't know if he should eat first. Already, the groceries were put away.

"I'm heading out, Dan."

"Okay."

It began as a patient drive out without the headache, he had the MP3 player hooked up, and when he was on the highway, he lit up a smoke. For once, he was breaking free from the apartment, knowing he mattered less in a typical duplex where he could only find trouble when left alone.

With the excitement of leaving the apartment for Omaha, Michael was aware of various people. In response to this, voices came from inside the air conditioner, excessive but quiet. It didn't affect him. Breaking the routine and heading out to a bar would bring voices, perhaps because it was the wrong thing to do. At the same time, for him, it was the right thing and the only thing.

Michael turned the air conditioner off, rolled down the window, and threw his cigarette out, but the voices shouted from every car. They returned behind the radio, so Michael turned the music up and was less aware of them.

He laughed when one said something funny. They were the same ones who disrupted him before his psychosis, speaking over the radio whenever a thought ended. It seemed unavoidable. He didn't know what he was allowed to think. Maybe he was going to hell.

Finally arriving in Omaha, the voices had left. He focused more on the road and felt right about being in town. He drove on wet streets, and clouds loomed low.

Then, it was as though he needed to get away from everything: the apartment and surrounding homes with all the people who had money, cars, everything--it always brought frustration. He needed the break.

His thoughts picked up as he passed busier parts of town, and he lit up another cigarette to function away from his worries. Eventually, his thoughts eased.

Then, he decided he was younger than most people, settling for what younger people could handle as though he was coming straight from the playground. He hated the feeling but laughed as he pictured kids playing and fighting in a park in fast-forward motion, up until they were dulled by school and tossed into adulthood. Childhood was hardly even an afterthought; it was so short.

He couldn't grasp any real ideas about people who'd influenced him. They simply were what they'd been, of a time which seemed to never have happened, but when it was happening, it seemed it would never end.

Voices again screamed. Or it was one voice.

Finally arriving on Fifteenth Street, Michael parked and walked alone. Early, he didn't have to pay to get in. He paid for a beer and took it to the tables in the back. Immediately, someone got up and sat next to him while he lit up another cigarette.

"How's it going?" the guy asked, seemingly wanting to meet someone, just not the rest of the people here.

"I'm all right." Michael felt used to the environment. He

was fixed on the idea he could make his own choices among people when in Chicago. Naturally, the club was no different than being in a straight bar in Chicago underage. He knew of this place from two bisexual girls who were involved with different men and each other at the same time, but he had never gone in before. He wasn't much a part of the lifestyle, nor did he identify with it. The place was dark and seemed suited for professional people older than him.

"I'm Malik."

"I'm Michael," he said over the music, and they shook hands.

Malik looked away, and it made Michael curious. Neither knew what to say. Then, Malik turned to him. He said, "What brought you here?"

"Well, I came to drink. To socialize. I didn't think I'd meet anyone. I'm up in Fremont."

"You get high?"

"Yeah."

"We can go to my place later if you want."

Michael nodded.

Malik then spoke to the people he had been sitting with. Michael drank the rest of his beer while the music surrounded him. Malik came back.

They held a demeanor like they already knew each other from another place and time, as though this meeting was a way to pretend they didn't know each other. "I'll get you another drink," Malik said, so he took Michael's empty bottle and went for the bar, while Michael stayed and felt the buzz carry his worries away.

As Michael waited, he considered his parents. If he knew how, he'd approach his mom and dad for them to better understand nothing changed his relationship with them, at least not for the worse.

Malik returned. "You'll like this. It'll work faster."

"Okay, thanks. How old are you?" Michael said.

"Thirty-seven."

"You don't look it."

"I know." They waited for either one to liven up but became interested when neither did.

"You live downtown?" Michael said.

"Dundee."

They didn't speak, and Malik seemed completely relaxed. For whatever reason, he clearly appreciated Michael. It was as though he wanted nothing to do with anyone else here. He remained quiet.

"Come with me to the game machine," Malik said.

"A'right."

They took their drinks, surrounded by the beats. "I play this all the time," Malik said when they sat at the screen. "We can play pool later if you want to, upstairs."

"Okay." When they first shared a glance, Michael was close to having a new friend. He could tell Malik felt right about him, too, perhaps as someone who didn't have the right friends.

CHAPTER 12

Extension

She arrived at the bank before it closed, then headed out of downtown for Westroads Mall. As she drove, she could remember only some of the past three days. She didn't know what to make of any of it.

The day otherwise brought a sense of freedom, away from the persistent nagging of her past and the responsibilities at the new place. She visualized more of the book and anticipated it to do well. Also, she could admit she was happy Jae called, even though it sped things up again. Maybe friendship was all he needed.

It was a quick week in and of itself, one she otherwise felt caught up to. Whatever reality was set for today, outside of being high, was one she couldn't keep herself from confronting. Her nights had been restful, and her work waited for her again as if she were at the end of another weekend.

As Laura drove further, she considered Marcel. He was like a distant memory fitting into her life long ago. She was calm in her waiting, and the drive was easy. She was down to three cigarettes and lit one, exhaling out the window.

For whatever reason, she thought she was predictable. She finished her cigarette before making it to the mall, and parked, knowing answers would come today.

Clouds covered the sky, and temps were mostly cool outside, near to another rainfall. Laura made a stride to one of the main doors before entering. Mindful of people as they passed by her, she walked through the middle of the food court into the mall and took the escalator up to the second floor. She was living in Omaha for once, and the change came almost too fast.

People surrounded her. She was dodging them toward a that store hadn't moved in over twenty years. Therein, she came to where she remembered the cards to be because she could maybe find one for her mom.

Instead of cards, she looked at journals with embossed covers and recycled paper. Laura picked through to find what was cheapest without the embossed detail. Also, she found a photo frame for the new photo of herself. Waiting in line, she wished she had a new photo of Marcel from when they first met. She would make a card for her mom sometime later.

After buying the journal and the frame, she returned to the dimmer-than-usual galley of the mall, much of it still lit by the day. Nearest to Younkers, she decided to browse clothes.

She didn't find enough reason in life to want more. Here, she was giving up at the same time she had to make more of herself. Laura needed motivation, and answers were far from obvious. Maybe it wasn't her calling to build up her life.

What made the attraction to certain men mostly came with wanting a change, however drastic it was. All her life, Laura had only known white people, so she wanted a connection to people with ideas not matching her own; it would change her feelings of isolation—to having a broader sense of the world.

Being more open to black people and having doubts about the people she already knew—had both broadened her view and separated her from her past. Laura only somewhat had a sense of it now.

Her original intent was what she envisioned happiness

to be: a process of understanding herself through different people, with freedom apart from a bitter loneliness long affecting her. She used to care about the people who made up her life.

Although Laura was nervous with people, she tried to hide it. If her family didn't approve, she would still go down this path because it was a matter of opening a door, and taking the first step could lead her anywhere. So far, she had had no regrets, even with Jae. With Marcel, it felt like another step forward.

Then, she was briefly in a trance, with concern for her future. Amid the shopping, she forgot. It was necessary to forge ahead.

Oftentimes and even now, Laura carried herself through the meaninglessness of it all, but she didn't feel vain. Ordinarily, she didn't have confidence because confidence was only masked if not sincere. To say what she felt was often truthful but came with inhibition. However, she could always reinforce her beliefs alone in public, just as she was now, looking at faded jeans. She had to be alone to connect with true aspects of herself.

Laura was free to express herself with weed; at least it used to be this. Without it, she was limited to what was only ever on the surface, and the back pain. Time and worry and gravity had long had its claws in her back. She couldn't get past the hurt, and she had remained less outspoken, believing surface matters were the only things to speak of. So, because she was in pain, she was less open to trusting others and speaking her mind. The response to people was always pain.

At the least, she had a united sense while alone in public with commitments to no one, like just about anyone in the mall. It pleased her being around people, though she had a limited wonder about them this day.

Laura found a pair of jeans and taupe corduroys. She was aware of a few people in the store, and it was not always a sense of pride in comparison. On the other hand, she was happy being alone and who she knew herself to be. It wasn't crowded, being a weekday....

She bought slacks with a shirt which would together make her appear taller and older at work, passing up the jeans she had tried. She left with her bag and what she had bought, intending to further shed her troubles. Shopping alone was empowering, and it revealed a similarity people strived for together.

Nothing came as an illusion but the fact America was at war as she walked through the mall. It seemed an idea only for a moment until she carried herself through the constant struggle again; if she ever got past her shyness, she'd know Marcel was worth befriending. Whatever came from Jae now would be his best intentions, as well. It was heavy considering both of them, not to be in a relationship but to remain friends for a while. It was all she could offer because she didn't know herself well. Suddenly, she didn't know herself well. She could only blame planetary shifts...

Approaching adulthood meant less could fail in bringing meaning to Laura. Many times, it was a challenge not having the answers, and it was still something she searched for. At the sight of herself in a mirror, she stood harshly repressed, and she wondered if she had grown up at all.

She started browsing a music store and kindly rejected help. It was easier to come back to the bands she already collected from, but this time she listened to some of what was new. She felt a sort of grandiosity come to her then; it always appeared something other people didn't identify but followed, themselves. Then, she couldn't get into the music. She was immovable, then shaken by the presence of a customer who stood next to her. He was younger, a white guy, and she didn't welcome the feeling he gave her. So she left the store and began walking toward the other end of the mall.

The day's outing was meant to be a short trip. She came

to a coffee shop and ordered a cup: too hot to taste, but she took it with her to the food court. There, she sat at a table and again tried the coffee.

It was a day to be free, though she had somehow lost her way to it. She knew pain had long kept her silent, but it was mostly just questions without answers. It was getting to be time for the road again.

It should be simple to talk with anyone, but Laura was so stuck between childhood and adulthood, she couldn't break free. She noticed people as they sat near and far, comfortably talking with one another. The place reinforced her as a worker on a break and nothing more, neither meaningless nor meaningful, and she had less purpose being away from home. It choked her up because it was a heavy, onward feeling to understand no one else could see it the same way. It was important for them to be happy.

Before she could cry, Laura got up and left out the doors to have a cigarette. And yes, for a moment, she knew herself well.

* * *

Satisfaction

Malik and Michael left the dark club and entered the later part of the day outside. They stopped around the corner when Michael offered a cigarette, and both began smoking with Malik leaning against the wall and Michael opposite him on the sidewalk. They didn't speak through the entire smoke.

Michael was curious about him the entire time and had the urge to say something, but neither had anything to say. His nervousness was slight, though it ran deep.

"It's cool not having to talk all of the time," Michael said. "You still want me to get high with you?"

"Yeah."

"I'm really feeling that beer, too."

They laughed.

Malik drove Michael to an apartment, giving mention of this or that. They came up an old set of stairs wrapping around steep with a banister, to the only door on the second floor. The boards welcomed them with creaking. They had entered when Malik led Michael in.

The living room floor was constructed with tile to cover up the wooden floors. Malik had nothing moved in yet and was living in another apartment across the street, having to decide whether or not to live in this one. A vintage apartment, it had appeal, but the floor was an absolute mistake, Michael had commented. Malik agreed.

With nothing apparent to do, "Should we do this?" Malik showed Michael the cocaine, in tiny glass tubes.

"Might as well."

Following Michael's lead, they kneeled and leaned against a wall as though to avoid detection. Windows were open, though it was silent inside. The walls were the original white, the windows had no curtains, and the original wood remained in the other rooms.

"You live with people?" Malik asked.

"I live with a friend." Michael nodded.

"And you want to move?"

"Maybe sometime."

Michael was looking out a window when he thought of Trish possibly living in Omaha, and he looked to another room at a window. He could hear people outside, and his first thought was voices. "I'm in deep shit with money; I hate it," he said.

"Join the club. Here."

Michael took the tube to his nose and sniffed the powder before snorting and handing it back. He continued sniffing harder, then swallowed a few times. The effect came to him. Daylight was still outside, but the apartment was dimly lit.

"I could never make this a habit. Do you?" Michael asked. He thought, at the look of Malik, he seemed to have a supportive family the way he was dressed. He drove his mom's Jaguar.

"No."

They didn't speak.

Michael finally said, "We're getting one of those times we don't know what to say."

"Yeah, I notice that," Malik said. He smiled.

"People think I'm too serious when I talk."

Malik nodded. "You maybe think a lot."

"You know I was in a hospital?"

"For anxiety?"

"Mostly, yeah, and I was stuck without work in Fremont. I'm *there* still."

"You think drugs had something to do with it?"

Michael thought. He nodded. "Sometimes...I started when I was young, so--then, I tripped acid in California once." Malik was preparing more of the powder.

"Yeah, they say you shouldn't use too early. I don't know anything about acid."

"Well, I was young."

"You want another line?"

"I'm fine with it. Sure."

"Alright," Malik said, smiling. Michael stared away at the thought of the police being here. A lot mattered. Then, all of his worries disappeared. He had grown up with more interest in the world than what he could show. "You want this?"

"Yeah."

Michael took it and relaxed.

Malik was someone who always felt in the situation to make others feel welcome to him, a matter of sharing a good influence. Spending time with Michael, Malik was the same way, but he almost had more respect for Michael than some people he knew.

"Join me for a cigarette?" Michael said.

"All right, I'll take one." They stood.

"Here," Michael said, handing Malik one. They lit, sharing a lighter. "I grew up on a farm."

"Yeah, you mentioned it. My family is Muslim."

"Oh? I haven't known anyone who—" Michael paused and switched gears. "I guess you would see people through a different lens."

"Yeah." Malik had an easy mind to the subject.

Michael said, "I've always felt like there's more than what there is." He smoked and exhaled.

"Yeah?"

"I think so," Michael said. Unless you consider Fremont." Michael smiled, only it was to be with someone who—well, maybe Michael would never get involved with anyone. Malik seemed to care about people, and if Michael also did, a simple hug would be one gesture to show it.

"Age comes fast; maturity comes slow," Malik said.

Michael hesitated. Even though he met plenty of people before, getting to know someone at first presented something beyond him, just as it did now. "So, what do you know? What's on your mind?"

"I don't really pay attention to it. You shouldn't prejudge people."

"You get that from me?"

Michael was different from the typical people who wouldn't find themselves in places like this, since their attitude would suggest they were above this old apartment, above Omaha, and above it all. "A little," Malik said. "I might accept people more than you do."

This didn't bother Michael. "Well, I have a fear of people you might not have," he said.

"True. I can see that." Malik nodded.

"But everyone has that," Michael added.

"You leave people to what they know and go for what you know. You can't have them on your mind because you become too aware of whatever bothers you...I was bored, too, shit. You said you didn't like Fremont. You do drugs. Simple."

Michael couldn't comprehend what exactly was being said. It only meant Malik knew more at his age than Michael. "Right," giving a half-smile. "You're a cool guy." Michael felt more open to talk as he smoked.

"You seem you don't know too many people like me," Malik said.

"It's cool. Everyone I know keeps to themselves. Honestly, I don't get to know people too much."

Malik relaxed his shoulder. "I know, it's like that."

"So, are you with a guy?" Michael asked.

"No. Used to see a guy, but we got sick with it."

"HIV?" Michael said. Malik nodded. "That's awful. You think it's strange how I act happy?"

"Yeah, a little. You'll grow out of it."

"It's anxiety." Michael glanced away. "I don't know what's wrong with me, actually. I think I'm just excited about meeting you."

"You want this?"

"Sure." As Michael took the cocaine, he felt he needed to somehow stop the doubt and torment. With nothing feeling right at this moment, the drug was a mistake, but it was too late. He began snorting it into the back of his throat. "We should just go. I don't think I like it here." Michael paused. He said, "It's not you. It just seems like we could get caught."

"A'right. I'll drive you back."

Michael felt back to himself again when they arrived at the club, calm with the effect of the coke. They hadn't said much on the way, yet they had the unspoken potential for being close friends.

"Let me give you my number," Malik said, as he reached for a paper and pen from the glove compartment.

"Actually, I can put it on my cell phone," Michael said. So, they exchanged numbers.

"All right. Now you got my number," Malik said.

They quickly kissed, just a peck on the lips, and if they were to know each other as friends, it started this day. Michael didn't expect it. Before entering his car, Michael watched Malik head out. Everything was calm. He was aware of traffic. Then, he pulled away and left.

Michael wished to have made a closer connection, but the feeling seemed right. There was no urgency in getting home. Anyone should feel this relaxed about something if they ever had shame about it before. He also hoped anyone could lead the way because it seemed he couldn't do it for himself these days.

CHAPTER 13

Originality

Dawn arrived. Laura was already smoking. She tried to remember anything from earlier this week, but whatever came to her was a blur. Then, Dawn was at the door. "Hey," Dawn said. "You ready?"

"Let's smoke first."

"No, let's not. Tonight, let's just drink."

"Fine. I'll get my bag." Laura acted quiet, even confused. She went back to the living room, put her smokes in the bag, and they were on their way out the door. Again, she didn't want to feel as though she forgot anything, so Laura turned off the light and shut her door without another thought to keep her in.

They started walking to the elevator. "Did you forget something?"

"No, I'm sure all I need is my bag," Laura said as she caught up.

In the elevator, Dawn said, "There's college kids at this one, mostly our age, though."

"As long as the beer is good, right?"

"Yeah." After a moment, "These elevators are slow." She looked at Laura. "Did you call Marcel?"

"Fuck, I forgot."

"That's ok. One of us will just have to drink less."

"I'll be ok." Entering the elevator, they were out of words. They waited, then left the building for the car. They had spoken less on the way to Fremont, but what they did share made them feel more caught up. Laura had doubts, expecting these people to be mean-spirited brats, which often was a fear. Being with Dawn helped.

Laura was less than amused by the place because it was small and dingy, practically a shack with people smoking outside and a group already drinking inside with loud music. Not trusting them, Laura locked the car and took her bag with her. The music rumbled through the building. It seemed a typical place set up in Eighties, Nebraska with what would often become a muddy parking lot.

"How's it going?" Dawn asked someone outside.

"I'm going in," Laura told Dawn.

Inside, Laura paid and took a cup. She weaved around people until reaching the kegs, and a younger guy filled her cup for her. "Who are you?" he said.

"No one. I'm just from up north." She wanted to believe these were good people, and drinking would help. Maybe not.

Dawn soon stood next to Laura. She waited to fill her cup, then yelled, "Let's go outside. It's too loud in here."

"Gotcha."

They went outside and eventually leaned against a car parked out front. People talked across from them. With the music, they went unnoticed.

"You and Marcel talk a lot?"

"Some. We were high."

"You know, you're going to be paranoid with too much of that. When did you last see him?"

Laura had to think back. "I only saw him Sunday and Monday."

"What does he do?"

"He told me he worked at a hospital."

"Cool." Dawn felt as though they were sharing a flashback. It was a lot like when Laura said nothing before getting involved with Jae. They were stuck. "You think he'll be good?" Dawn drank.

"Yep, a good influence."

Dawn looked up as she had been looking down at her drink. She took a swig. "I hang with guys, lately. I don't feel alone all the time." She stopped to think. "I think I'm okay." They drank.

"What do you talk about?" Laura said.

"We share time more than words."

"And you don't get high anymore?"

"At first. But I quit when I couldn't find any, and I couldn't sit still and read. I couldn't watch TV. I drink tea sometimes. And it's easier to read without wanting to be high or needing a smoke. Otherwise, withdrawal is way too much to handle." They drank. "What else did you and Marcel talk about?"

"I don't know, I sometimes get the idea people don't care. I think we talked about that."

"I know what you mean."

"Yeah. I called Rebecca, you know—it's never going to be the same."

Dawn said, "I had no friends when I was young."

"It seemed to work out for you."

"I don't know." Dawn drank. "I wasn't jealous of people, but I wanted friends later. You're there, too."

"Sometimes, people are all I think about." Laura shook her head.

"Yeah. Like a bad habit?"

Laura had to think. "I guess," she said. "Or a compulsion." They both drank the rest of their beer as more people were going in. Someone was out for air near the car and ready to vomit. The girl breathed and didn't want to throw up, but she gave it a go several times. Another girl and a guy were with her, standing before they kneeled there, drunk.

"We should go in," Dawn said.

Laura followed Dawn back inside, where the music was at a break, so the voices of everyone took over the room momentarily. Laura took her beer and sat at a table while somebody grabbed Dawn into another group. The music started up again.

Dawn had nothing to relate to any of them, but she still talked. At the moment, she was landing a buzz.

Meanwhile, Laura, for all she could tell, saw these kids as whorish lost siblings of her own small world. They wore clothes to show off their bodies. The girls were seeking guys, and the guys seeking girls. It seemed they could all agree to have one big orgy when Laura and Dawn would run the hell away. None of it brought any meaning to what she faced. A guy turned his glass in circles next to her.

"Who are you?" she asked.

He said something.

"Rick?" she asked loudly.

"Yeah," he finally said over the music.

"I'm Laura."

"Nice to meet you." They shook hands. It was enough for him to say just that, and he acted as though he wouldn't say anything more.

"You're from Fremont?" She yelled in his ear.

"Out of town," he yelled.

"Me, too. What do you do?" She drank.

"I just cruise around, mostly weed."

"I know, that's what everyone in Fremont does."

"Yeah, this town sucks."

"It's what everyone's attitude is."

"Yeah, what do *you* do?"

"Living in Omaha," she yelled.

"Ah," he said, nodding.

Dawn came to Laura, yelling, "Let's go outside." From behind her, Dawn was surrounded by intensity, people gathering at the keg, and everyone in motion, the music picking up. Laura followed her out and left Rick behind. She met someone she probably wouldn't see again.

Dawn led her to a car further from the door as the first one had already left.

"What did you guys talk about?" Laura asked.

Dawn gazed at the ground, shaking her head, and said, "Nothing, as far as I know."

They drank. Laura hesitated, then drank some more. "Guess who I talked to today," she said.

"Who?"

"Jae. You know he's in Omaha."

"Jae? What did he want?"

"He wants to meet."

"Fuck that."

Laura had to think. She said, "It would hurt his pride if I didn't see him. I figured I'd talk with him tomorrow after work."

"*Fuck* that." The music had Dawn. She stood straight, despite her swaying. "Let's have a cigarette."

"Oh, yeah." Laura took out her pack and pulled out two for them. "He doesn't bother me. I mean, as long as we're not living with each other. He says he's changed."

"People could tell you that's what they all say."

"I believe him. He was real nice when we first got together. All I had us do was drink, and he got angry–you know–and I could barely talk. That's what happens."

"You want me to go with you?"

"I'll be fine. You'll be at work." Laura anticipated more lies from Jae, but with what was said, he probably had less to lie about with the truth out. Laura was slowly leaving Dawn. "I'm going in for another drink," she said.

"Hold on." Dawn drank the rest of hers. "I'll go with you."

* * *

Solution

Suddenly, a long, rising yell.

It was as though Michael had the radio on low, but it was them. Michael sucked back more of the cocaine. At the idea of them possibly harming him, he slowed down, as if speeding was the problem, only he contemplated the voices even more by doing this.

One said something insulting. Michael had already gone through one trip with them, and he didn't make it known to anyone but his doctor before later denying them.

One yelled again. It sounded like an old friend.

Michael left Omaha into the darkness. He had driven through town for a good half hour.

Another voice said something he couldn't make out, so he was now accepting someone approaching him as a child would and was open to listen. She didn't return. Then, more yelling came and went.

He assumed if he were anyone else, he wouldn't have these voices. It didn't alarm him when it first occurred, because they were often kind. It changed, sometimes even brought him to laughter, and he couldn't share it with anyone because they'd question it. It became trouble for him because new voices crowded with the first ones, and the first ones were gone. Now, they were strangers, and he felt he was in the way. At the sound of them, he wondered if they were actual people.

They had returned too soon because they would only prevent him from getting another job and keeping it. Another voice offended him.

His eyes were wide open, focused on the road. He wanted them to either go away or meet with him as someone who would cooperate. Michael wanted what was right. Then, more yelling came.

He couldn't tell if it was one voice with an added effect or many voices together. It seemed to bubble out as boiling water would. Overly aware as he drove, he couldn't change his focus to be someone who wouldn't turn on them. They made it seem he already did. If they continued much longer, he could see himself going back to the hospital with no real answers and no reason to stay if he had no symptoms of a real psychosis. They didn't seem to be his imagination. He surely wasn't going crazy, because this was outside of him, and he wasn't causing this. He was his usual self, just vulnerable.

Michael arrived home and entered the darkness of the apartment. The only light was from over the sink in the kitchen, and the view outside was black besides a yard light to a neighbor's home and shadowy grass.

The voices still sounded like boiling water, seeming ready to shout. For him to be aware of them, he'd end up paranoid about a number of things, especially with the idea they'd physically harm him. They now sounded like elderly women.

Michael left for the living room. They stayed under the refrigerator, remaining quiet when he turned the television on and sat. The news came on with a blast, so Michael turned the volume down, flipped to a channel accidentally, and returned to the news. Still, it was talk about terrorism, like some crude metaphor to what was happening to him, nightmarish. They seemed to be people in a dream he was having.

Michael looked away toward the kitchen, troubled by the news and the refrigerator. As they populated the space, he was losing the time he had improved without them. Sitting in the dark with the television was just more isolation.

It was too early for Dan to be home. Michael lit a cigarette, a nonchalant focus during his troubles, though if he didn't, he'd be anxious.

The menthol smoke filled his lungs smooth and cold before he exhaled. He felt calmer, watching television and ignoring the voices as though it was normal and they'd already been tolerated for weeks. They yelled, but it was more of a sound than something directed toward him. Aware of them again, they returned.

He sat straight up and adjusted his shirt. '*This just in...*' and Michael lost his focus to the television. He would've made plans while driving home had the voices not disrupted him. Meeting Malik, having cocaine, handling voices--everything was moving too quickly.

Michael pulled the table closer as though he were taking up responsibilities no one would know about. He reminded himself of a man who was shown to be schizophrenic with math, and maybe his own paranoia would lead him toward ideas of conspiracy. He worried. It wasn't like him, and he should live his life just as anyone else should.

They screamed from the kitchen. Then, there was a long stream of different phrases from different voices, all offensive.

Michael got up and went to the refrigerator to maintain his space. His exertion getting up to do this made his neck and head swell in pain.

An elderly woman screamed long from the refrigerator as if she were angry on her deathbed. Michael would soon panic if they wouldn't go away this night, just as he had before.

He turned the light off in the kitchen and went to the fridge. He opened it to the sound of boiling water within it. Then, he closed the door and went back to the sofa, finishing his cigarette and lighting another one with nothing more in mind but the worries about his situation, being without a job. Anxious with another headache coming to him, he flipped through the channels, landing on a movie.

No.

Where is he?

He's out of town now. He'll manage.

Should we talk to him? He needs help.

The movie was undeniably immersive. He couldn't tell if it was paranoia. It had to end sometime, but he didn't know if it would soon enough to avoid being hospitalized. Maybe something was wrong with his head, to have this wonder. He worried as the movie unfolded.

Michael's eyes widened. One of the voices sounded like his own grandmother.

After putting the cigarette out, he decided he could smoke more weed. When he passed the fridge, the voices rose and continued. One shouted as he made his way down to the basement, something about 'dragons.' At the pool table, he loaded the pipe and lit up, holding the hit in. A calm came over him after the second hit, and he halfway finished the bowl, saving the rest for later.

For a moment, he went to the computer, the voices returned, and his head hurt in response. Sometimes with the high, it would backfire and set off this reaction.

Michael's mouth hung open, then closed. There may have been other people who felt this way. Maybe he didn't deserve a normal life. Sometimes he wasn't happy, but it didn't make him a bad person. And why would these people be so compelled to follow him if they would disagree with his every move?

He was impatient with the computer starting up, thinking again of Malik. Maybe Malik would have no time for him.

He went to his house plans on the computer. More yelling came, so instead of looking it over, Michael shut down the computer, and left for the sofa. The voices went away. He felt calm and dismissive enough to move his foot forward, fearing the voices would return, the more he was aware of them, whatever action taken.

He leaned back and decided to put on some music, too deep in isolation. He'd often think of the voices. With the music, he sat on the sofa again. They had to leave him alone because if they persisted, it would only stir up more fighting. He smiled because he was right, and he let go of the smile, knowing it hadn't passed yet.

Still, more voices came. Michael remembered he left the television on, so he turned the music and lights off and went upstairs. His behavior was a mistake, but what could he do? He felt electrified.

In the living room, he sat, waiting for Dan. Michael would simply watch TV high. Moments later, he was impatient, so he took a cigarette and went out to the front steps.

Outside, nothing felt wrong. But when he lit up, he realized this situation was far from normal; it shouldn't have been happening. However, the neighborhood around him was quiet as he stood on the porch. A car passed and voices came from its engine. Their noise continued and left with the car.

He had no plans, and this was a definite departure from one reality to another. His attention had been scattered in many directions, and he didn't want to go down any of the paths the voices would lead him. Michael had no real destination and little money. He could lift himself in thoughts of better things, but the vulnerability grounded him to the steps with his head full of matters of no importance.

He finally rested his mind. Although the voices made him nervous, it was right to be high and calm for once this night, even though he needed support. He also needed a purpose, and he had none.

Michael finished the cigarette and used the restroom before going to bed. He left his clothes on.

His grandmother had said, "Face it, we're stupid."

CHAPTER 14

Introspection

As Laura and Dawn drank their last beers, people hustled out to take the back roads either home or to spend time sobering up. Cops didn't patrol the area because the party came unexpectedly. They'd never patrol the back roads. "You wanna go with us?" a guy asked.

"No, we work tomorrow," Laura called.

Dawn said sarcastically, "Have fun."

"You have a good one," he said, drunk. "We're outta here." They left.

Two men were hauling out the remaining keg to their truck and shut their doors at once before heading off. Everyone was gone but Laura and Dawn at the car. They stood outside each other's doors.

"You know, if you're too buzzed to drive, we can just wait it out awhile," Dawn said over the car.

"I know. I'm too fucked up right now...get in," Laura said, unlocking.

They sat in the car together, facing north to a black nothing with light shining to the end of the dirt parking lot. Trees ahead were barely visible silhouettes. The two had their drinks to finish, and they rolled down their windows to the cool night with the radio on low.

They drank.

"I don't mind being here right now," Laura said, looking at the steering wheel, dazed. "You?" She asked.

"Nope. No humidity. That's the way I like it."

Laura looked at Dawn. "Do you even drink that often anymore?"

"Not like these kids do." Dawn shook her head.

"That's what I thought. It's been a while for me." They drank some more, and Laura lit up a cigarette. "Do you want one of these?"

"I guess." Dawn spoke slowly, giving it a moment.

Laura handed the pack and the lighter. Dawn arranged a cigarette to her mouth and lit it, then exhaled out the window. They were silent.

"I've got some water in the back," Laura said.

"No, I'll have to pee soon."

"You know I feel lucky to have you around. This past week has been something else for me. I'm losing myself, it feels like."

"Why?" Dawn asked.

"I don't know. Everything is too fast." Laura was looking out the windshield. "You know how to handle the world with its endless nothing and shit."

"Well, there is meaning in the world," Dawn said. "But you're right, you've gotta find it on your own."

"It's just nothing."

Dawn could see Laura needed people, and maybe she had no one lately. "We're allowed to feel that way sometimes. Just try to include more people in your life."

They drank, and Laura looked out her window. "Sometime, this all has to stop," she said. "I mean, everyone drinking–it does nothing for them later on."

"Let it be them and not you."

Laura nodded, then said, "But I don't know why they don't see the responsibility they have, and they think they're the ones to raise families. It's ridiculous. They get stuck doing the same shit every *day*. It's like you could tell them they're doing something wrong, and they'll maybe listen for once. But there's no way to have them see it the way you do."

"Like I said. It's not your worry."

"But it is. I worry."

"Maybe that's your problem."

Laura thought. "It *is* a problem because I don't have the solution. People don't have to be idiots."

"Just give it time. Like Jae always said, 'simmer down now.'"

"Yeah," Laura looked forward and then at Dawn, who drank again, so Laura drank until hers was nearly halfway through. Then she drank the rest and threw the cup out her window. Then Dawn threw hers out.

"These cigarettes are good," Dawn said.

"I know. The filters are cotton instead of plastic."

"Cool," Dawn said as she looked at Laura and they met a glance.

Laura was hunched forward again, so she leaned back with her head rested, only to become dizzy. "Fuck, we'll be up late."

"Promise me you won't fall asleep at the wheel?"

"We'll keep talking. You got caffeine pills, anyhow." Laura put her arm at the window and her head on her hand in her dizziness. She yawned, and said, "I promise. I'll just be relaxed."

They said nothing. Laura turned the radio up. Later, Dawn turned it down.

"Gotta pee." Dawn got out and went out of view behind the building.

Meanwhile, Laura was far from thinking about her troubles, relaxed and comforted by the idea of her home and bed ready for her, then remembering Jae. Dawn came back.

"I'm thinking about Jae," Laura said.

"He really fucked you up if you ask me. You were quiet after it ended."

"Really?" Laura paused. "I can't understand it."

"I can't either."

They smoked through the entire length of their cigarettes. Laura finished first and threw its butt out at the ground. Dawn flicked hers. Even Dawn didn't have the answers, and Laura tied up her hair while she thought again of a time she always got high. Maybe from getting high, she had these worries now. She couldn't talk to anyone like before. She didn't want to settle into what everyone predictably did because it wouldn't lead her far.

"You know my grandma just died?" she said. "I couldn't think anything of her. My mom called, crying."

"You didn't know her very well?" Dawn asked.

"Well, I did, but it was like nothing changed."

Dawn thought. "Yeah, it's like that." And she leaned back, shaking her head.

Laura settled her hands on the steering wheel. "You know I liked her a lot. Sometimes I shared a side of her, the way I talked. I don't know. Time is too fast."

"That just means you need to take it slow," Dawn said. "You're just not used to being alone."

"You think so?" It seemed Dawn had matured a long time ago. Maybe it was the alcohol.

"I think you're learning," Dawn said.

"Great," Laura said, drunk and doubtful. "How do you feel?"

"I'm so wasted. We drank the same."

"Fuck."

"So, how's your book coming along?"

"It's good. The woman is going to be afraid of black people all her life until this guy kills her." After a moment, Laura looked at Dawn. "I don't know what to say to you. I feel like I should be talking more, and that no one should care about whatever stupid book I write. And I can't stop thinking there's more to life, but what? You know?"

"What's on your mind?"

Laura relaxed. "I just made a comment to my mom that all people do is bullshit each other, and I still think about it like I shouldn't have said it."

"I know it's difficult to really get into talking sometimes," Dawn said.

Laura looked ahead at the darkness. "Yeah, everything passes by; everyone's superficial."

Dawn said, "But we're talking now."

"We're too distracted," Laura said, making eye contact again. "All these kids talk about nothing, and they want sex from each other. Based on nothing, they want to marry," Laura made expression with her hands. "If I see it in other people, the issue somehow falls back on me. It's like I wonder if this is a Nebraska thing, or an American thing."

"I don't think so. Just forget about people."

Laura hesitated. "Well, it seems like I have to think about the people around me. It's who we learn from, for better or worse."

"I don't know. Just don't let people get to you."

Laura thought. "I'm smoking another cigarette. Want one?"

"Sure." Then, Dawn sneezed.

Laura lit up and blew smoke out her window. She wanted something more to say as she glanced outside. Instead, she turned the radio up because she was in no position to speak her mind. Dawn would leave for Chicago. Laura couldn't keep starting over with new people.

"You think we've known each other a long time?" Laura asked.

"Yeah," Dawn said.

Laura looked ahead. "I can't remember a lot of it," Laura said. Then her face lit up. "There was that time we were making chicken noises at the cheerleaders when we were stoned."

Dawn laughed quietly. For a moment, she had thought Laura was depressed. "You remember that? I think it was you who started it." Laura was nearly laughing. Dawn laughed again. "They looked just like hens in those skirts."

Laura just smiled and took another drag. She let go of the smile to something serious. "You know I have cancer?"

"Laura, are you serious?" Dawn stared at Laura.

"Just kidding!" Laura said, laughing loudly.

"You know a lot of people wouldn't find that funny."

"Yeah, but your expression was," Laura said.

Laura turned the music up loud and smoked, staring at the ground outside. "I have to go now," Laura said as she turned the radio down. The song was over.

"Okay."

Laura got out, tossed her cigarette, and went to the back of the building while Dawn smoked and turned the music up. She gazed out her window and rested her head on her hand. It was past midnight. She was trying to remember something Laura said...

Laura returned. "Wasn't this party a complete waste of time?" Laura asked.

"Kind of. Drinking and BS. BS and sex."

After a moment, Laura asked, "Did you see your brother?"

"Yeah, but I didn't talk to him."

"I met this guy named Rick."

"What did you talk about?"

"Can't remember." Laura grabbed two bottles of water for both of them. "After this, we've gotta go," Laura said.

"You're all right to drive?"

Laura thought. "Give it another thirty minutes."

* * *

Articulation

Michael woke early. It wasn't past eight yet, so he remained in bed, staring at the ceiling. Then, he remembered the voices. Anticipating them, he got up. It was as though they were with him already. The morning light seemed different, and his bed lay low to the floor as he stood tall in the room. Clothes were sorted into colors on the floor and ready for washing. He was trying his best to avoid voices by being slow and cooperative.

He took a bath and went through the routine. He hadn't shaved yet, and the hair on his face had grown. It seemed more charming, and he looked a little older than his age. He dressed in his closet and filled a bag with laundry before taking it to the basement.

He got his supply, loaded another bowl, and smoked in the basement, then sneezed repetitively afterward, which may have cleared his head and gotten him higher. Then, he lit a cigarette and sat on the sofa. Both the apartment and the neighborhood were alive with him, and he was unsure of having their company.

Michael smoked. He focused on the leg of the pool table when his thoughts left him. The hum of the washer in the other room entered his mind. He was up late and woke early because he was getting sick. It may have been the caffeine or the constant smoking. He couldn't get himself to quit.

Nicotine definitely added to the mania he went through before the hospital, and here he was in the same situation as the last time: overly aware and alert. His body would need sleep after maybe a week of this. He'd be aware of things unrelated to what needed doing, and since it was making sense, he wanted to deny it. He could also end up rationalizing the voices.

To him, entering the hospital meant he wasn't adapted to living on his own. People would opt to leave him there someday, believing he was crazy. He couldn't explain himself because he didn't talk openly enough.

At least, this was what he was seeing, and he felt uneasy, cycling over it a number of times with the same end. Ideas were getting fast.

He finished the cigarette and came to the fridge for some milk. It was something he had never tried high. He wanted no breakfast because his posture at the table would bring a headache he was already feeling. If he ever had the money, he would get his back fixed. He stood near the silent refrigerator and expected more voices.

Since the voices left him the last time, the hospital was almost an option, but stay or go, he'd still need a job eventually. He could never tell even Dan about the voices because it would rumor out, and if Michael stressed it as a worry with the doctor, the doctor could give the wrong diagnosis. Maybe it was the acid. It was true some of the voices were familiar. Once, he tried recording them on a digital recorder when they first came around, and they didn't record.

Maybe he had to go through this because of a role he could take up. But he decided against it because his experience wasn't a positive one.

True, many people were in a position not to adapt to the changing world, a position he was in. He could relate. He was still young and didn't have the answers, but he didn't deserve to be sidetracked.

He rinsed the glass and slowly placed it on the dish rack. It was ill to think this much.

And it was no longer just getting a job. Now, it was complying with voices. Maybe he was already too sick. He couldn't decide if he was having a psychosis, but he *was* alert. It had to be too much coffee. His mentality was now close to what it had been the first time through. Since his time in the hospital, he had adapted more to avoiding triggers but being overly aware of what he was doing confused him. He was separated from people he knew before noticing he was more alone than he had ever felt.

He could see it now: soon, he would return to the hospital. Just then, noises rose again from behind the wall.

Michael wasn't always easy to see eye-to-eye with. He didn't have the sense many people had, but he also had avoidant tendencies. Most people adapted to others like anyone would, but Michael rejected this experience growing up. What he saw in all this was far too simple. But sometimes, Michael fell into both categories. Still, he'd have to learn from people he didn't know yet, because no further path could be seen with those of his past, as far as being a better influence went.

Sometimes his first impression of certain people was their hatred or an obvious bias. It was necessary to care more.

He breathed.

In the living room, he worried about all things. It was looking for a job, the voices, and the chance he could be losing his mind and self-control. Helpless, he paced around the room for something to do this early and decided he would start on the jobs.

He grabbed his bag from the sofa and left out the back door, unchained the bike, and rode off toward the gas station. He would apply at several places in the area. Simply, he would collect as many applications as he could, and fill them out at home, to return to those places the next day.

Riding through the neighborhood north, he saw himself to be a loner, dispatched to what any other loner would do in his case. It consisted of nothing anyone would pay mind to, and he appeared both distant and open-minded as though borne of the air this day. A car passed from the opposite direction, and the voices went with it. He thought he was different from everyone when he arrived at the intersection, and the voices yelled from every passing car like a stadium crowd. It would have overwhelmed anyone, and no one here seemed to know.

Michael crossed the street, parked his bike, and went in.

Under this scrutiny, getting a job was stupid. "Are you hiring?" he asked the woman.

"No."

He didn't know what to do. "Can I get an application?"

"Yes! Got 'em right here." She took one out and handed it over. "Here."

"Thanks." He was just anyone in public.

He left for a restaurant nearby. They weren't hiring, and neither was the movie-rental place. He rode on toward Bell Street, thinking about Trish again as he passed the gym. The voices populated Military Avenue. No one heard them, but they were many and loud. At the intersection, Michael worried because he was either getting away from them or deeper into it. He crossed and went to a street with less traffic. The voices remained on Military behind him when he went a block south and headed west to the unemployment office. Therein, he registered and took a few applications, but they had no immediate openings.

Downtown, he heard more voices from cars on a one-way street while he waited to cross. If these voices would always be aware of him, he'd have to stay calm. The more activity he was exposed to outside, the more overwhelming the situation would become.

Michael's back hurt when he continued across the street. He found a place with a large 'NOW HIRING' sign.

"You'll have to fill out an application here, and I'll have someone talk to you when you're done."

"Okay," he said.

His back hurt the entire time he filled out the papers until he handed them in. It was under whatever judgment of what was right or wrong. He was one or the other but being between the two was a balancing act he had little patience for. The second woman took the application.

"Thanks. We'll have someone call you if you are considered."

"Okay, bye."

Entering further downtown, his back hurt enough he didn't want to be riding around anymore. He needed a cigarette, so he stopped his bike at a bench and sat. There, Michael lit up and exhaled before the voices returned through the air. He tried ignoring them in a focus on the ground, but they surrounded him, quietly for now.

A familiar voice spoke up. Michael looked around and had the sense he was being watched. Then, everything was wrong with him. Maybe he wasn't the worst of people, but he felt far from being the best.

The pain in his back had him standing up and smoke. He then sat down and impatiently stretched from side to side, and continued smoking. He wanted a job if it meant everything would return to normal. The voices came and went. It felt uneasy being watched, but he ignored it.

He thought of the younger guys he used to live with in a house on Military. The same voices surrounded him then, and he had chosen to overdose on pills before waking up in a hospital. It didn't matter what those guys were doing now because life was easy for them.

Michael couldn't decide why he had once chosen to end his life. He was no longer on a clear path. Something had to be done...

In the first hospital, he had taken the IV tube from his arm, left the room with no one in the hall, and stood waiting, not knowing what to do. He went to the elevator. The voices were with him, and he needed a way to kill himself. It would all end.

After he was out of the psychiatric hospital in Omaha, life returned to normal. He'd been curious about the voices, yet often calm and avoided the TV. At the time, he was living at home. Without a car, his mom started buying cigarettes with his money. Before the apartment, he was often searching for opportunities allowing him to move on. Meeting an end with no new beginning, his inner world missed a few beats.

He flicked the cigarette to the idea none of this was fair.

Someone was responsible for it happening.

Michael got onto his bike and rode to a few more places, unworried. He threw his empty pack of smokes away and was happy to be through with the menthols. After he got everything he needed from downtown, he went to the smoke shop.

"Hi, Mike," Sharon said.

"I'd like a pack of Spirits if you got 'em."

"The organic?"

"Sounds good."

Sharon grabbed a pack and came to the register. "Three, eighty-two."

Michael handed her four dollars, took his change, and eagerly took out a cigarette just to give them a try. He leaned against the building when he was outside. No one took notice of him under the awning as they drove past, but the voices came and went. He had concern all over his face. They got the best of him the last time, and Michael couldn't simply be in his surroundings without being followed.

At this, they started yelling again. Michael felt deeply troubled. There was a time he thought he should die. They were driving him away from everyone and everything he had known. If it was anyone else, they may not have withstood the trial of it all.

Once, he had a loaded shotgun to his mouth, lying in a bed at home, and he couldn't go through with it because he would feel the shot all through his nerves left in a dying body. At this memory, Michael was glad to be alive. His thumb had been right over the trigger.

At the psychiatric hospital, he had to explain why he was trying to kill himself. Avoiding mention of the voices at first, he simply said it was too difficult with his bills and seeking a job where there were none. No one was hiring him because of his record.

"Fuck." He had to go in for a urine test.

Michael put the cigarette out on the sidewalk and rode

his bike to the side of the probation office. Therein, he signed his name and waited.

"Hi, Michael," his probation officer, a kind gentleman with glasses and thinning hair, said as he walked toward his office. "How are you?"

"Fine."

"Next," a person called.

Michael walked to the back and helped with the papers before giving a sample. The office was suddenly taking him away from his thoughts and bringing him back into the world. Apparently, there were some people offering help in Fremont, and maybe it was more than just a job.

He later returned to his bike outside and rode through an alley he had all to himself.

CHAPTER 15

Devotion

It was Thursday, and Laura arrived home from work, heading for the phone. All day, she had planned to call Jae. She checked her caller ID, then dialed...

"Hello?" he said.

"It's me. I just got off work." His TV was an abrupt noise, just as anyone's was.

"Laura, hi!"

"Do you still want to meet up today?" *Of course, I do.* "Okay, where?" she asked.

"The mall at Seventy-Second?" He was pacing now. *Okay, coffee at the bookstore.* "Sounds good, Laura."

"I'll be there as soon as I can," she said.

"I'll be there."

"Okay, bye."

Soon, as she made her way to Dodge Street, she found herself revisiting the same memories she always had of him... Often, he'd be back to being her friend after all the threats, and she never knew the reason for it, even now.

She came to see people differently after all the fighting, suspecting some had the same troubles he did. Now, she more or less avoided the public to more privacy, which wasn't like her.

Mostly, she saw the public oblivious to what needed to change. Everyone seemed too occupied in the brief, amusing shit to take notice of whatever else should be. He was one of the few closest friendships she had ever known, and his behavior concerned her.

Jae sometimes seemed afraid of what she may have thought of him. He had bad experiences before her, so he had a lot of hope for her at first. Back in the days at the studio, Laura quickly grew to respect his generosity and uncommon thoughtfulness, sincerity, and a habit of defending her. His efforts were sometimes even heroic. Yet, she had long suffered through mundanity and rejection, and she couldn't see into his efforts anymore.

She wondered what the day would bring. Living together would be awful; she preferred he stayed with the girl even though she probably wasn't right for him. She could handle bills. Frustrated, she lit up a cigarette, exhaling smoke to the rush of air outside her window. He'd be okay because he had a place.

Still new to her these days, Laura had freedom away from him. Maybe they'd finally talk friendlier since they both faced something different. She smoked and felt lifted by the song on the radio.

As she smoked, she remembered the various times he threatened her. It always seemed he wanted her to be afraid of him, and she couldn't just run out the door because it was often late at night. It always worsened how she felt about being home...

Further west on Dodge, she relaxed. True enough, this day, her emotions were at her side.

Laura arrived at the bookstore and parked far from the front doors since the place was busy. At the entrance, she kept the door open for a few people before entering. She didn't see Jae, so she went to the cafe register and ordered a coffee. Then, Jae came to her. "I was just sitting down over there," he said, pointing further to the back where they'd be alone.

"Oh, hi, Jae! You look good as usual," she said. He was dressed in clean clothes, but he had always kept a sharp appearance.

"I'm really happy to see you, too."

She then added a coffee for Jae, and when their order was ready, they sat where he had been, initially speechless. He was in front of her now like someone completely different. At first, they both drank from their coffees and looked at other people. "Besides the girl you're with, how are you?" Laura asked.

"It's tough." He thought, man, he wanted to live with Laura again. He tried to laugh it off. "What are you doing lately?"

She hesitated. "I'm trying to write a book."

He smiled brightly and gave a slight chuckle. "Ah. Well, I'm just keeping up with the bills, doing the same old shit."

"Are you drinking still?"

"Yeah." He didn't want to admit it.

"You should stop," Laura said, "I drink sometimes, but mostly tea or coffee, and water. I also get high."

"Haven't been high in a while," he said, nodding.

"I usually have some."

"Really?" he said.

"Yeah. Dawn tells me to stop, though." She wondered if it was a mistake to tell him. He could go to the police about it.

"Shit can make you paranoid."

"I'm noticing that." She sipped. Then he did. She leaned back with her legs crossed. "What movies are out? You want to see a movie?"

"Oh, nah. You know I don't have patience for a movie. What's your book about?"

"Well, it's about two separate people."

"Okay. How far are you?"

"I'm outlining it."

"It's good you're doing something." He felt slightly jealous but wanted to encourage her. Yet, to him, she seemed to have no interest. "You know, I wish I could write."

"You should get rid of the girlfriend and start a journal."

"Hmm. I need the extra money to save," he said.

"Well, you should write anyway." She nodded. It was in her most encouraging voice to say this, with her memory of him and all she could see in him. He deserved to be happy.

"Are you journaling?" he asked.

"Actually, I just bought one yesterday. This week has been different. Lots of ideas." She gazed off, wondering what it all had been.

"Like what?"

"I don't know," she said. "I'm having a hard time finding words to say to people. It's too complicated." She shrugged her shoulders.

"I know." Much of what came difficult for him was out of jealousy. Not always, but at times it kept him from saying what he wanted to. With the new girl, he was more to himself, absorbing matters out of his control. He used to think he had to control everything. Now, he felt he couldn't.

"They've got journals here," she said.

"I didn't bring money with me." He was nervous.

"I'll buy one for you."

It seemed just the same with the other girl. Laura was only concerned about herself. "Okay," he said.

For a moment, she thought, despite his age, he was still with the same understanding carried from his youth. She knew it to be true of herself. "Don't you think we're young?" she asked. "It's like we should understand what adults understand. And yet, it just doesn't come to us by itself."

This was new to him. "Oh. I don't think about that shit."

Maybe she was exerting too much. True, her thoughts

were elsewhere. She sipped. He followed. They were stuck again.

"I met a guy. At a bar on Sunday."

"You two together?"

"I wouldn't say so. No."

"Black?"

"Coincidentally," nodding her head.

He grinned. "You sure do like black, huh?"

She had to think. She sat back. "White guys are like brothers. I can't get past that."

Jae laughed and liked the attention. "I got ya." He wanted to be right about her liking him.

They began to look at other people, or at least Jae did. Laura briefly watched him before she sipped more coffee. She said, "I'm serious, though, do you want me to buy a journal for you?"

"Yeah, I guess I'd write." It was like her to do something like this for him, and he didn't always see it was her best intention, though now he could tell it was.

"Okay. We could get together and share what we've written." She wondered what had changed with him.

"Yeah. That would be cool."

They waited. Laura said, "You know I like it when you're happy?"

"Yeah, but the bills suck." He let out a breath of anxiety. "I hate this coffee," he said.

"You can dump it."

"But you paid for it, Laura." He wanted to make a connection here, but she was already with another guy. What was he trying to say? He thought he could only say the wrong thing. He thought, fuck this.

Laura thought for a moment. "You know, living alone is pointless. People need people."

"Hmm. I don't know. I'm not here to theorize."

"Okay," Laura said. She sat up.

He said, "Say what you want, but it doesn't apply to me."

"It's probably good you see it that way because all we'd end up doing is agree with what I have to say, and I go in circles all the time," she said, shaking her head.

"Whatever." He was jealous and impatient; he deserved more than she seemed to.

Laura was helpless in the conversation. She thought she was somehow wrong again. "You know I think about you?" she said.

"Great, you think about me. Whatever."

"That's not fair." She knew their friendship. "We should get that journal for you."

"Fine." He thought she had more important things to do than talk with him, and he knew himself to be worth more than what was fronted. They got up, and she led him to the journals. "These are it?"

"Yeah, pick any one of them." She watched him look through a rather diverse collection, some fitting to his taste.

He browsed for a moment. "This one's good." It had a cork cover.

"Yeah, Jae, looks good." They soon went to check the book out and said nothing. Laura thought a lot about the journal he chose. She knew he'd be happy with it, but she was close to crying. "We should have a cigarette before I go."

They were back to being friends, and it felt right, he thought. "You wanna leave already?"

"It's not that. Just, I'm insecure in public," she said as she looked at him, concerned, reminded of their past with the feeling it had placed in her, this need to escape.

"All right," he said, looking at the doors with his eyes wide open, suggesting he was with someone losing her mind, yet he didn't feel responsible.

They walked out to the landscaping in front, and Laura shared one of her smokes. She sat, and he faced her.

"You know, just like everyone else, nothin's gonna work out for you, bitch," he said, endearingly. "We're like penguins climbing an ice hill. We never get to the top."

But Laura took it as an offense. "I try."

"I know, and it doesn't work," directly at her with eyes wide open.

"I'm doing fine, I would say."

"Whatever." He wanted to take control. He wanted to be the one to help. "You're faced with the same shit I'm dealin' with, and it doesn't work. You know it."

"I question it sometimes," she admitted.

She was denying him. "Just run along back home with your parents." He had motioned with his hand and began laughing.

"I've gotta go." She put her cigarette out on her shoe. "Call me sometime when you've got some writing done," Laura said. She started walking to her car.

He followed her. "You know you need me!" he said.

She looked back. "Jae, not here; not now."

"I know you're gonna need me someday." He was angry at her for meeting someone, with thoughts of the guy she met. "It's not enough living alone." He was aggressive, saying this. He wasn't thinking of the girl he was with.

"I'll be fine." She got into her car and locked her door, afraid. Then, she rolled her window halfway down. "Just get it together and call me sometime, okay?"

He kicked her car. "*Fuck* you!" He thought, how could this girl turn her back in every way? "Bitch, I *hate* you!" She pulled out and mouthed the words 'Call me' before driving off. He cried as he walked toward the bus stop, fearing she was proof he could fail, and she'd fail without him. The new guy didn't love her like he did. "God."

At the intersection, as she looked in her rear-view mirror, watching him, Laura had already pulled together the idea Jae needed her friendship. She feared inviting him over, but somehow she was in the position to find herself alone with him again. After this, he'd apologize and want to come over. As she had before, she considered it to have been a mistake meeting him, to begin with.

Still at the stop sign with traffic, Laura could do nothing for him now. She knew nothing about what he needed. He cared for her, had done a lot for her, and he deserved more. It would have to be the kind of love no one could give him.

She cried and felt it all through her body. Life could be difficult for him.

✳ ✳ ✳

Grace

Presently, Michael watched TV. Nervous but steady, he went through the applications this afternoon at the dinner table. The voices were with him as he wrote the same information down several times, though much of it had been memorized from the last time. Not far into it, he worked in haste to leave the kitchen.

Watching television was hopeless, because he had little else to do to stop the voices and lacked any confidence in it. In reaction to one voice, he felt as though he were a parent neglecting a child while trying to make sense of what was on, but the voice had his attention when she spoke. He watched and waited, so she'd leave, and if he would laugh with the sitcom, she would. The idea made him laugh.

The voice said two things at once, it seemed. Then came another elderly woman. Then, another voice was a familiar one, and Michael refocused because he thought she would stay with him. She left. Here was just one more opportunity to be high, so he turned the TV off and went for the basement.

From the pool table pocket, he took his supply up to the kitchen table, where he smoked, then took out a cigarette. Aggravated, he stared at the applications, knowing a job wouldn't be the solution.

Again, they came from within the refrigerator, screaming together like water starting to boil. Dan came up from the basement, and Michael just looked at him.

"Do you hear that shit?" Michael asked.

"What?" Dan asked.

This made Michael nervous. "Never mind."

"Is there any left?"

"Yeah." Noises rose from under the refrigerator again. "That. Do you hear it?" Michael said.

Dan thought, what was wrong? Michael seemed otherwise okay, but distant. What if he was hearing something? Would he be the one to call the hospital before something bad happened? "It's just the refrigerator," he said.

"Okay." Dan then smoked a bowl as Michael smoked a cigarette out the window. "Do we have incense?" Michael said.

"I've got some."

"We should light one."

"Sure." Dan went to the basement, and Michael took his cigarette out the back door, where the outdoors tormented him. Fremont was awake with its own noises. A man was running a loud mower, so Michael put the cigarette out altogether and returned inside. Dan set up incense and lit it on the table, moving it to the center while it burned. He went to the living room, and Michael followed. They both sat.

Michael waited for the high to set in. "I think I'm having another psychosis."

Michael didn't like the look on Dan's face. "Did it just start today?" Dan said.

"This week." Michael nodded.

Michael didn't appear panicky. But he didn't appear himself, even though maybe he was struggling to. This was new to Dan. "What's happening?"

"Voices. I don't know."

"Fuck." Dan looked at the floor, speechless.

"You want coffee?" Michael asked.

At least Michael was handling it. "Nah."

"Okay." Since Michael was high, he was reminded of needing a job, the town, this apartment, and needing to clean and cook again eventually. Talking would maybe help, but what was there? "I might have to go to the hospital."

"For how long?"

"Maybe just a few days to get on medication. They had me on something before. I don't know what's happening with me."

"Fuck," Dan said long.

Michael felt going to the hospital was the only real responsibility he'd have in this. "Mostly nobody's hiring yet, but I got applications filled out. I also went in for a urine test."

"They're gonna find weed?"

"They might; I don't care. They're only testing for alcohol, I think."

"You think they'd search us?"

"I wouldn't worry about it."

"Fuck," Dan said. He sat up, shaken. "They're gonna search us." He said this like Michael should've known.

"Just don't worry about it…it's the last thing I'm worried about, okay? We'll smoke the rest of it before they get here, and we can hide the pipes."

After a moment, Dan slouched again, and said, "Can I get one of your smokes?"

The pack was on the sofa, next to Michael. "Yeah, here." Michael handed him one.

Dan lit up and exhaled, leaned back, and rubbed his eye.

"What are they saying?"

"They mostly just yell…It happened the last time."

"Fuck. I don't know. That's fucked up."

"I know. I tried recording them once."

"And you think it's from drugs?"

"Maybe acid." Michael lit up a cigarette and moved the table and ashtray closer. He felt more in control now, having been through it before. But his anxiety was taking hold, and he lost track of anything they could share. "How's your job?" Michael asked.

"It's all right…Fuck, I've gotta get ready…I'll talk to you later." He put the cigarette out and left for the basement.

With the remote, Michael turned the TV on. He flipped through the channels to the news, which came with intense sound effects before an anchorman greeted viewers. Michael wanted something more to do in his high and thought hard as the intensity of the TV filled the living room, bouncing off every wall. More yelling is what came of it…

One-two-three and a jab at his wrist. The voices were all around him with no end anymore. They followed him everywhere, and he had no choice. Already, he had been scratching at his wrist with a broken piece of glass and had a bloody jumble of lines. Michael aimed the knife at his wrist and motioned in the steps toward a jab, but he couldn't do it. Instead, he remained awake through the intensity of the voices in his old bedroom. His parents were gone. *How?* A day later, he returned to the apartment with vodka and pain pills.

…The news still blasted through the room until Michael turned it down. The voices screamed along with the noises of the refrigerator. Michael looked toward the kitchen.

The incense ended its burn. The room was full of smoke he couldn't see, and he breathed it. At least, he wasn't in a panic. Light came in from the north windows; the room was dark, uninviting, and uninhabitable, in a building needing immediate replacement. He smoked, watching the TV.

He could go anywhere without a job, and before he would meet another night with the voices, he'd admit himself. It would only be a few days if he admitted himself, and he'd get on medication.

With an actual plan, he could do anything. They'd take care of him. He was comfortable smoking. He had to live, but for some time, he seemed to lose purpose. He would get bored smoking cigarettes and had no way to speak to anyone like he used to, at least not in this condition. Dan had already left out the back door when Michael put the cigarette out. This all must've been the weed.

Michael took his bag and went to his car out front. Inside the car, he held the steering wheel, wondering if things were moving too fast. The voices weren't following him for once, and someone drove past quietly. He privately whispered ridicule at the car, anticipating ridicule himself. The neighbor was still mowing next door as Michael started the car and drove off slowly.

Silent without music but with the sound of traffic outside, he was coming down. It wasn't easy to be so near to his youth one day and find himself entering adulthood without experience. This was a huge responsibility. It would only get worse, watching TV day in, day out, aware of the voices. Without question, he didn't believe they were his imagination.

Michael could only pretend to ignore the next voice. It was as though they intended to cut him off, and the feeling of being watched and criticized was far from what originally was. What he had known no longer worked for him. He blamed them for his behavior at home. His response only further disrupted everything.

Approaching the interstate in Omaha, he was ready for whatever medication would rid these voices if it actually was the mind's work. Pain shot up his back to his head, and he couldn't concentrate. He stretched up his back and felt a warm flow at the center of his spine.

Much later, Michael entered the hospital lobby and asked where he needed to go to admit himself. They directed him, and he approached someone.

"I've been here before, and I think I need to come back for a few days."

Soon, he was in the hall of the unit he would be staying in, already in hospital clothes. His pride dismissed itself, and the voices were gone. The hospital wasn't a great place when it came to thinking about how worse off anyone else was. He was aware of those in situations similar to his own, but he wouldn't admit to hearing voices. He sat at a table where two people were playing cards.

"Hey, man. What's your name?"

"Michael."

CHAPTER 16

Seduction

Time passed. In this time, people drove, and not always because they had to. It could've been the unfolding of their days alone and of the race to the next thing to keep afloat. Or it was the offensive workings of their fellow man: the wealthy offending the poor, the poor offending the wealthy–in whatever car either side drove in.

This was Friday. Laura was on her way out of the bookstore where she worked. On her break, she searched her bag for Marcel's school photo with no luck finding it.

"See you Monday?"

"All right, Laura. Take care," Jeff said.

She left, arriving back outside where the sun was hot. As she walked, she knew her mother would be going to church on Sunday. Laura had already made plans to make it out to the farm on Sunday, at the latest, and would spend the afternoon there. It wasn't necessary, but she liked the feel of her apartment when she returned before the workweek (and there was the fact she didn't go to the funeral today).

Pursy would be fine.

Overnight, she thought of Jae, at first unable to sleep, and it all came back to her now. Maybe she saw him too soon.

Marcel seemed a distant memory, not someone in her life, or somehow a person she couldn't reach out to at the moment. Jae had sensed something wrong about her. Perhaps, without him, she acted stronger, but it was all an act. Thinking this didn't put her any more at ease.

As for Marcel, she could call. If she needed anyone in a situation like this, maybe it was him. Of course, losing his picture terrified her today. If it wasn't in her bag, maybe it would be in the car, but the other day she looked there, too. If it wasn't in either place, it could be anywhere.

It seemed the day never offered time to stop and understand a purpose to it all. She wanted a resolution before she got home because everything else was too much to bring there. Her family was getting older, and she remembered wanting those years back.

She entered her building feeling little self-worth, and she climbed the stairs to the hall of her apartment. Here, she was just anyone, but it was everything she had wanted. With the rattling of her keys, she opened her door and went in.

She left her bag and keys on the table before taking her supply from the shelf, then took a bulge from the weed and loaded the pipe. Maybe she was using too much of this, but she'd smoke it anyhow.

Laura lit the weed, watching it crisp as she inhaled a hit, then slowly exhaled. She took another hit, and a moment later she lost all tension in her back. It'd be funny if there was no brain and all there'd be was air. Whatever right ideas she could come to wouldn't last.

Even still, she faced the matter of not being more open with people, to recover what used to be, although in whatever instance this didn't come together, she could still find happiness. She almost cried as she looked at the blank TV. She wasn't ready to call her mom.

Jae had kicked her car, and he could've even kicked her if she wasn't already on her way out. She went for a cigarette, decided she wouldn't smoke, then took one anyway. Sitting there, staring at the table and her bag, she had nothing to do. This wasn't an inescapable feeling, but she wanted to do more than she could. She took the phone and dialed Marcel's number...

"Hello?"

"Marcel, it's been a while." *Laura?* "Yeah. You wanna do something tomorrow?" She smoked. *I guess.* Urgently, she said, "What about today?"

"I'm sorry, Laura," he said. "I actually have to work tonight because they needed me more on this shift."

He had just mentioned something about work. "Okay," she said.

They paused. "We'll do something tomorrow; I have to get ready for work here. Talk to you then."

"Alright," Laura said. She hung up.

Laura stared around her apartment. Everything had stopped. She wasn't in school, she wasn't busy at home on the farm anymore...What was she doing? Taunted by the phone, she felt a sting of paranoia. Jae could call again, and her thoughts were in too many directions. She was in no mood for music or her journal. This moment, she wanted some company and had no one. The high held her there until she fell to the sofa.

Maybe Jae was right about things not working out for her eventually. Then, she decided she was capable, just not with him.

Laura dialed and waited.

"Hello?" *Hey, Mom.* "Laura! How nice of you to call. I'm at a break."

"I am, too," Laura said. "Is this what adults do?" *What?* After a moment, "Nothing," Laura said. "I mean, I've got nothing today. I just think to myself, and it's nothing. Work was nice, though."

That's good, or bad. I'm sorry you're bored.

I am. I bought a journal, so I might write. "How was the funeral?" Laura said.

"Well, Laura, it went well, but you know I cried most of the time. I really wanted you there." *I know.* "I've been at the school, getting things together. We've got a few Hispanics this year again," Renae said, delighted.

"Oh? You think they're just bored down there?"

"I don't know," Renae said. "Maybe that's it. So what have you been doing?"

"I drank with Dawn at a party; then I saw Jae." *Laura.* "I know." *Are you okay?* "Mom, he turned on me again. I don't know how to talk to him." *I understand.* "I don't know what it was." *You leave him alone. He'll be fine.* "But I care about him, Mom."

"You be careful, and you shouldn't be drinking with Dawn. When was this?" *Wednesday night.* "That's not what you should be doing on a Wednesday night. You didn't drive drunk, did you?" *We sobered up.* "Good. So you had a nice chat?" *Yeah.* "That's good. You know, it's been a while since I spoke with anyone. It's just been a quiet summer here," Renae said.

"Are you coming to Omaha this weekend?" *No.* "I might be at the farm Saturday or Sunday." Laura refocused. There was a pause. "Was it hard raising me, Mom?"

Renae was confused and thought for a moment. "No, Laura, it wasn't. You grew up fast."

"But isn't it difficult talking to me?"

"Oh, I like talking with you. No, Laura, of course, it's not a problem."

"But don't you think there's something more that needs to be said? It's like we don't have enough time."

"Yes," Renae admitted. "You are right. But I know eventually we know what needs saying."

"Even now?" *Of course.* "But it's not enough," Laura said. "There's more to us than what's said. I don't see myself going anywhere."

"You'll make it. You just have to be patient."

"I am."

Laura had her hand on her head, her elbow on the

table. Renae had been fussing over dishes, now looking out the kitchen window to the road she watched Laura drive away on. "We all love you," Renae continued. *I know.* "Are you worried about anything?"

"Just not being able to talk," Laura said.

"Well, it's the same for all of us, I think."

"I don't know. There's nothing, you know?"

"Yeah, we'll talk more when you get here. I don't wanna run up your phone bill." *No, it's okay. I just can't think of anything.* "Well, I love you."

"But don't you think we should be doing more?"

"Yes." Renae was close to crying about this already a number of times before. *I don't give enough,* Laura said thru the phone. "Oh, it's okay," Renae said, fighting herself. "I was almost planning on coming out to Omaha."

"I know, but I miss the farm. Save yourself the trip this once." *Okay, Laura.* "I'll see you then. We'll talk." Laura was happy saying this. *Okay. Mm, bye.* "Bye."

Renae was already teary-eyed before she returned to her dishes. Having spoken about this, it was as though she'd been keeping herself from some truth. After all this lost time, what they were for each other had weakened. Laura was right, they were both faced with a change.

✳ ✳ ✳

Grounding

Michael and three other people had started a game of spades. The hospital couldn't allow smoking indoors anymore, so Michael grew anxious. Although free of the voices, he couldn't do much more than walk the hall.

An older girl, Stephanie, sat across from Michael, her white hair braided back tightly, her glasses reminding him of someone he knew. She had a deeper voice than she appeared to have. Perhaps she was twice Michael's age, but she seemed to be in her thirties. One of the guys, young and black, had a grin on his face; he had something funny he couldn't tell but wanted to, or maybe he found everything in front of him humorous. The third was an older white kid, who Michael would forget because he didn't speak much. He had pale skin and dyed-black hair, and holes riddling his face where piercings had been.

Stephanie started the game. As they played, they spoke of things Michael couldn't comment on. He quietly watched them, convinced they knew a lot more about life than he did at this point.

"Why are you in here?" Michael asked her.

"Why am I here?" They hadn't made eye contact before this. "Everything was too much. I couldn't do anything, and I had to work. It had been on me for a while, actually. I let myself in. I got here yesterday."

"Cool."

She laughed fully with menace. "It's cool being here?"

Michael paused. "Cool that we met."

"Oh, okay," she returned with a smile, nodding.

They continued their game when the black kid, who didn't share his name, said, "I'm in because I was using drugs too much."

"Just for drugs?" Michael asked.

"No, I argued with my parents, and I wasn't making any sense--telling them off. I didn't say anything right...they asked if I was okay...I just screamed at them."

"Who brought you here, your parents?"

"No. Cops brought me here, I threatened them as a joke, you know, so they'd laugh with me."

As Michael dealt the cards, he said, "Oh. How long have you been here?"

"Just got in two days ago; told the doctors all about the drugs."

"And they're putting you on meds?"

"Something; I don't know what it's for."

"I'm sure it's an anti-psychotic because they couldn't really diagnose me the last time, and that's what they gave me. I also did drugs, and they wouldn't believe I quit for a year," Michael said.

"Oh."

"What about you?" Michael had turned to the other kid. "What are you in here for?"

"Depression." He was quiet.

"Everyone has that," Michael said, as if almost to bring laughter out among them.

"Yep," Stephanie said. "That's the truth."

"Your deal," Michael said.

Moments later, snacks were being handed out, so most of the patients were in line for decaffeinated coffee and an allowance of a few crackers each. A few were talking, but most were not. The group playing cards felt rushed, or at least Michael did. Their attention wasn't so much on the game when those few talking were this loud. They played until it was over, and Stephanie's attention went to the others in the room as she leaned sideways in her chair. The black kid left in his hospital clothes for the hall, and the other kid remained but didn't speak.

Michael got up and left the room for the hall. He had taken note of the newspaper on the counter.

In the hall, it was a stretch in both directions with the lunchroom being central where he was. Standing there, he opted for the fountain down the left hall. He walked alone and reminded himself of the voices, and he returned his attention simply to the fountain with the nursing staff in mind as he passed the office.

Michael thought of a cousin because his intellect matched hers at this point. It was in his eyes, how he looked around and gathered everything around him. He walked tall with a defined jaw, mouth shut, seeming unable to speak, multi-tasking his mind with the presence of everything around him. He'd been in this same unit with the same doctor, disoriented the last time, dreamy and seeming to talk from his imagination, so the doctor had a lot of questions and notes.

For once, Michael felt happy. He was beginning to recognize the challenges others had. There was no immediate method to change it, but being among the patients helped him accept his own troubles.

Maybe he needed to remain in the hospital until he was on the right medication. He could return if something else was wrong with him. With little expectations for when he got out, he felt lost. He needed a job, and it was no guarantee.

He quickly took a drink from the fountain.

"I need your vitals," someone called from a room Michael was near.

"Okay."

"Brown?" the nurse asked, as Michael entered.

"Michael Brown. Yep." He sat.

Michael's arm was set up, and the male nurse was waiting for Michael's diastolic. "You just got in?" He was about to check Michael's temperature.

"Kinda." They shared a moment, silent. Michael was fearful of many things but resisted the sense. He didn't want to go home to the apartment if the voices were there.

"Okay. Got it. Thanks."

"Sure." Michael left the room.

Another nurse approached him. "Michael?"

"Yes."

"Doctor Kyle is ready to see you. Third room on the left," she said as she pointed.

Michael approached the room where his doctor was at a table with the case file ready to add notes to.

"Hello, Michael. Please have a seat." Michael sat across from him. He said hoarsely, "Could you tell me why you let yourself in this time?" His eyes showed concern and disbelief at how so many people could have these troubles.

"Well, I'm out of a job, and stressing a lot."

The doctor began writing. Michael feared he was in too deep but remained calm. There were cars below, outside, the only sound in the room. "The last time you were here, it was for a suicide attempt. Have you had any thoughts of hurting yourself?"

"No."

"Any thoughts of hurting others?"

"No. Never."

"Do you know what day it is?"

Michael thought. "Friday."

"Do you know the date?"

He thought again. "The fifteenth?"

"What's been happening?"

"Just, it's difficult watching TV."

"How?"

"They'll say something, and I have a reaction to it."

"You feel the TV is talking to you?"

"No. Well, sometimes. I just follow it too much."

"Have you been hearing any voices?"

Michael couldn't answer. Then, "No."

"Are you taking the medication you were last on?"

"No. I quit because it was expensive."

"Have you been doing any drugs lately, Michael?"

Michael thought. "Just marijuana. Cocaine, once."

The doctor began writing and underlining. "Are you paranoid?"

"Yes." The doctor wrote and underlined once more.

"Are you paranoid right now?"

"No. I came in because I thought I needed medication. Sometimes, it's difficult to think normal."

"You described hearing voices the last time. You don't hear any voices?"

Michael didn't want a long stay. "Well...does that happen often?"

"We have people who hear voices, yes."

"What does it mean?"

"We believe it's a chemical imbalance."

"For me, I just can't think straight, or I think too hard and too much at once."

"It could be that you're taking in too many toxins. Do you drink and smoke?"

"Yes. Both. And coffee."

"What happens with too many toxins is it can overwhelm your mind. Your routine may get complicated, which in turn could lead to paranoia."

"Yes."

"Is it more intense with the marijuana?"

"Sometimes. It's just difficult getting a job where I am, and I thought medication would help."

"It will make looking for a job easier, of course."

"I know, but I need the thoughts to stop."

"I could prescribe the drug you had the last time. It's an inhibitor—do you want to try that again?"

"Sure."

"Make sure you have some sort of insurance that will help you. You probably won't be here long, but your symptoms, I assume, are consistent with what they were the last time. We'll start it at three milligrams a day."

"Okay. What was my diagnosis the last time?" Michael breathed.

Dr. Kyle sighed. He said, "Paranoid schizophrenia. Now, the thing I would advise is to *not* use marijuana or alcohol, or any other drug while you're on this. It's meant to help you, and the recreational drugs will only make your situation worse. I'd also suggest avoiding coffee or just don't drink too much...Will you agree to that?"

"I'll try."

"How do you feel about being in the hospital right now? Do you feel better?"

Michael thought. "Yeah."

"What do you plan on doing when you get home?"

"Well, if getting a job doesn't work out, I can live with my parents."

Dr. Kyle wrote more. "With your parents?"

"I could."

"It's likely you will leave tomorrow."

"Okay."

"Well, I'll start you on the meds tonight. Will you follow through with a doctor in Fremont?"

"I can."

"We can set you up with a doctor and a therapist at Family Services. Do you have any questions?"

Michael thought. "No."

"That's all, then. You take it easy, Michael."

"I will." Michael got up and left the room for the hallway. He breathed. The voices weren't with him for some reason, but they could return when he got home.

They had less room for Michael at the hospital at this time. People were coming and going, but the rooms were full. It was more guys than girls. Michael had noticed it was a lot more activity than before. He sat where he once worked on his house design, in the hall near the day room.

A girl sat across from him. She said, "I took five hits of acid before they put me in here."

It was somehow entertaining to her, being here.

Michael said, "That's not good. When?"

"A month ago. I was fucking crazy, saying all types of shit. My mom took me in."

"Oh, I'm Michael."

"I'm Jan. Why are you here?"

"It's nothing," he said. "I'm out of work."

"Yeah, I couldn't find a job for shit in this town," she said. "Everyone and their dog has a job."

"Right," Michael said, smiling.

They kept each other's company, sitting on vinyl upholstery, but they couldn't share much before someone sat next to Jan, which interrupted them.

Michael had tried acid and maybe this was why he was

here. It made the hospital seem like a potentially long stay he didn't want. His options were less than what they'd been after leaving high school. Back then, he had a job, and it was easy. Everyone had jobs.

He left the chair and came to the fountain for a drink. Then, out of boredom and curiosity, he walked the hall again, passing a nurse and watching the faces of patients, who were thinking to themselves, one laughing uncontrollably.

Michael laughed. Meghan had said 'beat the bedpost' taunting that girl in sixth grade.

CHAPTER 17

Influence

I t was already dark when Laura woke from a nap on the sofa. She got up, checked out the window, and watched a car park below, people laughing when they got out and entered the building. Happiness looked too easy.

She seemed to rebalance herself at the window. Television was unbearable. As she watched the town this night, everything had stark meaning, like something old and filmlike in the air, not quite real.

She considered her journal but didn't want to get into it right away. Maybe thinking of herself was all she ever did; she couldn't express much without people around. It was even true with Marcel, as though they'd only continue to know each other as acquaintances.

Love was a complicated idea, a tricky concept, a precarious step. No matter who she knew in life, it had meaning.

Before Marcel, hopes for better situations were met with disappointment, so she had done nothing for a few months except watch TV stoned. A couple of weeks ago, even TV was too bothersome.

Meeting someone had often been on her mind, despite the avoidant behavior. Severing ties was once a matter of protecting herself, because trying hurt too much. School was too much of the same as well.

Laura decided on the first lines of her journal. She went to the table and lit up a cigarette, standing there. Then, she returned to the window and smoked.

She couldn't turn back, and the days hustled her: walking, driving, keeping the loft up, and everything else. It was all so meaningless and had to stop.

Soon, Laura finished her cigarette and dumped the ashes out the window. She set the ashtray there in case she'd have another. Having heard Laura, Pursy raced down the steps and meowed for attention. Laura vigorously rubbed Pursy's fur, as if she had just asked to be teased. Pursy then ran off like a wild furball to escape.

Laura took her journal out of the bag and sat at the table. She took a pencil out and wrote the first lines without stopping.

Intuition has always led me away from everything I have known. I've been less able to talk to other people.

Nothing is ever enough to settle. I think always. It pleases me to recall time with others, but alone, very little matters. Also, some things matter when I'm alone, whereas, with people, nothing matters.

It feels desperate, as if there's more to say than what I can let out, and I see the same is true for many people. There is less purpose than what I had imagined. Typically, everyone seems driven by money.

I had very few aspirations, and it was natural to let go of things that didn't come together for me. I find myself with more time but nothing to do with it.

Always, there has been the question as to what I am supposed to do. I want to love people like anyone should because I see it as necessary and lacking. I don't see too many others understanding the meaning of a relationship.

Although I have friends, it is difficult being alone without a real path. For now, this is my path, what I am searching for, and I have nothing meaningful to say. I owe it.

Life has sped for me, and it's difficult to remember what was significant in becoming who I am. I believe it's the same for anyone: we don't find a way but fall into one, and what we are for others, we don't always know until we start to open up. Those I know don't communicate anything for me to know and stand by, at least not openly.

What I have proved myself to be, apart from others, dictates what I mean to myself. After what has now been a long time of separation, I know I need people. I grew up with honesty, and there isn't much to expect, since that time is over.

She took a cigarette, lit it tiredly, and returned to the window. What she wrote was forgotten, but she felt composed of a mood. She simply smoked and hated the habit.

No plans for tomorrow, other than to get back with Marcel. Things were changing, she just needed to slow down.

❊ ❊ ❊

Mastery

Michael woke with a few people talking outside his room. The voices had visited him in the air conditioning, louder than before, but he slept well. He changed into his jeans, T-shirt, and sandals, and went toward whatever this day would be, outside his room.

The patients were all waiting for breakfast, and he was right on time for his tray before he sat at one of the tables. He looked at the buttered toast, some jelly, milk, and orange juice covered with foil.

He sat across from a Hispanic, whose peculiar accent was stressed but articulate. He was shorter, older, and slim with perfectly curved hair in a morning mess, and tired eyes, which Michael noticed when they shared a glance. Someone had offended the guy. "Why are you here, man?" he asked Michael.

"I just think too much."

"You think too much?"

"It's the same thoughts over and over."

"Oh...yeah."

"What about you?" Michael said.

"Me? I'm here because I was fighting too much. I did drugs. Do you do drugs?"

"Just bud, and I've tried things, yes," Michael said.

"I did cocaine?"

"Anything is bad if it's too much."

"No, I did too much." He became disinterested in Michael, so they continued eating. The man left abruptly because he felt he was being ignored and didn't feel it was due to his race, although maybe he often suspected otherwise. "See you," he said.

"Okay."

Later, the day room opened, and most of the patients participated in a drawing game. It was a large room with a small TV, a ping-pong table, a crowd of chairs, some exercise equipment against the back wall, a lone computer, and books along the exterior, below the windows. Michael had joined, sitting near the windows facing west. He looked out some of the time.

He loved Omaha. His attitude brightened in their company, away from the apartment. Michael stood composed with thoughts of famous people as he drew a picture and sat down.

Somewhat concerned about the wellbeing of those around him, he made up ideas from their looks and demeanor.

He wasn't going to be as talkative as the first time around because he needed a plan. At this, he could see the patients in the same battle.

After the game, they each filled out a paper regarding their support system and whom they would keep in touch with for help. They were sharing their answers when Michael thought of Dan. He was one person Michael could talk to.

Michael couldn't return to the apartment right away. He'd spend a few nights at his parents' house and let them know he'd been in the hospital. He wasn't aware of the voices so much because the meds were helping him. He felt relaxed, but he knew schizophrenia was a serious illness.

The headaches had been brought on by cigarettes, coffee, and beer; maybe not enough water, so he excused himself from the room and went for the fountain, drank, and breathed.

With his memory of the car accident, he walked the hall to the entrance of the unit, looking out its window. Only Dan knew where he was. His headache sharpened, and it had to be from the accident. At the same time, withdrawal from cigarettes was setting in.

The patients loudly left the day room, Jan being the most vocal. Michael watched from where he stood and followed the group as it dispersed: some to the lunchroom, a few for items from the nursing staff, and some kept to the day room privileges. A nurse was sitting in the hall, talking with a patient near the lunchroom where Michael now was.

He approached the newspaper. While concentrating on a photo and description, he feared the voices would return, so Michael let it go. He simply looked at it and knew he couldn't read anything yet.

It was almost time for visitors, so Michael left the room for the television. In the lounge, he looked through a window to the nursing staff before sitting down. He'd mentioned his drug use, and it was on his health record. Maybe they only assumed he had schizophrenia. He didn't know if it was developing into something worse or not. At least he was on medication, but he badly wanted a cigarette. Sitting further in the corner, he wasn't watching TV but listened to it and tried to focus at the same time.

He needed a plan. It needed to be more than a job, a real way to earn money, and he had nothing. He dreaded going back to the apartment, but he had a commitment there. It was possible just to have a part-time job, manage his living expenses, and eat at home with his parents. But it wouldn't save any money to leave.

His time in Chicago fit into this. He was used to fast times there. Then, Michael forgot what he'd been thinking; it was almost like he *was* in Chicago, as though it would last. He rested his chin on his hand, staring at the floor to his side. A bird's shadow swiftly flew across the corner of the room, followed by a few more.

Studying to be an architect was an option if he got a loan and worked somewhere with help from his parents. He knew nothing about loans, but he'd aim to get help. He returned his attention to the vacant lounge.

Just then, a girl came into the room and switched the channel before leaving. She appeared to be a staff member.

A horror movie was starting, so Michael was thrilled. Stephanie came into the room with another girl, and they were each excited because they knew it to be a classic. It was like their first time watching it as it went through the opening scenes before the commercials. During this time, a nurse was monitoring the group and making a note of the movie they were watching.

Stephanie was brushing her hair out. "Don't you just hate the commercials?" she asked.

"Yeah," the other girl commented. "It's like everything's quiet, then boom, commercial time. Crazy."

Stephanie laughed as though it entertained her. "Oh, it's absolutely bonkers sometimes," she said.

The girl laughed in her black voice. "Right, right."

Michael could tell she was smiling, so he smiled. Each of them were smiling.

"They could at least try to be normal," Michael said. "You know, and straight to the point."

"Yeah," Stephanie said. "And be professional but with some freaking common sense," her hand cutting into the air to be simply stated.

"Something," Michael said.

"I follow you."

"Yeah, commercials are too much sometimes."

"God. It's like hold on to your seat, you know?" as she leaned back.

"Yep," Michael said, smiling.

The movie came back on, introducing a few characters. They focused on the movie, and Michael became anxious for a cigarette. A tall guy came to the door. "Michael, I'm your social worker. I'd like to talk with you."

Michael and the social worker, David Wells, walked the hall to the room at the end and sat at the table.

"So, Michael, we're ready to let you go, and I'm supposed to ask you where you're headed off to. Do you have a home?"

There was often something luring about black men when he was fed up with white people. This guy had Michael's immediate respect, though there was still resistance and uncertainty. "I might stay a few nights at my parents' house, but I've got an apartment, just no job," he said.

The social worker noticed anxiety. He wanted to encourage Michael; Michael seemed to respond well to encouragement. "So, you're working on finding a job?"

His voice was deep. He was far more of an adult than Michael. "Right," Michael said.

"Do you feel you should stay longer?"

"Not really."

"Do you have any questions about the follow-up?"

Michael hesitated. "Not that I can think of."

"Okay, we'll let you go this afternoon then. Soon."

"Okay."

Michael walked back to one of the nurses on staff. "Can I help you, Michael?"

"I wanna smoke. Can I go outside and smoke?"

"Yes. I believe you have a pass. I'll have someone run down for your cigarettes. You've got cigarettes, right?"

"They're up here with you guys already, I think."

"Okay, I'll send you out with one of the nurses," she said, as someone who was making a deal would say in a way to also be nice. It seemed she'd hate him for liking guys but admire him for being with a girl. "You feeling all right?"

"Just anxious to smoke."

"Well, we do have nicotine gum."

"No, I gotta smoke."

Michael was soon walking outside with one of the nurses, and they hadn't spoken yet. Michael lit up and exhaled to the sunlight, which he closed his eyes to. The smoke was partially to blame for him going to the hospital, to begin with, and he wanted to quit. At least, the pack of Spirits didn't have the added chemicals.

"It's really good for people here to go places and be outside if they want," he said.

"You're probably right. There are rules here, though." The nurse was handsome. For whatever reason, Michael thought he couldn't open up anymore to white people, and it was strange to be met with so many blacks in his time when he wasn't even searching for them.

After a moment, "No one's hiring me now with my misdemeanor."

The nurse said, "I went right into school. It's the only way to stay out of trouble, man."

"Right." Michael smoked and the nurse started smoking as they walked further out and stopped near some landscaping where the sidewalk forked out. "I wish I had money, you know. Everyone needs money." The nurse said nothing. "People seem to ruin it for the next guy with the rules that have to be made," Michael later said.

"You do drugs?" The nurse asked.

It seemed they were already plotting against him. So what if he did drugs? He already admitted to them, but—"I used to a lot," he said. Michael had to hide any attraction, but he was happy to be outside.

"They're no good if you're having problems."

"Yeah."

"I'm serious," he said, as they smoked. "It's what everyone does before they end up here. Some of 'em, it's more than just getting a job."

"Yeah, but there isn't anything to do about the jobs. I think I'm screwed."

"Just get into school," he encouraged.

After a moment, "Sometimes, I get a lot of anxiety from cigarettes, too."

"Oh. I hear ya. Anybody who smokes will eventually hate it. I'm Marcel."

"I'm Michael. I knew you already from the last time here." They were actually talking for once. They hadn't spoken before.

"Yeah? I wish I had the answers for you," Marcel said.

"Well, I don't know what to say about why I'm here."

"I remember you coming in the last time for a suicide attempt. What happened?"

"Just too many things at once. I had voices."

"Ah." Marcel was taken aback by this. Michael noticed. "You seem normal to me."

"I am." Michael worried this was the wrong thing for him to have said.

"What about now? Do you still hear them?"

"Not now." They both smoked.

"Did you tell the doctor?"

"No. The first time I did, it wasn't right to share it. It was outside of me, you know. It wasn't my imagination." Michael's headache returned, but he smoked anyway. "I've got a headache, though."

"Could be you're smoking too many cigarettes, bud."

"And I'm not drinking enough water or eating enough food," Michael said.

"Water is important." Marcel smoked again.

Michael wanted to ask something, and he didn't know what it was. "You might see me again if the drugs are my problem. I did acid once."

"Yeah? Lots of people messing up. Believe me."

"I've also got scoliosis and a lot of anxiety," Michael said and laughed. They smoked. "You want one of my smokes? They're all natural - no additives."

"Sure, my friend smokes these," Marcel said.

Michael dropped the pack, picked it up, and quickly opened it before handing Marcel two. Michael then said, "I think people like you here."

In the hospital, they had never shared a glance, nor had they been overly aware of each other. There was much Michael read into about Marcel at times when he was last in for a suicide attempt. Marcel appeared to be a part of the world he didn't know yet, one apparently existing in Omaha.

Somehow Michael's innocence and the influence people had on him would bring him to the right people, though it was always brief, even though Michael could have felt he was being cut off from the world by entering the hospital, what he felt the first time around.

Marcel made it seem people truly were considerate of others. Yet, there was no way for Michael to take any steps with people with the idea they may not like him, for whatever reason. He sometimes felt his inner self come out with some people, though not extensively masculine or feminine. Michael was just a guy: he felt like a guy, thought like a guy, and acted like a guy most of the time. These experiences with people were his own, and he felt ahead of many. But he wanted something to change.

"You think so?" Marcel asked.

"Yeah, you're different from the other nurses. I like Cheryl, though."

Marcel smiled. "Yeah, Cheryl's something else."

"Right...you know I'm leaving today?" They smoked.

"Yep, I know."

"It was cool seeing you again."

They were finished with the cigarettes. "Sure. Hey, don't worry about anything, okay?"

Michael thought, in all this trouble he'd had, this was one thing he needed to hear. "Sure," he said, nervously, in light of this doubt. Had he any sense of value toward himself, he wouldn't lose sight of what others were to him.

Michael was greeted by one of the nurses when he returned to the unit. "You ready to go, Michael?"

"Yeah." Michael was confidently reassuring himself about what Marcel said.

"We've just gotta get your things out for you, and you'll go. If you could just sign these papers that say you'll meet up with the doctor in Fremont—we've got you scheduled. And we'll give you a copy."

"Okay."

"He's also given you a prescription, so I'll let you put that in your bag."

"Sure." He took the bag and the prescription, then signed the papers. After waiting over ten long minutes on a chair in the hall, he was on his way out. "See you, Marcel," he said, as Marcel was getting ready for a break. It was like Michael, the nurse, and Marcel were together on the job.

"Yup, take care," he said.

The time was short with everyone. Already outside, where it was different from before, Michael walked through the parking lot. He needed to go to school, though it should've been an idea already. He came to his car.

He arranged his bag in the passenger seat like the bag was a new responsibility he needed to care about, and he looked out the windshield at parked cars. Was there a place in Omaha he needed to go? Here, in his car, there was nothing he needed in Omaha. He was alone again, but the voices were still gone as he looked around at the scene. Finally, he started the car and drove off.

CHAPTER 18

Transcendence

Rebecca headed downtown in Omaha's busy, eastbound traffic. She'd have to wait a few light changes before she'd cross the intersection here. It was exciting to get out of the routine on her way to Laura's. To go to the lofts for the first time, she'd have to take a tour! They'd probably get beer and talk since there was nothing else unless they'd go to the Old Market, drunk together, of course. There had to be something they could do, something fun.

She had both hands on the wheel and leaned forward without her cigarette now, the window still open to traffic outside. Cars ahead were finally making it through. Laura was someone who'd never turn her back on Rebecca; they had their friendship from the start...

Sitting at the table again, the supply out, and a pipe loaded, Laura would only offer the smoke. Rebecca hit the buzzer, and Laura let her into the building.

Rebecca arrived at the door, smiling there after knocking; smiling still after Laura opened it. "I can't believe you're staying in such a nice place," Rebecca said. "I'm jealous."

In their younger days, Rebecca had often spit out while laughing. It was her f-sound laugh. Laura smiled wide to have her friend over at the thought of it.

"Thanks, Rebecca." Laura had a smirk. They went further into the apartment. "Do your friends in town get high?"

"I've never actually been high, I don't think I should," Rebecca said.

They came to the table and sat. "Well, I've got this ready to smoke, so I'll just sneak in a few hits."

Right or wrong, there were side effects, some major, some minor. "Do you smoke every day?"

"I only smoke if I've got it. Lately, I've got it."

Laura already had the pipe to her mouth and began lighting it, wanting only to be able to speak her mind. She exhaled.

"You know what it does to you?"

"Not really. I mean, I know what the high is supposed to feel like. Sometimes people feel paranoid with it—I don't know. It only takes a few hits before I'm high with this. A little won't hurt."

"Okay," Rebecca spoke long.

Laura continued with another hit. She said, "I have some anxiety afterward, but I think I've always had it with my back pain."

"Really? I don't have the trust in it that you do."

"I'm used to it, but I could give it up if I get paranoid. Could happen." She took one final hit, moving much slower. "I'm already feeling it; it's fast. You want a cigarette?" Rebecca was more than a good friend. But it was hard for them to see it remain what it once was.

"Sure."

"Try one of mine. They're all natural." Laura handed Rebecca one, along with her lighter. "Let's sit on the sofa."

"Sure, okay."

They had taken off their shoes and now sat across from each other against the arms with their feet in the middle.

Laura turned the TV on with the volume down.

Rebecca wasn't uncomfortable, smoking now.

"You feel *okay?*" Laura asked.

"Sure." Rebecca nodded.

Laura said, "It's been too long."

"I know! Time goes so fast." Rebecca was aware of herself this once. It wasn't the feeling she wanted.

Laura took one of her cigarettes and lit it, mindful of the ashtray at the window, so she got up and brought it over. "There isn't much we can do about it," she said as Rebecca watched her sit back down.

"It's like we should still be in high school. All of a sudden, we were out. You know?" Rebecca added.

"Yeah. I think about school." Laura was reminded too much of everything this past week, and for it to be on her mind was on her mind. "I don't know, the things I say are never right. It's not how I feel."

"Yeah. I think it takes a while before we're used to it." Rebecca had never given thought to this. Why was Laura saying this?

"It's all I think about," Laura shook her head, and she had to think. "I met a guy this week."

"Oh. Is he nice?"

"Yeah. He gave me the only photo he had of himself. It's his kindergarten photo, and I don't know what happened to it. Before you got here, I was looking in the car for it, and it's not there. You know, I don't want to tell him."

"Oh no! With school, it's gonna be a while before you see me with anyone. I ditched the last guy."

Rebecca smoked. Laura was trying to think.

"Such a nice place here." Rebecca wanted to say more. "How high is the ceiling in here? Twenty feet?"

Laura thought for a moment. "Close. Something around that. I often wonder what the point of everything is because nothing matters like it used to."

"I don't know. There isn't much in Nebraska to go by. It's pretty simple here." Rebecca animated this as if she wanted Laura to be more positive-minded. Laura didn't appear to always appreciate people, at least with what was said.

"It could be the same feeling anywhere," Laura said.

"Yeah. How's your job?" Rebecca was suddenly sincere, with lasting influences behind her.

"It's fine. Nothing to it."

"You should go back to school."

"I've thought about it. I've been studying astrology and everything." Laura was irritable. She said, "You know people talk too much on the surface?"

It was difficult for Rebecca to consider this. "I don't know, we should just say what's comfortable. Do you remember swimming in Dodge?" Rebecca asked.

"Yeah." At this, Laura seemed to lighten up.

"I miss those days. Don't you?"

"I do!" In her mind, she watched kids playing in the bluest of pools.

"Soon, we'll be old," Rebecca said.

"Yeah. I don't know. I always have to be doing something, and I've got nothing."

Rebecca was her usual self, saying, "Tell me about it. All I do for fun is drink."

"You go to the bars?"

Rebecca thought. "No, I hate going there. I drink at home sometimes, but only with friends."

"I think I'd drink too much if I drank at home, but I like vodka mixes," Laura said.

"Me, too. But I go for rum more than vodka."

"Yep." They saw they couldn't say anything. The TV was on low.

Rebecca wanted to say something. She said, "You know, we all care about you. You shouldn't feel like this."

Laura laughed with an agreeable smile. "I agree. I don't always like how I feel."

"I don't know, I'm sometimes self-conscious, but you think too much," Rebecca said.

"Yeah, it's the smoke," Laura said. If only she could feel as good as Rebecca did. "People take in too much TV," Laura said, pointing at the television.

"Yeah, true," Rebecca said.

Laura adjusted and seemed back to her usual self. "You want another cigarette?"

"Sure," Rebecca said, as she put hers out.

"Okay." Laura handed Rebecca one, lit another one for herself, and they both smoked. "You know, I went to Fremont the other day. All I could think about was not being able to talk. There's just nothing," Laura said and smiled. "I thought about people and Marcel."

"That's the guy you met?"

"Yeah. He's someone to talk to, someone I can trust, someone who will listen—."

"It's what you need."

Rebecca seemed to be one of the fewest of people to openly trust, and a necessary friend to stay in touch with. Now she could see how brokenhearted Laura was. Maybe Laura brought it on herself. As a child, she had so much trust, but the reality of the world constantly challenged what they knew as kids.

"Yeah," Laura said. "Kind of. I'm alone a lot of the time."

At the sight of Laura saying this, Rebecca believed it was true of herself. "I am, too, but I can handle it."

Laura said, "Me, I just keep thinking no one knows me really, and they haven't for years now."

"I know you well."

"I think things are changing."

"How?"

"There's so much I want to say, and I have no one around. I'm away from home, and we don't exactly have the family thing going on anymore. There's just something beyond what we know as kids. In between, it's the same shit day after day." Laura smoked. "This whole adulthood thing takes us away from everything we've known. I think it's dangerous."

Rebecca thought. "With me, I'm just used to not much changing. I think it's gonna take you awhile. You can't just expect it to fall into place." Rebecca's childhood influenced how she said it.

Laura said, "I mean—what we want might be different, I don't know." After a moment, "To me, nothing really matters though. You know?"

"It should. You should have better feelings."

"Yeah, but when it's easy, it all passes by."

Rebecca was surprised. "Yeah, that's right."

"Yeah." They smoked. Laura hesitated. "I mean, it's like we're all strangers."

"You'll get past that, I think."

"You think so?" Laura said, desperate.

"Yeah."

"Maybe…I don't know. There's nothing, you know? I could say anything, and it's nothing."

Laura spoke quieter, but it was obviously the high. She said, "It's like, what do we say when there's nothing?"

"You have a lot of people who love you."

"Of course, but I don't see it. They don't see it from me, either. I'd at least like to try."

"You're smoking too much."

"Cigarettes?"

"No. Weed."

Laura's eyes were glazed and emotional, appearing overly affected like she held a lot of pain in but couldn't let it out. She raised her eyebrows. "Maybe you're right."

* * *

Innocence

Michael pulled into his parents' driveway, left his bag in the car, and locked up. At the front of the house, he was aware of an unwelcoming Fremont. His father came to the door, quiet and unsurprised.

"You having dinner with us? I'm making spaghetti," Dale said.

Michael felt worlds apart; they wouldn't understand. "Sounds good. Mom here?"

"She's in the basement."

Michael entered and went to the stairs from the kitchen. This was home, and an apartment was a pointless burden. "Hey, Mom?"

"Yes, I'm here. Why are *you* here?"

"I was in the hospital and got on some meds."

"You *what?*"

Further down the stairs until he could see her at the computer, he said, "I was seeing a doctor in Omaha." Michael may have been a victim, but he'd been through it before. "He prescribed a medication for me."

"Why didn't you tell me before you went?"

"I knew they wouldn't keep me long. I don't really wanna talk about it." There was a sting in Michael's throat over having to explain this. She was busy with the internet or something, maybe a game of solitaire.

"So you have a prescription for me to pick up?"

"Right."

"Okay, I suppose I'll do that now."

"I'll go with you."

"Give me a minute and I'll be right up."

Upstairs, Michael's father was leaving. "Where are you going?" Michael asked.

"I'm going to the store. You want me to pick up some beer?"

"I guess."

Michael sat and turned the TV on, to wait. Dan would soon be at work. It felt to Michael like he was being watched, so to turn his attention away, he paced over to the phone, dialed, and waited.

"Dan, it's me. I'm back out, and I think I'll stay at my parents' house tonight." *Okay, cool.* "See ya."

Michael left the house for his cigarettes and prescription. He returned to the front porch, where he lit up. School seemed as much out of reach, if not more than an apartment working out. A car passed without any voices, so he probably needed these meds.

Sitting where he was, without the noise of lawn mowers, voices, or trains, he had a new vantage point, or an original one: calm at the idea of the apartment. For too long, he'd wanted more than he had. It wasn't a feeling he liked, but it seemed anyone would feel the same. Then, he looked toward Omaha.

He was thankful. Halfway through his cigarette, his mom came out. "You ready?" she asked.

"Yeah."

They later pulled up to the pharmacy. Michael waited in the car. He sat up and glanced at the place next door, staring at some of the faded merchandise at the window. He was disinterested, then curious about the cigarette butts on the ground outside. Everyone was getting by with nicotine, or not.

When they drove back, they didn't speak. He couldn't cope with ideas about voices, so he simply watched the houses pass by. He loved his mom, but he was ashamed he couldn't take care of himself. They arrived at the house.

"I'm going for a walk," he said at the front door.

"Oh, okay."

Michael took a cigarette and walked around the garage on the sunny side. A distance up the street, he thought of his cousins again. They often went for walks.

This had been a home. The minimum wage was somewhere around five or six dollars an hour. The shit many took interest in didn't amuse him. He wasn't settled. There were too many limitations to surpass this, and he could see it: he'd been losing his way either because everyone had it made, or they didn't. His life was a balancing act between it all.

"Fucking hell," he said quietly, deflecting pain.

Free of the voices and the hospital, this was a time he didn't take for granted. But he loved and hated himself, and loved and hated others in his impatience. His past had no lasting influence, so he smoked and carried with it a momentum of both pride and shame.

Michael felt confident knowing he had an advantage some people didn't have, but it only opened him to the idea there were always those with far more confidence and advantage. And facing the fact there were some without an advantage, he deserved less.

A few people were behind him. As he finished his cigarette and turned back, he said 'hello,' and they said 'hello' back.

He wasn't ready for the apartment. He'd stay at home with his parents for the week. Then, he'd be ready to search for a job. Maybe the apartment would be ok.

Returning to the house, he came to the room off the kitchen where the TV was on, and he turned it down. He wanted to be alone before his dad got back with beer.

Aware of the voices on TV, Michael had everything to hide. Here, he was going to drink again, and he was on meds. Soon, he'd just have to quit. He looked out the window, not to be overwhelmed. This was home.

He stared at a neighboring house. There were times smoking meth with friends before school at the cemetery, and it was an even worse drug after he quit. He was amazed to have gotten out of it, and to be alive after having a gun to his mouth. In bed.

He laughed for a moment, and his smile was his inner child.

CHAPTER 19

Versatility

Marcel arrived. After buzzing him in, Laura anxiously stepped out into the fifth-floor hallway to wait for him. There, she lit a cigarette, smoked, and kicked at her heel until he came around the corner.

"What's up, Laura?" he said as if she were a child.

They both smiled and hugged before entering.

"Do you want one?" she asked, handing him a smoke. "I know they're pointless when I've got bud."

"It does kind of feel like a smoke break at work," he said. "Since I've been working."

"Yeah," she said, smiling. "Let's sit."

"A'right," he said, as though he didn't know her too well yet. They came to the main room, sat on the sofa, and waited a moment, thinking the other would talk.

She said, "I can't get myself to remember much."

"Yeah, I know," he said. It seemed he believed she was right for him. He maybe had intentions and would say all the right things to keep it together.

She smiled. "I think about you."

He smoked as though he preferred not to. "Great. I think about you, too, Laura," he said, smiling.

She said, "Before we me, I was really starting to lose

myself." She didn't want to feel she was taking advantage of him because he seemed much too good for her.

"How?" he said.

"Just nothing to do, except watch TV like it's the only thing. There are more important things."

She was just as he remembered at the bar; obviously, she'd been through something. He said, "Right. I sometimes watch more than I need to. Sometimes TV is good to keep your mind off of things."

Laura nodded. "Yeah, I guess."

Laura crossed her leg away from Marcel while he leaned against the other arm of the sofa, and they both smoked, looking away from each other for a moment and away from the TV, both wondering what to say. "I like your plants, Laura; I didn't notice them before."

"Yeah, thanks."

"I need some."

"There's a place just down the street, east of here." He was more grown and adapted, and it could've been the marijuana to remind her. Maybe she smoked too much. She said, "It's painful, thinking I should say more."

"Well, you're just getting your confidence back. You aren't outspoken because you've been hurt. You'll come out of it."

"Okay." She was aware of being quiet.

"Really. Don't worry about it. Sometimes I have it, sometimes I don't." The room was too quiet.

She adjusted herself. "Maybe I'm impatient?"

"Nah, but you've got plenty of time ahead to make more of yourself," he said.

They finished smoking. "Do you wanna smoke?" Laura asked.

"I guess we could."

They sat at the dinner table, and Marcel started, then passed it to Laura. He saw it to be the sort of crafty process a woman and her husband would do together, taking turns. They didn't have to talk.

She passed it back to him, and they passed it back and forth until it was cashed. Both felt the high and remained at the table. It all felt slow, and they behaved well with each other.

She said, "An old friend came over today."

"How'd that go?" He then sneezed loudly.

"She's just like I remember. I want to believe that's a good thing. I can't go back even if I'd like to."

"See what I mean? Big thoughts."

She said, "I think that's why the last guy hit me."

"You made him think a lot?"

Marcel wasn't typical of anyone she'd met. It was in his voice, maybe his eyes. "No. I didn't talk with him enough," she said.

"But you're coming from a good family."

"Yes. They're separate from it, though. I think a lot of people bullshit each other. I don't know if it's the TV or what, but I've never liked it."

"It's what you'll love about them. You should try to appreciate people more," he said.

"Nothing changes, though."

"You know you're changing, and whatever changes them--leave it up to them."

"Yeah. Today with Rebecca was good. I just fight it all the time now."

He said, "This is enough, being together."

"Yeah, you want another smoke?" Laura had the pack in her hand.

"I don't mind, but you smoke too much, Laura."

"I agree," Laura said, handing him one. She lit hers, and he took her lighter, lighting his. "It just, I don't know–it encourages conversation." She was grinning.

"Yeah, I get that," he said, looking out for her.

"I'm serious about the bullshit." She was shaking her head and seemed tired.

"We all just need each other, that's all it means." He said, "You don't have to prove yourself to me or anyone."

"But it's like I don't even know anything."

"You do love," he said. "Everyone is just trying to find a way."

She nodded. "I worry that I'm alone."

"Nah, you've got people."

"They don't understand." She shook her head. "And that's the problem."

After a moment, he said, "If I were you, I would just try to be patient," looking at her, smoking.

Laura could say nothing, though she wanted to. Both were aware of the conversation going nowhere, and here they could do nothing.

"I'm glad you're here, Marcel," she said. "Don't get me wrong."

"No. I know."

She spoke slowly then. "I mean, you're the only guy I know, and when I'm trying to be—I don't know—it's too distant." She shook her head. "I mean, I know you care. But I want you to know I care, too."

"Well, I know you do, Laura." He grinned. "That goes without saying."

"It's hard finding the right people." She was surely losing her chances with him since she lost his photo.

"Laura, it's okay if we don't know what to say. Let's just be high."

After a moment, she said, "We should try relaxing." They went to sit and said nothing through the rest of their cigarettes. "We could watch a movie," she said.

"No, it's all right. I'd rather just visit."

"Okay."

"Laura, when was the last time you got a back rub?"

"I haven't ever."

"Well turn around, and I'll fix that." A sitcom was on TV, and he glanced at it. He began rubbing her shoulders.

"Thanks for this. It gets so boring here."

"Right? I've just been busy working." He smiled.

She said, "Could you see us living in Chicago?"

"No, you don't want to live there. You've got a nice place already."

"You wanna move in with me?" She was quiet but to the point of just going further with him. She didn't care about anything else.

"We'll give it some time." He wanted her to not feel rushed, and could tell she was affected. Maybe everything was a shock to her.

After a moment, she said, "You know, there's just something I wish I could say, and I don't know what it is."

"Well, I could tell you I missed you."

"You did?" she asked.

"Yeah, I was thinking about you at work. There aren't too many people like you."

"Thanks," she said, smiling. "I think the same about you." She wanted to keep a calm high. "This feels good."

Marcel smiled. "We'll see a time we have more to say. I've got friends who talk all the time, but you can say more with less. So don't worry about it."

"You think it's funny," she smiled, "but it's—"

"You seem really affected by your relationships," he interrupted. He finished rubbing her back.

She shook her head. "I've just had a long week, and it's like this is the end. I mean, I don't see anything changing--or I do--and it doesn't look good." She felt too aware of herself, and it seemed what she said didn't matter. She wondered about Jerome and Jae.

"You should see it as a beginning, not an end."

"But I should know where I'm coming from. And I can't

identify with it. It's like I've forgotten."

"You'll be okay," he said, shaking his head.

After a moment, she said, "Yeah." And she finally exhaled and leaned back. "Thanks for the back rub, Marcel."

He nodded his head.

They watched television, and she leaned against his shoulder, unable to speak, though she wanted to. "There's just something wrong with me."

He felt this wasn't a good time. "Maybe I should go. You should really try letting go of the weed because I don't think it's done you any good."

"Are you sure?"

"You need to get used to being away from people, Laura. Try to enjoy your place, and relax more, but don't rely too much on that other stuff."

She thought. "Well, you're right." She didn't know what to say as they got up, went to the door, and stood together. She said, "Oh, I almost forgot!" It appeared she got a dose of reality. "I cooked something the other day, and I have it ready for you."

"Laura, you didn't have to."

"Well, I did." They were in the kitchen. She was getting something out of the fridge. "This is a tomato tart with lots of different cheeses and herbs. I think you'll love it."

"It looks really good, actually."

"I promise I won't always be like this," she said.

"Yeah, same here." He wanted to be alone.

"I'm sorry." She could cry, but it didn't show.

He hugged her tightly in one arm. Again, it was as though people didn't ever hug her.

"I'm going to be at the farm this weekend. Let me give you the number." Laura got a pen and paper, wrote quickly, and returned to the hall to give him the number.

"All right. Cool, I'll call you." They nodded. "Bye, Laura." He left toward the elevator.

She entered her apartment, shut the door, and returned

to the TV with her feet on the sofa and her arms around her knees. Quietly, she cried, just tears and a look of concern while she gazed at her plants. She should've offered one of her plants since he needed one.

Laura would endure time alone for too long, and she already missed having Marcel's company. He could only become disinterested if she kept this up. She breathed, rubbed her face, and quit crying.

❋ ❋ ❋

Artistry

Michael and his parents had eaten together. His father took a few beers out while his mother finished clearing the table. She stood there at the sight of them. "Guess you don't need me here," she said. "I'll be downstairs."

His dad began reading the paper, and Michael took a beer for himself. He didn't know what to say or why he was being ignored.

His father skimmed the front page but didn't want to talk without a buzz. Life here was tedious, and he knew of Michael's friends. Michael would read him in any discomfort. Both had stiffened at the sight of everyone not understanding the world as they did.

It was clear they had nothing urgent to say. Michael drank and looked toward the living room as he leaned back.

He rested the chair. "I was in the hospital."

Dale gave Michael a glance around the paper, then set the paper down. "What for?"

Michael shook his head. He said, "I had too many things going on."

"You've been doing drugs?"

"Some." The look his father had was somewhere

between not wanting to hear any of it and choosing to be a father to the situation, somewhere between choosing discomfort or confidence.

Dale said, "You never know if they're giving you the right diagnosis."

"I told them everything. They put me on what I was on the last time. It helps."

"How much will that cost?" Dale said, confused.

"I don't know. I think I'll apply for assistance since it's difficult getting a real job here. You know it was the same as the last time?"

"Are you sure you need medication for anything?"

"It was crazy," Michael said, shaking his head. "It would've only gotten worse."

"I doubt you'll pass for disability."

"I did stuff in during school, and I think that's why this is happening. That, and maybe the car accident."

"And you smoke marijuana still?"

"Well."

Dale meandered through his thoughts. "You know, we didn't do that when I was young. I don't know what to tell you. We let you do whatever you wanted because we thought you were being responsible. We couldn't do anything about the drugs when we found out."

Michael drank. "Beer is just as bad. Worse when you've got people driving with it."

"You used to drive around drinking with Ronny and those kids all the time, out on the country roads," acting as the father, somehow not relating because Michael was still young.

"It was honest fun. They drove slow and parked."

"You were with those kids when they crashed their car that night during the winter. Did you mention it?"

"No, but I did have a concussion."

"I think you're just making excuses, Michael."

Michael wouldn't tell his father about the suicide attempts because he could use it against him whenever making a statement with the doctor, on a visit. Michael made certain steps away from the situation the first time, and it was enough being in the hospital to never want to go back. At one time he wanted to die. It could reach a point where he'd have to tell his doctor about the voices, but without them now, he was okay. He breathed and took another drink, waiting for his dad to say something.

Michael was getting anxious, though he looked rather calm. "You wanna try one of my cigarettes?"

His father gave something of a smile. Michael was trying to be funny, though quite honestly offering one, with a grin. "It'll only make me sick." Dale had never smoked. Michael opted for one, said he'd step out, and took his beer to the porch.

Outside, he lit up and exhaled into the invisible breeze. He wondered if it had an added risk taking the hit with the lighter flame. He wanted to quit, but he'd have anxiety without them. He sat on the steps.

He felt typical being outside with a smoke and a drink, considering the future, so he didn't want to think about it. He smoked and looked down both ends of the street, alone again, connecting with previous years he waited here, just as he was now. Nothing came to him then. It was a question of whether he was okay being alone. His loneliness came from a tendency to be quiet and serious with people. People always told him to smile, and he often felt he couldn't.

Everything was urgent. He waited.

Maybe smoking kept him from getting oxygen. He could be dehydrated, not drinking enough water, and he'd maybe have a stroke when he got older.

He drank and let it sit in his mouth. He didn't want beer brain because he already understood the feeling of vacancy, nothing mattering. It could get desperate.

Studying architecture would mean he'd have to quit all the drugs. He could get more exercise...He drank again, knowing he had materials from his doctor to go over, including a scheduled appointment with someone in town the next week.

Michael couldn't see why there was so much crime and what led people to it. He had grown up knowing most people didn't commit crimes. He'd known just as many adults as he did peers because his parents had several groups of friends.

He wanted to be more than what he stood as, and it was hopeless when time was limited to what could be done within a day. If he got into psychology, he could work in the hospital as a social worker or anything to give him the credibility he needed apart from it as a patient.

Last he knew, a close friend was doing this. Everyone was so iconic. He remembered the time he stopped at a blinking yellow light after she had specifically told him not to. Of course, they were high, it was late at night after seeing a show at Sokol. Another time, they ran over an old parking bump they used to have at the mall, and it was the funniest thing. So silly, she would say.

Maybe with a doctor and the right questions, Michael would better understand this disease, but it would be difficult to translate any sense as to why he was hearing voices. The doctor would only suggest it was something of the mind. It had no other logical reason. Michael could appear to be in a more serious condition if he admitted to them, and he didn't want to be routed through the wrong way. He could be led to believe he *was* crazy. At this, he wondered why he was under such force to think about it.

Michael finished his cigarette and went inside. His father was still at the table, waiting, it seemed. Dale appeared to have been abandoned to where he now found himself, without many of the people he knew in his own school. He was a suitable father, but Michael didn't want to let go of past experiences with people like he did.

"What's in the paper?" Michael said.

"Nothing."

Michael sat and drank. "I don't know what I'm supposed

to do but get a job in this town. I would maybe go back to school."

"We can help." He seemed he didn't appreciate the first time Michael dropped out, but he accepted it.

"Maybe architecture," Michael said. It seemed his father could say 'fuck you' to the improbability with whatever else aggravated him. It wasn't normal for him to say this; it just seemed he could lose his patience with Michael someday. "There isn't much else I can do."

"I think that would be good. Or you could even design furniture. You have a good eye for it."

He was a father, a position it seemed he didn't have a choice in, but he was a good one. He'd never be told otherwise, and he deserved something to bring him away from what was all too usual for him. He was informed, and from what he learned, he did what he thought was necessary. He could admit, at times, he would assume something different from what actually was and went by what things appeared to be. "I don't believe you're crazy," he said.

"I know I'm not. It's just not easy. Everything seemed easy before. Chicago was great, but I didn't have time to get to know them. It'd be different now. We should go sometime. I'd show you around."

"It was easy sending you out there."

"Yeah, too much partying, though."

"You always assume we know what's going on."

Michael waited before he knew what to say. "It's just easier to leave me to deal with it."

"You need to accept help."

"I'm doing all right. You know, living with Dan is cool, I just need work. I can meet people and get back into the routine I need before school."

"All right. You consider the meatpacking plant?"

"Yeah, they're not hiring yet." They both drank. Michael finished his beer, took another out of the fridge, and sat again. "I might try Chicago again if it's better than Omaha, but I won't be drinking like I used to. That was a mistake."

"And the marijuana?"

"With the meds, I might not be able to anymore."

"It could be a problem," Dale said.

"Yep."

Dale's appreciation for Michael actually talking for once showed. Michael seemed fine. "Just try to stay off it while you look for a job now. You don't want to take it with these meds you're on anyway, I don't think. You've got to be careful."

"Yeah." Michael drank and knew he should pass up the beer after the one he already had. It felt good. After a moment, "We should have more conversations like this."

Dale thought. "Well, I'm going to Omaha later. Would you like to go?"

"Not today."

CHAPTER 20

Electricity

With a light buzz, Michael put the beer back, because driving somewhere would help calm him. "Think I'll drink this when I get back." It seemed an open afternoon.

"Where are you going?" his father said.

"Out for a drive."

"You be careful."

"I'll be fine."

"All right." Dale smiled, hard work behind him.

Michael was out the door and around the front to the car. It was another defeated moment to have known he must've forgotten something in the house when it was nothing. In the car, he looked around. He could visit the apartment.

Halfway through the neighborhood, he turned around because he wanted to drive out of town. He'd go as far as his grandparents' vacant farm, for one last moment with the place, before someone takes up residence.

He had a feeling with no thoughts to match it, except it happened many times before, to understand and feel nothing was wrong. Music on the radio brought him to cry intensely before he stopped in the same quickness.

He left town on Luther Road, making plenty of dust

behind him before he reached the highway and waited for cars. He had to follow through with his health. Michael merged onto another highway, northbound, thinking of a movie. Maybe with events past, he was losing sight of things, but it didn't matter.

Fields surrounded him again. There had been nothing to do in these towns for kids his age. He never had the feeling he could do anything more than drive places, meet up with friends, drink--The country needed to change, it was so fucked by greed. People knew nothing but to work for a buck before they died, their lives dedicated to something so meaningless.

Of course, there was a girl, who he could've known further, as friends. They both went to school in West Point, and he had completely forgotten about her, just as many other faces had already been forgotten.

Had he been thinking about her? Something changed about him when they met up with Michelle at Village Inn late at night, after the rest left.

He opened the window to smoke, but he had had enough; he'd be smoking at his grandparents' house, so he rolled the window back up...

It seemed too simple going into architecture. With what he knew of feng shui, he might do well. It meant he'd see less of the people he knew and make friends he'd either keep in touch with, for once, or let go of, again. A person normally wanted to keep friends.

Michael could've easily left the other direction to see Malik in Omaha, but there would be another day. He thought of Michelle, who might've acted curious about him. They would remain good friends. Once, driving together around Blair, the hunt for some weed lasted all day and through the night with various people. She had quick, honest judgment.

Anxiety set in, and back pain. Michael wanted a cigarette as he careened down the four-lane, divided highway, so he opened the window, searched his bag, took out a smoke, and lit it with the car's cigarette lighter. He exhaled a large cloud of smoke that dispersed quickly, and the road was long ahead of him. A car could just break down in the middle of nothing but fields here.

Michael wasn't the only one driving. Someone sped past him in the right lane, so he switched lanes and was moving down a hill until passing Maple Creek.

He had trouble being sincere and realized it was always something weighing heavy on his mind. After a few miles, he decided he'd make it a slow drive on the country roads back to Fremont when he'd finish at the farm.

Had anyone confronted him with anything, he would've taken them seriously, but often he was met with it alone. It wasn't now, but there was the night when the voices returned. He had bad feelings about it.

People could've known he was interested in men. Then it was something vague, something he didn't want to think about. Maybe people hated him for it, and maybe most wanted nothing to do with him. It was true he had to live further than what he'd been through, and there were people he didn't know yet. He had the urgency to get back with old friends, only now it needed more than what he knew how to give. He had a fair amount of respect for people he felt had been mutual. Maybe he was wrong.

There was the possibility people didn't care. Maybe he shouldn't care either. Before he'd quit alcohol, he was ready to drink his worries away.

Michael finished his cigarette and focused on the road as he approached another town. This perspective was all he had known. He knew some things in the same light his family and friends did, yet there seemed always something more.

Driving through Hooper, he had nearly forgotten all of what came to mind. He wanted to know more than what he had answers to. Growing up, he had confidence he'd someday be something for somebody, but adulthood proved woefully uneventful, with responsibilities he wasn't prepared for. He passed marshy ditches as he sped up out of town. It was all falling apart.

Michael later turned onto another highway. No one would bother him at his grandparents' old farm. He was impatient with the drive. But then, his focus descended to what was ahead of him, and he passed a stretch of road meandering through hills, until finally leading him to the top of a hill with the town in the distance below.

Moments later, he parked at the gas station and entered, saying 'hello' to Holly and Teresa as he passed the register, went straight to the aisle with the alcohol, and grabbed a forty-ounce beer. A man on the radio was discussing methamphetamines and police cracking down on it. Waiting in line, he noticed the movies for rent, as he stood surrounded by merchandise before buying the beer and leaving. He had said nothing because enough people around quieted him.

Michael arrived at his grandparents' old farm. He pulled up slowly and parked, facing the driveway with the house to his right and the barn in front to his left. Patches of weeds covered the lawn. He watched a semi drive by, its dust carried by the wind, and before he could think, he opened the bottle and began drinking.

✻ ✻ ✻

Reform

Laura had nothing in mind apart from the worries of her apartment. She lit up the quick fix of a cigarette and started watching TV, simple nonsense to see past. Had anything helped settle her, she'd better speak her mind, and with every cigarette, these issues persisted.

Her time with Marcel was passing by too quickly. But the problem was more than that: time went too fast for everyone.

When she was back at the farm, staring out the kitchen window, she was trying to remember--something: an acquaintance, from high school. (He could've been a great friend.)

Television was barely watchable. Its chattering came as a reminder of being holed up in Omaha with too many strangers. She flipped through the channels, patiently, until landing on an afternoon movie. She breathed, but her mind was falling apart.

She smoked and flicked the ash off. In her position, starting out in life, people ahead of her could lead her through it, but no such thing was happening. In a way, she was proud to be finding her way, but it all came traumatically slow. Just a week ago, she didn't have this trouble. It started with boredom. It could've been coffee, marijuana, or cigarettes. It wasn't enough to live alone. She needed Marcel. They could live together sometime, maybe even feel settled. But it had to wait.

The choice to live here had abandoned her altogether. People knew her better than this. She couldn't match ideas because they'd be thinking something far different from her, and their length of following her these days was short. If she was going to be alone for the length of it, she'd be depressed with no end to it.

She tried watching the movie to ignore this, then put the cigarette out to leave. Standing at the TV, Laura switched it off and grabbed her keys and bag from the table. She was shortly out the door and in her car.

Her problems followed her out. She sped off to Dodge Street. Laura just wanted to see her mom.

She quickly switched the radio on before turning onto Dodge. She'd someday be an influence on others who had these issues. It was all up to her.

She didn't know what she would share with her mom at home. She'd mention Marcel. She'd see Siva and give her a good hug.

Careful in her driving, she feared these ideas would stay with her throughout life because they had almost always been with her. She didn't feel she could relate to anyone anymore; relationships were too severed.

The radio continued but didn't sway her. Here she was, in busy Omaha traffic again.

She could recognize people didn't have the answers. She recalled a time chatting online when the men talking to her at first seemed like normal guys but turned the situation around, only to be interested in sex. They were likely strangers to even the people who knew them, so communication lacked as far as Laura could see. She took no part in it after that.

She passed the university.

True, some things people said didn't matter. The guy she met through Michelle seemed to know some of the things she did. She wondered why they had never known each other in school. He was younger though. She wasn't ever interested in getting to know younger guys.

There was no going back, and she would not have been any different had she known then what she was confronting now. Maybe she wouldn't have had strong feelings about anyone. Laura drove in disbelief. She wanted to think the best of her friends.

Was she abandoning them, or had they already forgotten her? Those she had known besides Dawn and Rebecca weren't keeping in touch, and it had to be Laura to even call Rebecca. Rebecca was giving herself too much to her job, yet she wasn't to blame. Laura was helpless in turning her in any new direction, but really she was okay. Maybe Rebecca was disinterested in her, but it was fair.

Laura's being rejected seemed to put her in a place where others would come to do the same. Maybe Marcel would even find a girl if she couldn't go further with him.

From all this confusion, she thought she'd eventually free herself from the worry. It was just holding her back. She had to stop and breathe because her thoughts were quickly coming and going, and she had no control over them.

CHAPTER 21

Modulation

T he house at his grandparents' farm had always been painted pistachio green, matched with some rose-red brick, and its color had outlasted the time they lived there. Michael had been there many mornings growing up. A tree between his car and the house was recently struck by lightning, its branches cut off while the base of it still stood. Behind him was the sad, once-lively chicken coop.

The scene was a dramatic change, not being surrounded by Fremont. There was too much activity there. Maybe he was more suited for this. Since Chicago, he'd gotten used to going places by train or bus, sometimes taxi, always moving. Returning home, he could barely sit.

The farm had a lasting presence, though he believed it was something of the past that would never happen again. The house belonged to the family still but looked like someone else would take over. He impatiently drank, and the only sound was the breeze through trees and the swig of beer. Maybe he'd always come to undermine whatever else could be.

He was witnessing his own estrangement with no understanding of what his family had meant to him. Back at the apartment, the computer might help him. He could e-mail people. He turned the radio on to stop him from thinking as he drank.

Around the farm, the beats of the music became the world. The old white barn knew this music, the insects knew it, the house knew it, the grass moved to it...

Maybe all this trouble came from smoking. But it was a matter of still being young, and his youth wasn't enough support for everything he was faced with now. Some changes should be right ahead.

Over time, he could be much older with the same lack of connection with anyone if he were to continue avoiding people. However, he was serious but also didn't come across as having a problem. Whenever it came to getting to know someone, he'd feel it wouldn't last; he'd give up on trying to make it anything more than a memorable encounter. Now that he understood it, he wanted to deny it .

He wasn't taking his meds yet, except for last night's dose. This would be his last chance to drink. Ditto with weed. His health would be more important.

He drank repetitively again. These troubles he'd likely carry a long time. It would be difficult to ever return to a sense of being genuinely happy. He couldn't deny he hadn't felt happy for quite a while. To express any happiness was often followed with doubt.

He simply didn't want to let go of everything and become what was assumed of adults—the job and family— meaningless in comparison to what he'd been through with friends.

Everyone seemed distant. The house no longer breathed life. Even all the stray cats were gone.

The time he had apart from people would change him. He didn't want his life to continue consisting of this. In any interaction with people, these ideas weren't even an issue, so maybe he was thinking too hard. He stared at the road. Without stability, he lacked the confidence he saw in others.

The beer wet the inside of his mouth and throat, and his

eyes were moving slower to the scene as he contemplated the junk in the garage, staring for a moment before drinking again. Maybe he'd take a souvenir.

Then, it was as though he could talk with anyone, and it would be fine. If it was depression that had him, he could make sense of everything over the years it would be with him, and he'd grow from it. He had the patience for it, yet he'd know most of it alone.

He drank repetitively. The only sound in the car was the beer when he drank since he had the radio off now.

He didn't want to forget his grandparents, but they were still around. It was either way: he could feel they were at the end or were people of his world who he should be more involved with. He continued drinking because he wanted to alleviate the usual anxiety.

Suddenly, everyone he knew populated his mind. He hadn't taken up the responsibility when he moved into the apartment. He wasn't ready, moving from place to place this frequently. And he had had a feeling of giving up each time. Now he needed the break .

When he remembered the cigarettes, he pulled one out and gladly lit up, feeling like his roommate in Chicago, a behavior as he held his cigarette and leaned toward the open window. Then, his cell phone rang, and he brought it to his ear.

"Hello?" he said. *Michael?* "Yeah. Malik?" *Yeah. What's up?*

Malik had the sort of behavior suggesting he'd known Michael a long time already. Michael said, "I'm at my grandparents' old house, drinking. Not much." *Okay. You wanna meet at the club tonight?* "Sure." *A'right, see you there.* "All right, bye."

Michael put the phone away. This was all some future he had never expected and nearly forgot. He'd keep in touch with Malik because there was something about him Michael appreciated. Despite the drugs, he seemed a good influence.

This moment, he wanted to walk around outside with whatever excitement was taking over. He was almost ready to drive off with the beer but decided he had plenty of time. He stayed in the car.

Already, he had had a long week with many questions. He should be able to say more to people. Of course, he had spoken with Meghan and Dan, but it was short of what could be said. He wanted to feel he was a friend they wouldn't turn away from.

Michael didn't feel properly suited for whatever lay ahead. It could be anything good or bad, and not knowing which made him uneasy. Alone, he complicated everything, and it was difficult to understand what people meant when they said something. He couldn't relate. He breathed in the surroundings. Maybe it was just him. Perhaps everyone was perfectly fine with what they knew and could say.

Whatever confidence Michael had was missing now, leaving him exhausted. He couldn't relax, but he leaned back and smoked until his cigarette was through, all the while keeping his mind tasked.

He took another cigarette, lit up, and exhaled.

Michael had nothing of an itinerary—no place he needed to be—still, he could come to no ideas about the family. He had a lot he wanted to say to them and was quick to think he had many opportunities ahead, but he should know now what it all was. What did he want? A job was one thing, but work wasn't necessary for him to develop his relationships.

He drank. It had to be something anyone was going through. He just wanted to be okay, and maybe he wasn't. He had a severe lack of purpose. He often thought more of people than what he could prove of himself, so his expectations were rarely met.

He was losing patience, so he needed a different focus. Thinking too complicated could bring him to the hospital again.

After a moment, he thought of Chicago and all the walking around to find himself at unlikely places. Once, he left the train on the Brown Line to reach Cornelia, northwest of his apartment a distance, in search of a Buddhist temple. He missed Chicago: the stops off the Red Line, school, and the people.

He'd be alone much longer than he had planned. However, he had always carried himself through loneliness. The idea of it came as a responsibility, and he didn't know where it would take him.

Never had he been this ready to understand more. He wasn't making progress with the family. If he had full trust in them, he wouldn't have found himself in the hospital. With people, what could he say? If he didn't have full trust in his family, how could he have trust in anyone?

As he smoked, he knew he needed to slow down. He didn't want to think anymore. There had been times already when a single idea led to too much when none of it needed any consideration. If he'd have one of those thoughts, it wouldn't stop.

He finished his beer and started the car with his cigarette held at the window and threw the bottle out hesitantly near the burn barrel. Someone would have to pick it up later.

He waited at the end of the lane, where there was no traffic. So, he started up the hill and gazed at the fields to his right, refocused, glanced at the road, and stared again at the fields, to where he had walked before to an old, abandoned farm, which was barely there.

This instant with the radio playing, he thought, whatever way he would see things was in the light they needed to be seen. But he could've thought more of his family had he considered them.

* * *

Passion

Meeting with people, whenever the chance came--whatever the outcome--would allow more to happen, not just for Laura. People seemed as oblivious to the truth as she was. Keeping tied up with people she'd known seemed right.

As she left Omaha, she couldn't decide: she was either spending too much time with people or not enough. Maybe she needed to focus more on doing well alone. She'd prefer not to meet with anyone and feel this anxious. In what way was right to say she cared? She thought of Jae. Why their friendship didn't work out for them, when he was so kind on the phone, concerned her.

She traveled Highway 275, calmer now but with no real answer as to why she couldn't get herself to open up more. It quieted her and held her back now more than it ever had. With the perpetual game everyone was in, she wasn't making the connection she wanted. Marcel knew she cared. Maybe he didn't.

She wanted to just smoke, so she breathed and tried to relax away from it all. Time was too short for her to influence anyone with the understanding she had. She felt settled with the idea people may not care about her as she cared about them. With no real answer to it, she was ready to let go for a while. She could be alone much longer with this, and here it began.

But nothing was wrong. Nothing was happening except all this thinking. The outdoors were the same, and the people the same. Everyone got by.

If Laura could have just not involved herself with Jae, she'd have been without these ideas. But to feel this young and misinterpreted was her life in summary. To herself, she was much more than what others saw her to be. And maybe it was the same for anyone. No one seemed to know each other.

She had known from Jae she wasn't the friend she

thought she was, and it was with her now unquestionably. But then it wasn't an issue as she approached another highway and merged.

Again, she worried. Never in her life had she been this stuck. Of course, she had always perceived these matters, and it always called for her to be something more than what she knew how tp. She expected it would come with experience. It was too much on her mind.

Laura seemed to be losing past friendships. Maybe they weren't the right people for each other anymore. Maybe they were too far from what Laura was facing and wouldn't understand. They used to live for drugs.

But her friends were important. She would likely feel alone for a long time, yet she had Marcel, although he could quickly lose interest. She feared it would be the same challenge the next time, but he understood her.

There was no emergency. She could recognize this as something she had long known, but it only got deeper.

Anywhere she went, it was alone. Often, she wasn't met with anyone who could sway her, so she didn't want to turn Marcel away. Perhaps there was a side of her that made her less of a friend than people wanted.

She drove further, eager for it to make sense, and to be a more obvious friend. There was no way to be what most people were, in their complacency, and she'd have to live with this burden before she could understand it.

Laura was approaching Fremont and bypassed it without another thought. For a moment, she had considered her book.

Maybe the tarot brought her to these complexities. It sometimes offered a reminder of what should've been.

Her opinion of Rebecca played against Laura, even though the time they shared was pleasant. None of what Laura was coming to seemed to bother anyone, but to care enough to talk openly, she was afraid of being too inadequate. This was exactly what led Laura to be on her own away from people. She wasn't good enough.

Soon, she was traveling north at a faster speed on a four-lane, divided highway. Fremont was behind her. She followed the speed limit because there could've been cops approaching from behind.

This next week, she'd have less to busy herself with, but thoughts could overwhelm her. She could also find herself in the routine of things and ignoring it, but she was sure she'd always know, whether alone or with company. She couldn't see what was beyond this.

Her life was just beginning at the same time her past was dismantling. She didn't know how to interact with anyone when there was nothing left to say. Laura could see what it meant to care, so what would it take to talk beyond what didn't matter?

She finished her cigarette but left the window open as she came near a bridge over Maple Creek. It was an easy drive and not late in the afternoon yet, so she'd have plenty of time with her mom. Laura didn't know how it would be said, but she wanted her mom to know how she felt. She didn't bring the weed this time.

It may've been true anyone she knew was secretly unhappy in relationships. She wanted to know she came from a strong family with a strong purpose.

She exited onto another highway headed for Hooper. There, she passed everything without noticing more than a parked train she saw each time, and the peculiar hotel. She left Hooper and sped up.

On the highway, Laura was impatiently driving behind someone slow and passed what was an elderly man with a ridiculous cap—but she was behind someone slow again. Then, she lost her train of thought. Whatever means she had in expressing herself would come once she cleaned up. She sneezed suspiciously.

She was starting to lose her way with people around the time she met Jerome. It had been several years ago already. She was once living in an apartment while studying before finally giving up on school, then Jae, before moving back to the farm and helping her aunt. The time with them was enough to believe there was no way to enter something new. She didn't feel closure.

Maybe she was the one abandoning everyone, the more she came to know them. She wondered more about people when she had to turn away from it all. It was never enough just knowing someone. There was simply something more she didn't know, even with people of her past.

Again, it came to her as her fault she didn't relate well to people. She was often the one who never knew what to say to anyone because she had long ago given up. People had a reputation for ignoring her.

Returning to people would be difficult. She didn't know where to start over with anyone.

Laura drove through Scribner and reached another highway. It was her fault no one knew her. All this time, she barely said anything for them to know her as well as she knew them. And here she was, on the edge of going without a home, someday being without her parents. Her grandparents were already gone. Her brothers didn't know her. Marcel probably thought she was a mental case after today. Rebecca had other people. Dawn had other people and would leave for Chicago. The public was nothing to Laura but the very people who'd reject anyone. And here she was so used to silence, she may never be able to talk.

She was remembering a room in the hospital. While sitting there, she was visited by a nurse, who told Laura she had tested positive for HIV. Upon leaving the hospital, Laura immediately forgot. All she knew was that Jae had cheated. He sometimes brought people over who they hadn't previously met. Sometimes, she suspected things. She had convinced herself at the time it must've been a false-positive.

How could she forget? How could she afford it?

She had to tell Jae. He didn't even know. He would kill her. There would be no convincing him it was his fault. She knew. He would find her. It could be full-blown now. Maybe she was already getting sick. His girlfriend had it.

Laura couldn't tell anyone. She had to tell Marcel. She could tell Dawn. Anyone else, and news would spread fast. She couldn't believe this was happening. She hardly listened to the nurse when she was being told. All that was on her mind was getting out.

She swallowed against the pain in her throat and violently turned onto the dirt road. It was a heavy guilt to have been quiet all her life and feel there was no way to get it back.

As she drove, she sobbed quietly. Something was isolating her from people. She drove at a fast speed when she came up a hill, and a car was speeding toward her when it came from over the top.

She had to end it. She couldn't handle this.

She felt an electric fear of death and turned into the path of the other car before impact. The cars hit hard, and she remained in her seat, unconscious with her head hung forward. The seatbelt loosened slowly, and her body leaned forward until her head rested. Her hair covered the sides of her face, and she didn't move.

CHAPTER 22

Renae was on her way out the door to buy ground beef in town. Earlier, she had made plans with her friend. But she didn't go with her. It was a trip to Omaha, and she decided to stay at home. Her husband was already there at the house, and she'd grill outside. It was all on her mind this instant, getting into the van. She drove down the lane and onto the road. Public radio was on, but she wasn't listening to it yet. She was reminded of Laura, knowing she would arrive tomorrow or perhaps today if Renae was lucky.

She turned and had the feeling she wouldn't see Laura this weekend because she could be busy, but Laura said she would. Renae smiled. Several people in the area had kids Laura's age.

Renae was proud of America, thankful for her bottled water, her old sunglasses, and especially the new van, though gas prices were getting high. Then, at the top of the hill, she had to slow down at the scene of a car accident, short of believing its presence in the road in front of her. Urgency filled her. She was the first person at the scene, and it had just happened.

She stopped behind the first car, and the other car was Laura's. "Oh, God," she said as she stopped.

Smoke rose from both cars, and the wind was taking it. In a panic, Renae was about to get out of the van to see if

Laura was okay, but it occurred to her she needed to call for an ambulance. This instant, with the sight of a head-on collision, cars that could burst into flames, she didn't know what to do. They needed to understand her on the phone, but she thought she wouldn't get the words out. She turned her cell phone on and dialed, and she tore off her sunglasses.

"My daughter's just been in a collision!" she yelled at the dispatcher. "I don't know if she's okay! I need an ambulance right now!" Renae wiped her face, disgusted by the dispatcher. She managed to give the location, trembling at the scene. "There are two people! Two people need an ambulance!"

Renae hung up and hastily got out to the scene because she couldn't just sit there and do nothing. Outside, surrounded by fields, no one else around, she could be losing her daughter. She went around the young man's car, its airbag deployed, the radio still on, some crude mockery of the situation.

She thought she could've prevented this.

The emotion of both being mad at him and the chance of losing Laura built within her a struggle to breathe.

She went to Laura's car. Laura was leaned forward with her hair around her face. Renae cried uncontrollably, no longer in a panic but helpless, and she knocked at the window. She knocked harder and harder. "Laura!" she cried, but Laura wouldn't move. Renae covered her mouth, crying as though she were with her sisters at the sight of this. The door was locked.

Renae looked down the road, shaken and holding the pain in her throat. In the distance, the ambulances were coming. Renae looked back at Laura, then watched the ambulances and a police car coming up the road, almost slowly as if unsure of the country roads and not believing this to be an emergency. She stood there, both trembling and crying. They finally arrived, and the crew got out.

"We need you back at your car, ma'am."

"Don't tell me what to do, I'm her mother," Renae managed to say. "I need to know she's okay."

"Back to your car, ma'am. We'll be at the hospital shortly."

Renae went to her van and stood facing the scene. Three men and a woman dispersed to help.

"I haven't got a pulse from this kid yet," one yelled against the wind at the young man's car.

"Oh god," Renae cried quietly.

The other man had broken the window and was already checking Laura's pulse from her neck. For a moment, there was silence. Renae covered her mouth with her hand.

"We've got a pulse!" he yelled.

A gurney was already at the door, they broke the door open, and unbuckled Laura. Two men carefully pulled her out of the car as Renae watched. She was no longer in a panic but calmly sobbing. At this time, she had to call her husband, so without hesitation, she went to her car, wiping her eyes and coughing. In the car, she dialed home, and Laura's father answered.

Hello? "There was an accident." She paused. "They're taking Laura to the hospital right now." *Oh god.* "I'm going there now." She hung up because she couldn't talk, and she cried much harder. He would be home without her while this was happening.

As the road was blocked, she had to turn her car around and take the back roads, so like a sport she couldn't play, she hurried and got the car in the other direction before driving off. They had taken Laura in the opposite direction to the highway.

Renae passed an intersection. The drive would be longer than ever before, and dust flew behind her. She breathed to stop crying but couldn't.

Renae knew Laura was on her way to see them and began blaming herself for the accident. It was better with Laura in their care, but it was a head-on collision; she could have lots of difficulty.

For a while, Laura seemed to be going through a lot of difficulties. Renae didn't know how to help. Laura was out of reach for so long, Renae barely knew how to talk to her anymore. It was simple being a mother, but something of a friendship was only beginning. "God." She turned and drove east to another road, still crying with the same focus.

Renae turned again, headed north, and she knew Laura had problems talking either out of shyness, or rejection by other people. It seemed life was more of a challenge for Laura than it had been for Renae. Still, Renae had no way of facing it with her, and she feared she wasn't the best mother for the situation. It appeared there had been time ahead of them to face it together, but in the meantime, nothing brought them to it.

Renae thought of herself as a simple mother with few words to ever get across. Laura had once told Renae she felt life was meaningless; Renae had fought with the idea, never speaking of it with Laura's father. He was more Laura's father than he was her own husband anymore. Her relationship with him *was* sometimes distant, since their children were gone, and she watched TV, often making it an invitation to watch it together.

It was all on her mind as something she'd been ignoring but was a wave of truth that triggered her impatience with the drive, causing her to cry more.

Coming to the bottom of a hill, she knew she'd take the opportunity with Laura after it was all over. Laura was alive, and nothing was stopping Renae from being the mom she needed to be. She cried more. It was necessary to promise more for her daughter than Renae ever felt she could've. She was still with the possibility Laura could die.

Laura lay unconscious in the ambulance with someone tending to an oxygen mask, which seemed to be the most they could do. The ambulance was driving fast, and the sirens sounded.

Renae sped on, still crying; all she could think about was her daughter. Renae was met with another car but didn't slow down.

After Laura had said that, Renae felt useless with people, and the rescue team brought this feeling back to her. They were all somehow more adequate. It was never voiced, and it wasn't overly against her but made her more talkative otherwise, to make up for those feelings. Sometimes people didn't listen to her at all. There was often something keeping her from saying what she wanted because most people didn't seem to care. She thought of it often because she wanted to be more for people. Without Laura, she would feel further isolated, when this was something they had in common. She needed Laura to survive.

Renae knew she could've called Laura before, which could've simply kept her from leaving Omaha.

Marcel was phoning the farm because he couldn't reach Laura at the apartment, and Laura's father answered. "Hello?"

"Hi, is Laura there?"

"She's just been in an accident." He wasn't dramatic. He had been privately going through some of the same thoughts Renae was going through, with some difficulty. He was, in his own way, in a solemn panic.

"Oh god. She's going to be okay, right?"

"I don't know yet. It sounds bad. *I'll call later.* Laura's father's face was extreme; he also took the blame for this happening. After all, it didn't involve him, blame or no blame.

Renae knew Laura often got high, and she couldn't confront it. Maybe it was keeping Laura from talking. Renae wanted for once to hear Laura loved her family because it would be a step forward. It'd be any day to just come to the house with nothing said. Laura started having trouble talking and keeping friends after Jae. She had said it was always easy to make conversation with someone at first but it died down, and just last week Laura said it was bullshit.

In disbelief, Renae cried while, in her mind, she still could see Laura leaned forward with her head down, unresponsive after the force of colliding head-on into someone, with no one else around. Renae swallowed against the pain in her throat. She could barely see the road, so she slowed down. She cried louder since she wasn't making good time, and it meant she was losing Laura. Finally, she reached the pavement and sped on without stopping at the intersection. She accelerated when her cell phone rang, but she didn't answer it. Likely, it was one of her sisters, which caused her to cry more.

Renae made it to the highway, all the while knowing she'd be the mother not to be there yet, after trying her hardest to make it before the ambulances. She again regretted not calling Laura earlier because it would've prevented the accident. She entered the town with these thoughts and visions of the two cars.

She drove fast in a low-speed zone, until she was behind a slower car, so she turned into a neighborhood and drove faster through it. West Point didn't know what was happening. The town held the most vacant appearance as though its people wouldn't console her if she lost Laura, and would move on as they always did. She reached the main road and crossed. Finally, she made it to the hospital and parked in the back, feeling very much alone, unwanted, that this was business, and she couldn't help but know what she had seen.

Renae quickly got out, wiping her face, locking up because she always had the sense she had to, and crying still because she wasn't making it in good time, as the ambulance had already arrived and taken Laura in.

She walked past the ambulances into the doors to the lobby where a doctor, known through church, was already waiting for her. He had been present when Laura arrived. Here he was, a friend to anyone, and Renae, but not now.

"Renae. I'm sorry." He held her hands. He shook his head and nearly cried at the sight of her. "I'm sure they did everything they could." He said this and rubbed her back.

The nurses on staff made eye contact with her before she realized nothing could be done. They together brought her closer to it being too real. "How can you just tell me that?" She sensed people cheating against her.

She soon left for her van, bawling. Her mother and daughter were gone, and she knew Laura's father wouldn't handle this well.

She got in the van slowly with some difficulty, because she could barely see, and dialed home to Laura's father. Her crying had quieted but was intense. She waited for him to pick up as it rang.

Renae?

At the sound of his voice, Renae cried aloud, unable to tell him anything. She thought she could at least say his name and was about to. The thought of it made her cry even more.

This moment, she remembered the time when Laura was first leaving for school, and Renae believed it was too much, too soon for Laura to even go to kindergarten, with the look of her in new clothes and shockingly aware of people she had never known. Renae felt she missed a chance she could have saved her while she remained that girl.

Her crying was the only way she could tell him before she finally hung up...

BIOGRAPHY

Rian Meir

The author resides in Nebraska, where he grew up. Meir spent two years studying and working in Chicago before severe illness from drug and alcohol use caught up with him. As such, he would suggest to anyone experiencing hardship or difficult thoughts to avoid the various addictions. This may include caffeine and tobacco, which had long challenged him. He felt it necessary to display what addiction meant in the time he was experiencing it for himself. He is successfully on treatment for paranoid schizophrenia and general anxiety disorder. He wrote Parallel Opposites at age 24, soon after the events that inspired it.

AUTHOR'S NOTE

High school journalism, persuasive speech writing, and artistic abilities greatly influenced my initial ambition to write a novel; film and television were an even greater influence, but disaster and setbacks outside of schooling further impacted my decision to do so.

Currently, I'm still involved with an old friend from Chicago, after two years studying and working there. Coincidentally, we left in a moving truck the day after the attacks on the WTC. It wasn't until after money trouble that I was revisiting the effects of excessive drugs, alcohol, coffee and nicotine, and I suffered through setbacks similar to the story before suicide attempts brought me to be hospitalized. To look back on my high school experience, not knowing the effects of drugs until it was too late, and meeting the people I've known through all that time, it calms me to read my novel, not for the events that transpired, but for my moral disposition through all of it.

For Parallel Opposites, I utilized feng shui, astrology,tarot, and the I-Ching to create something further and more efficiently structured from a basic outline. The story itself brings the two characters into separate real-time paths, on many levels this way. The kinetics of inner and outer workings uniting together continue to amaze me.

Following the first novel, I plan to someday return to methods of creating stories that hold up as spiritually meaningful while being innovative, different, and unexpected.

Besides writing, further studies in interior design and feng shui interest me, but architecture and drafting practices are also important. I haven't in a long time considered writing to be a top priority. In fact, currently I am considering thematic overviews of my house designs.

THANKS

I care to thank the few English teachers who got me interested in writing, as well as the early ones who taught Phonics. (Sally R, Mrs. Jaunke, S Peters, and Marlene W). Not until high school had creative literature interested me, once I was familiar with the technicalities. Learning to type was also crucial, and I have Mr. P to thank very much for that. The most notable influences on my writing and creativity in school were Michelle K and Kathy M. And even though I flunked Creative Writing, I remember enjoying Cheryl K's class. I cannot thank you all enough. Also, thanks go to Lori S. Outside of high school, I greatly enjoyed the lessons with Sarah K in Chicago. Of course, I would say all the teachers and their work was appreciated. David, Craig, and Linda, thank you. Nilda, Kristy, Wendlendt, and Benson, thank you. Furstenau, thanks! Carlson, I cannot forget 6th grade. Many thanks for those memories!

I care to acknowledge Michael Cunningham and James Baldwin for their creative efforts.

I want to thank Yvonne for inspiring me creatively. Although I was a mess to deal with, your intentions made a lasting impression on me even still, whether directly or indirectly. I think as a family, we all guided each other respectably, and I'm sorry for the mistakes I inevitably made.

I need to thank my immediate family for dealing with the whirlwind I was at home during high school. I want to also thank Maurice for putting up with all of it in my slow descent.

I feel there are numerous people to thank, and they know who they are. The people I've known have all been meaningful to me.

I want to thank Rima in Beirut, Nichole, Tish, Dave, Jennifer, Rachel, Wayne, Marcia, Curtis, and Melissa; Aaron, Angey, Keith, Amy, Billy and Joe, Brent H and Hannah, Brock, Diana, and Burdell, Alex and Marlys (and the cousins). Thanks also to Shaniece W. Brent R, Jared D, Michael A, Michael B, Nate, Adam, James, Toad, Sam, Beth and Barb, Angie S, Angie P, Melinda H, Melissa F, Miranda, Suzy M and the friends at Furst, Brooke (and family), Tamara (and family), Angie F (and family), Lisa and Kim, Lynn and Mary, Brad, Frank, Alyssa, Erica, Kyle, Steve, Jason, Alex R (and family), Alison (and thanks go to the rest of the class, including Katie M and Andrea R), Suzie and Rodney, the acquaintances in Vegas and the Bay Area and on Greyhound. The parents of my friends. Heather B and Kristy F. There are others I fail to mention: Jeanette and her family.

The friends and acquaintances in Chicago. Maurice (and his amazing family), Alonzo, EJ, Robin, Robert, Keidra, Abbe, Amanda, Naomi, George and Sherae, Ace, Deonte. Folks at the recruiting job.

Bendjo and the rest of the Yahoo friends, including Vivian and Ossy. Donna in Chicago. Beth P, Jodi P, Reggie "Putt" and "68," Cara, Leslie, Bonnie, Erin, Carly, Alvaro and Alejandro, Elizabeth, Bree; I know I'm forgetting people, but you've all been huge influences.

The nursing staff at Douglas County those few times. Chicago Read will always be remembered. Thanks go to the nursing staff (and patients) there as well as Mike who played UNO with me.

The friends at Furst Group, Omaha Steaks, and World Market: thank you all. Marcello, thank you for welcoming me to your church family in Chicago. Thanks also to the handful of people I hung out with one night on Damen. Also, thanks go to Sharon and Monica, and Bruce, whom I'll always remember. My two sisters-in-law. Thanks go to my family, most of all. Thanks also, to Pat. Thanks go to the Mini Mart.

Many thanks go to everyone at St. Paul. I have some of the most vivid memories from those days. I can't help but feel sorry I haven't mentioned Trinity. Thank you. Thanks also to Ben and his family for directing me back to the lessons of the Bible. Many unspoken thanks (as of yet) to the Creator. I want to thank my lawyer also, since I was once faced with jail.

Last but not least, I want to thank Pam and my other doctors. My health is much better than it once was. I'm so sorry to the ones unmentioned, but many thanks, just the same! And many thanks to Rose, Roy, and Brett for both the amazing memories from so long ago and the interest (and feedback) from this. Thanks also to the delivery drivers. Thanks, Meredith, Jeff, and Daryl.

Now, I have to admit, thanks also go to Gary Goldschneider for his extensive work with others on the book The Secret Language of Destiny, which enabled much of the direction of the writing. I recently purchased The Secret Language of Birthdays and am astonished by the readings of the random birthdays I chose for my two characters.

Thanks so much for reading. People meant the most to me.

Made in the USA
Middletown, DE
21 September 2024

61210125R00176